P9-DBT-794

PRAISE FOR
HELEN HARDT

"I'm dead from the strongest book hangover ever. Helen exceeded every expectation I had for this book. It was heart pounding, heartbreaking, intense, full throttle genius."

~ Tina at Bookalicious Babes Blog

"Proving the masterful writer she is, Ms. Hardt continues to weave her beautifully constructed web of deceit, terror, disappointment, passion, love, and hope as if there was never a pause between releases. A true artist never reveals their secrets, and Ms. Hardt is definitely a true artist."

~ Bare Naked Words

"The love scenes are beautifully written and so scorching hot I'm fanning my face just thinking about them."

~ The Book Sirens

CHASE BRANCH LIBRARY
17731 W. SEVEN MILE RD.
DETROIT, MI 48235
313-481-1580

FEB -- 2018

CH

Twisted

STEEL BROTHERS SAGA
BOOK EIGHT

This book is an original publication of Helen Hardt.

This is a work of fiction. Names, characters, places, and incidents either are the product of the author's imagination or are used fictitiously, and any resemblance to actual persons, living or dead, business establishments, events, or locales is entirely coincidental. The publisher does not assume any responsibility for third-party websites or their content.

Copyright © 2017 Waterhouse Press, LLC
Cover Design by Waterhouse Press, LLC
Cover Photographs: Shutterstock

All Rights Reserved
No part of this book may be reproduced, scanned, or distributed in any printed or electronic format without permission. Please do not participate in or encourage piracy of copyrighted materials in violation of the author's rights. Purchase only authorized editions.

Paperback ISBN: 978-1-943893-24-9

Twisted

STEEL BROTHERS SAGA
BOOK EIGHT

WATERHOUSE PRESS

For Dean

WARNING

This book contains adult language and scenes, including flashbacks of child physical and sexual abuse, which may cause trigger reactions. This story is meant only for adults as defined by the laws of the country where you made your purchase. Store your books and e-books carefully where they cannot be accessed by younger readers.

PROLOGUE

Ryan

I'd saddled up my horse, Sergio, and gotten ready to go for a run, when I realized Sergio, as fast as he was, wouldn't be able to give me the speed I was craving.

I patted him down. "Another time, boy," I said.

Then I wandered back up to the detached garage at the guesthouse where I kept my pride and joy—my Porsche 911 Turbo. Sleek navy blue—custom paint job—and posh leather seats, the convertible sat under its chamois cover. His name was Jake.

I removed the cover and stared at it in all its glory.

Neither of my brothers were into cars. They were more comfortable in their pickups than in the luxury sedans they both owned. Me? I loved them, though I didn't take Jake out as often as I would have liked to.

Right now? I needed speed. I needed the wind blowing through my hair as I sped a hundred twenty miles an hour down deserted country roads.

My life was in shambles.

The woman I—

The woman I what?

Loved?

Fuck. I shoved my fingers through my hair.

I fucking loved her.

Ruby. Ruby who'd kept a secret from me. She'd taken my punishment for that. A woman who had only recently opened her body and mind to sex had let me take what I needed from her.

Damn.

My life was a mess.

I couldn't have a relationship, and I had no idea if she felt the same way anyway.

So for now, I'd get Jake out onto the open road and scream through the next couple hours at top speeds.

My phone buzzed.

Shit. It was Joe.

"Yeah?" I said into the phone.

"Hey, Ry. Tal and I just wanted to..."

"What, Joe? What the fuck do you want?"

"To make sure you're all right."

"All right? Of course I'm not all right. My life has been shattered, and I just spent the last hour listening to my biological mother spin all kinds of tales."

"You went to see Wendy?"

"Yeah. You got a problem with that?"

"No. Of course not. But we should have been there with you."

"Ruby went with me."

"Good. Then you weren't alone."

"Alone? I got news for you, Joe. I'm fucking alone. I have no idea who I am anymore. I have no idea who my brothers are anymore. It doesn't get much more alone than that." I ended the call, furious.

I got into the Porsche, put the top down, and backed out of

the garage. "Let's go, Jake," I said. "Show me what you can do."

I drove through the private roads and off our property and then headed into the deserted country roads. Route 78 was straight and narrow with the ups and downs of the foothills.

Perfect.

The first one hundred miles an hour came easy. Jake's engine roared with power, promising me more speed, more thrill. The sound of his tires screaming along the road began to disappear as I eased him toward one forty. The rubber clawed at the road.

I resisted the urge to close my eyes and drift away with Jake.

Closing one's eyes at a hundred forty miles an hour was never a good idea.

I edged toward one fifty, and Jake drove as smooth as a gazelle running across the savanna. One fifty-five. One sixty.

Oh, yeah.

Lift. I felt the oxygen tunneling under the engine. Much more speed and I'd get into the air like a fucking plane.

Of course not, but I felt it. Truly felt it.

Jake's engine had now drowned out all road noise, what little there'd been.

My blood thumped in my ears in time with my heartbeat.

One sixty-five.

One seventy.

Vibrations. Vibrations against my thigh.

Just the engine. Just me flying through the goddamned air.

No.

It was my phone.

Answering the phone at a hundred seventy miles an hour?

Not a good idea. But what the fuck did I care?

I put the phone to my ear, a smile on my face. "Hello?"

"Ryan," a male voice said. "This is your father."

CHAPTER ONE

Ruby

What next for Ryan and me? Could we even have a future now?

If only I hadn't fallen in love with him.

Clearly he wasn't in love with me, and right now he had way more to deal with than anyone should have. Bothering him about our "relationship" was not something I'd do.

What could I do?

More research on the future lawmakers. Another visit to my uncle, maybe. Another visit to Larry Wade. At least the two of them seemed less crazy than Wendy. Still crazy, though.

It all seemed so futile now. No matter how hard I worked, I never seemed to get anywhere. Questions didn't turn up answers. Only more questions.

What would make me feel better?

Being with Ryan, but that wasn't in the cards.

Then it hit me. I'd call Shayna. Just check up on her to see how she was doing. Maybe she'd heard something about Juliet and Lisa.

I searched my contacts and pulled up her number. It rang a few times, and then a female voice answered.

"Hello, Shayna? It's Ruby Lee, from Jamaica."

"Ruby? I don't know any Ruby."

"This is Shayna Thomas, right?"

"Yes."

"We met in Jamaica. Remember? When your...friends and you went off on those Jet Skis?"

"I'm afraid I don't know what you're talking about. Please don't call me again."

The line went dead.

What?

I called the number again. This time I got no answer. It went straight to voice mail. "Listen, Shayna," I said. "I'm not sure what's going on, but I assure you there's nothing to fear from me. I'm a friend. I want to help. I want to—" The line went dead.

I called again. No voice mail. She had blocked me.

Why?

What was she afraid of?

My nerves prickled as I eyed my glass of water on the counter above me. I wasn't thirsty. I wasn't hungry.

I wasn't...anything.

And then my phone rang. A number I didn't recognize.

Shayna! Perhaps she'd been afraid someone was listening in, and she'd tried a different phone.

"Shayna?" I said into the phone.

"No," an eerily familiar male voice said.

"Oh, I'm sorry. Who is this, please?"

"Ruby," the voice said, "this is your father."

The phone slipped from my hand and clattered onto the floor.

Ruby, this is your father.

It was him. Once he said my name, I'd have recognized his voice anywhere. Its sleaze was etched in my brain.

Show Daddy how much you love him.

Still, my cop instincts kicked in. Background noise? Where was he?

Nothing. All I heard was the deep rasp laced with evil.

Theodore Mathias. Depravity personified. Inhumanity personified. I swallowed, inhaled deeply, picked up my phone. It was already set to record all my conversations. Good thing.

"Where is she?" I demanded.

"Where is who?"

"Shayna Thomas. You got to her, didn't you? You're telling her not to talk to me. You're involved in all of this somehow."

"Involved in what?"

"Trafficking. Human trafficking. I know all about it. You're involved in the disappearance of those two girls from the resort in Jamaica. You got to Shayna. That's why she's refusing to talk to me."

"You always did have a vivid imagination." He chuckled.

"And you always were an insane piece of shit."

I waited, listening to his inhalations over the phone, for him to respond to my comment.

He didn't.

A few seconds later, "You think you're worth that badge you wear?" he snarled. "Prove it."

My body went numb. He had always kept one step ahead of the authorities. Never left a trail. My father wasn't just evil. He was brilliant. A noxious combination. Only recently had he begun contacting me—once when he came to town with his girlfriend, and now...after his partners had been taken out. Something was definitely up.

"We've got Larry Wade. And Tom Simpson is dead."

"They were amateurs."

"Oh? And you're a *professional* criminal?"

He laughed—that sleazy, corrupt laugh. "Of the three of us, I'm the only one who's eluded you and that boyfriend of yours."

Boyfriend. Of course he knew about Ryan Steel. The Steels had been trying to find him for months now. I wasn't in the least surprised he knew about my relationship—if I could call it that—with Ryan. My father watched me, just as I watched him. It was a sick little game he liked to play. I'd only seen him once since I ran away from his home seventeen years ago—just recently, in the company of Jade's mother, Brooke Bailey—but he left little clues letting me know he was observing. I'd been compiling a profile on him for years. Now that I had a witness who would testify against him—Talon Steel—I was more determined than ever.

For a while, I'd lived in fear that he'd come for me, but he hadn't. Once I'd become a cop, it hadn't taken me long to figure out why he scrutinized me but didn't come after me.

He might be a psychopath, but he was also a father. In some bizarre way, he wanted to see me succeed.

Yet for me to truly succeed, I had to take him down. He and I both knew this. It was part of the fucked-up little game we played. I had to remain calm. Keep my cool.

"I suppose you'll be tracing this call...and recording it," he said.

"I will. It's procedure. But you and I both know it will come to nothing."

My father was way too smart to put himself in any danger of being caught.

"Indeed it will," he agreed. "Come to nothing, that is."

"So why are you calling me? You obviously know I was trying to get in touch with Shayna Thomas."

"I don't know who you're talking about."

"Don't play that game with me. You know damned well who I'm talking about."

"Think what you want, Ruby, but that's not why I called."

"Why, then?"

"I want you to call off the Steels." The line went dead.

That wouldn't happen. As much as I'd have loved to protect Ryan and his family from the horror that was my father, they would never stop until they'd brought him to justice. And neither would I. But the Steels had something I, as a cop, didn't. Unlimited funds. If I couldn't find him with my resources, they could with theirs.

Besides, my father knew I'd never ask Ryan and his brothers to stop their manhunt. This was just another little ploy in his game.

We were getting closer. Two of his cohorts were gone, and my uncle Rodney Cates had started talking. Wendy Madigan was also talking, and though the bitch was batshit crazy, she told the truth every once in a while. Now that Ryan knew he was her son and not the son of Daphne Steel, Wendy had fewer reasons to keep quiet.

My father, of course, knew all of this. I worked on the assumption that he knew everything that happened before I did. He had eyes and ears everywhere. He wouldn't have survived this long without them. Such watchers cost money, and my father had that in abundance. Human trafficking paid exceedingly well.

Acid crept up my throat.

Human trafficking.

I'd had a working theory for several years that my father was involved in the sex slave trade, but I'd only recently found out I was correct.

In the back of my mind, I'd been wishing I were wrong. As despicable as my father was, I'd hoped he'd stop short of selling people. But what could anyone expect of a man who kidnapped and raped a ten-year-old boy, murdered another, raped his own niece, and attempted to rape his own daughter? And those were just the crimes I could prove.

Human trafficking would be nothing to him.

I'd recently returned from Jamaica, where the older two Steel brothers, Talon and Jonah, had been married. I was the guest of and honor attendant for Melanie Carmichael Steel, Jonah's wife. She and I had only recently met but had become close quite quickly because of our ties to the Steel mystery. Having left home at fifteen, I'd gotten used to flying under the radar. I'd never really had a real friend before. Melanie was a friend.

She was also a psychotherapist. She'd said she'd be willing to talk to me anytime I wanted to. I was comfortable with Melanie, and I trusted her. And God only knew I had a lot of baggage I needed to unload, not the least of which was figuring out what was going on with Ryan Steel.

I'd betrayed him. I'd been the one who gave his sister a strand of his hair so a DNA test could be run to determine whether Wendy Madigan was his mother. Results were in, and Ryan was only a half sibling to Jonah, Talon, and Marjorie, the three of whom were full siblings, children of Bradford and Daphne Steel. Ryan was Brad's son, but his mother was not Daphne, contrary to what he'd always thought.

I'd owned up to my part in it when he confronted me. I owed him that much. I'd even let him take me to bed in the rage he was in. Then I'd gone with him to see his mother—his biological mother. We'd parted after that, and he'd promised me he wouldn't do anything stupid.

I sighed, worried.

What if Ryan Steel's definition of "stupid" didn't match my own?

CHAPTER TWO

Ryan

I dropped the phone.

My father?

My father was dead.

My mother was...not my mother.

My whole world had been shattered with one revelation. What the fuck?

Shit! My eyes weren't on the road. I'd gone off the shoulder and was close to Brown Canyon. The speedometer now said one twenty. I floored the brakes.

My life didn't flash before my eyes, but I knew I was toast. Dead toast.

The tires screeched on the dirt as I swerved to the left.

Thonk!

My head hit the dash as the car halted.

I raised my head, woozy. The car didn't feel stable. Quickly, I opened the door and hopped out, my head still swimming, my vision blurred.

Two seconds later, Jake toppled over the cliff and into the canyon below, taking my phone with him.

Ever seen a grown man cry? Try watching a Porsche fall off a cliff. But I didn't shed a tear.

I fell to the ground, my head in my hands, recalling the

conversation with my biological mother only hours ago.

"My father's dead."

"That's ridiculous. I just talked to him this morning."

"What did he say to you this morning?"

"He said he missed all of you kids. He said he missed me."

"Really?"

"He said he'd come home as soon as he could. As soon as it was safe."

My biological mother, Wendy Madigan, was certifiably nuts. I hadn't believed her when she said my father was alive.

But the phone call...

I looked around. I was miles from home, probably two hours by motor vehicle. I had no car, no phone. No one would come around here looking for me, and darkness would descend soon. November was here.

My body ached, and my head swirled. A minute later, I hit the ground.

★ ★ ★

I squinted against the sun high in the sky. Where was I?

I looked around. The redness of the canyon clued me in. The last thing I remembered was flooring the brakes. Where the hell was my car? My phone? What time was it?

I wasn't wearing a watch, and I had no idea how much time had passed. Something had happened that I didn't remember.

I'd lost the last few minutes before I'd hit my head on something. I touched my forehead and found an egg-shaped knot. Definitely had hit my head. My vision was blurry. I tried to stand, but my legs wobbled like jelly and I fell.

Tried again. This time I stayed standing, but fought

dizziness. I breathed in and out a few times, trying to gain some steadiness. I obviously had a concussion, and I had no idea what had happened.

I got a sick feeling in my stomach when I looked toward the cliff heading into Brown Canyon. It was a shallow canyon, but Jake wouldn't have survived it. I walked slowly toward the edge, fighting vertigo. I didn't trust myself to stand near the edge, so I sat down and looked over.

And nearly heaved.

My beautiful blue Porsche lay there, crashed at the bottom of the canyon. I checked my pockets. I wouldn't have gone anywhere without my phone. Since it wasn't on me, it must be in the car. It might have survived the fall. On a normal day, I could easily scale down the shallow canyon, but with a concussion? I probably shouldn't try.

Not like I had a choice, though. With no phone, I wouldn't be able to get help, and I needed help. I raked my fingers through my hair. Now what?

Screech!

My nerves jumped as I twisted my neck. A pickup had halted, dust flying up from its tires. My brothers, Talon and Jonah, raced out.

"Ryan!" Jonah yelled. "Thank God!"

They ran toward me.

I should have known my brothers would find me. They always took care of me. Of course, they were only half brothers now.

Now? Christ. They'd always been my half brothers. I just hadn't known until now.

They knelt down beside me.

"Are you okay?" Talon asked. "That's a hell of a bump on

your head."

"I can't remember what happened," I said. "But Jake is gone." I pointed down into the canyon.

"Jake can be replaced," Jonah said. "You can't. Whatever happened, I'm glad you didn't go down with the car."

"How long have I been gone?"

"Depends on when you left," Talon said. "We got an anonymous phone call this morning saying you weren't answering your phone, so we went to the guesthouse and found you and the car gone. We figured you'd gone on one of those road benders of yours. Ry, you have to be more careful."

"I had a rough day. I needed a little speed."

"We understand it was rough. But," Joe said, "you're still our brother."

"*Half* brother," I said.

Talon vehemently shook his head. "Bullshit. You're our brother in every way that matters."

I believed them. They still loved me like a...well, like a brother. That didn't change the DNA. I was their half brother. Nothing diminished that.

"We need to get you to the hospital," Joe said.

"I'm fine."

"You're not fine. We're not even sure how long you've been out here. Did you leave yesterday?"

Yesterday... Yesterday I'd seen my real mother. Ruby had been with me. God...Ruby. I'd gone to her place. We'd made love...if I could even call it that. I'd damn near forced her. How could she ever forgive me? But she had. She'd gone with me to see Wendy. And Wendy had told me—

"Christ!" I stood, stumbling.

Jonah grabbed my arm. "Easy, Ry."

"I got a phone call."

"You remember something?" Talon asked.

"I got a phone call. From...Dad."

"What?" Jonah nearly let me fall to the ground.

"At least he said it was Dad. He said, 'Ryan, this is your father.'"

"Was it Dad's voice?" Talon asked.

My mind was muddled, and my head felt like someone was jackhammering it. "I don't know. I was going over a hundred miles an hour. I almost missed the vibration of my phone."

"You answered the phone at that speed?" Joe looked toward the sky. "Jesus, Ry."

"I know. I...wasn't in my right mind." I still wasn't. I might never be in my right mind again.

"Ryan, think," Talon said. "How long have you been out here? When did you leave?"

"I saw Wendy. Then I got home."

"And?"

"I went on a drive."

"Shit. You've been gone since yesterday. Did you spend the night out here?"

I had no idea. My head hurt like a mother. Had I spent the night out here?

"He's been out here all night," Joe said. "Look at him."

"You're lucky you didn't freeze to death," Talon said. "This time of year, the temperature can go either way. It was mild last night."

Sweat emerged on my brow, yet I shivered. I looked from Joe's face to Talon's, to Joe's again. Hair, jawline, eyes...so like my own.

Blurry. So blurry.

Then, blackness.

★ ★ ★

I opened my eyes, my body jiggling.

"What the fuck?"

"He's awake," Talon said from the front seat.

I was in the back seat of Joe's pickup.

"You okay?" Talon said.

"What's going on?"

"You passed out. We're taking you to the hospital."

"I don't need a hospital."

"The hell you don't," Joe said in his classic big brother voice. "You've probably got a concussion."

"I don't need a doctor to tell me that."

"You need treatment, Ry. So shut up. We're almost there."

"I'm fine. I'm not sick to my stomach."

"You passed out." Joe pulled the truck to a stop. "We're here."

★ ★ ★

A few hours of paperwork later, I was set up in a hospital room.

"We'll need to keep you overnight for observation," a doctor had said.

I'd told him he was full of shit, but my brothers had wrangled me into the room. Now I lay in bed in a hospital gown, my ass hanging out, eating Salisbury steak and Jell-O. I was surprised at how hungry I was, though in reality I hadn't eaten in over twenty-four hours. I'd actually spent the night passed out in the middle of nowhere. As Talon had said, luckily it had been mild weather.

My brothers—*half*brothers—had gone out to get me some real food and a new cell phone. I slurped another spoonful of lime Jell-O—yum...nothing like artificial flavoring and coloring—and then looked up at the doorway to my room.

Pure beauty greeted me.

CHAPTER THREE

Ruby

Even in a hospital gown, his hair a mess, holding a spoonful of green glop to his lips, Ryan Steel was still the most gorgeous man on the planet. He looked up at me, his eyes wide.

"Hi," I said.

"Hey," he said.

I walked swiftly to his side. "Are you all right? Melanie called me."

"I'm okay. Just a little concussion."

I took the spoon he was still holding and set it on the tray. "What were you thinking? Taking your car out and going completely nuts. You promised me you wouldn't do anything stupid."

"I didn't—"

"Uh-uh." I placed two fingers over his lips. "You scared the shit out of all of us. You don't get to talk yet."

"Ruby, I—"

"What the hell did I just say?" I'd had a hell of a night, dealing with my phone call from dear old Daddy, and I wasn't about to let Ryan off the hook. "I know you've been through a huge turning point in your life, but that doesn't change how the rest of us feel about you. Your brothers and sister and sisters-in-law were scared out of their minds when they couldn't find you this morning. And when Melanie called me..." I broke off, tears choking me.

I gulped them down. Ryan didn't need to see me like that. He didn't deserve to see me like that after the stunt he'd pulled.

"I'm fine," he said.

"I hate to break it to you, but 'fine' people aren't usually lying in the hospital."

"Doctors are overly cautious. They don't want to get sued by the Steels."

"Oh, for God's sake, Ryan!" I stood and paced around the sterile room. "The doctor was right. I talked to Melanie, and she agreed with his assessment. In case you've forgotten, she's also a doctor."

"I don't want to argue with you, Ruby."

"Fine. Then don't."

He paused and then picked up the spoon, swallowing the Jell-O and hovering the utensil over the plate. "About yesterday..."

"What about it?"

"I'm sorry I was so..." He sighed.

"Like I told you. I don't do anything I don't want to do. No apologies, Ryan. No regrets."

"But I do regret how I—"

I shut him up, this time by pressing a light kiss to his lips. "Enough."

Jonah and Talon walked quietly through the doorway.

"Food's here," Jonah said. "Oh, hey, Ruby."

"Hi."

"Hungry?" Talon asked. "We brought enough to feed an army."

"I'm hungry enough to eat that much," Ryan said. "The

gray meat and Jell-O isn't cutting it."

I couldn't help smiling. This was Ryan being...Ryan. The Ryan I had come to know was, until recently, always jovial. Always smiling, despite the tragedies that had befallen his family.

I inhaled. Garlic and basil. Italian. My mouth watered. But I didn't want to interrupt their brother time. "I'll be going."

"No," Ryan said. "Please stay."

"I don't want to intrude."

"If you feel like you're intruding, I'll boot these two out," he said.

My cheeks warmed. He'd rather be with me than his brothers? Maybe he had truly forgiven me for my part in the DNA test.

Jonah and Talon exchanged a glance.

"We'll go," Jonah said, "but only if Ruby promises she'll see that you stay put until you're released tomorrow."

Way to put me on the spot. I opened my mouth, but no words came out. Ryan had asked me to stay, but it sounded like his brothers wanted me to spend the night here. I was pretty sure that wasn't what Ryan had meant. Besides, I had work the next day.

"Give me a break, guys," Ryan said. "I'm staying put, okay? Give me a little credit."

"Glad you're feeling better, Ry." Jonah looked to me and then pulled a phone out of his pocket. "Here's your new cell. It's all activated." He tossed it to Ryan.

Ryan caught it easily. "Thanks, man."

"I guess we're off then," Talon said and then looked to me. "He's all yours."

How I wished that were true. I was in love with Ryan

Steel. Of course I hadn't told him that, and until I had an inkling of how he felt about me and my part in his DNA test, I wasn't going to.

"Tell Melanie I said hi," I said to Jonah.

"Will do." He and Talon left.

I turned to Ryan. "Let's see what they brought you." I opened the bag of takeout and took out a container and opened it. "Yum. Spaghetti Bolognese. Want some?"

"I do, actually."

"Okay." I picked up the plate that had the remnants of his hospital food, took it into his bathroom, and rinsed and dried it off. I returned and filled it with spaghetti and a slice of garlic bread. "Eat up."

"Aren't you going to join me?"

"I hadn't thought about it." The guys had brought plenty of food. "There isn't another plate."

"You can use this one," he said. "I'll eat out of the container."

I smiled. Offering me his plate was kind of chivalrous. I wasn't used to chivalry. "That's okay. Go ahead and eat. I'll just take a few bites."

I grabbed a plastic fork out of the bag and took a few bites of the spaghetti. Spicy and delicious. And it kept me from having to talk for a couple of minutes.

I'd promised myself I wouldn't pester him about our relationship out of respect to everything else he was going through. Not that I would anyway. I'd never had a relationship with a man before. This was all new to me, and I certainly didn't relish the idea of talking to him about whatever this was between us.

He continued eating, and the silence became deafening.

I took another bite of spaghetti just to have something to do.

"I didn't tell my brothers yet."

Ryan's words startled me. I swallowed my mouthful of food and looked up. "Tell them what?"

"About my father. Your father. What they were into."

Right. Wendy Madigan had confirmed my human trafficking theory, and it had made me sick to my stomach. Ryan hadn't had such a theory, so I could only imagine how the new knowledge affected him. Still, we had no proof his father was actually involved in it. My father, however, definitely was.

"I don't blame you. It's not really a topic for everyday conversation. Especially not when you have a concussion."

"I'm sorry," he said.

"About what?"

"That your father is... Hell, I don't know."

"It is what it is," I said matter-of-factly. "If I could change my DNA, I would. But I can't." *Jesus, Ruby. Did you really just say that?* "I'm sorry about the DNA comment. I wasn't thinking."

He shook his head. "I have to accept it. Believe me, I'd change my DNA if I could too. I hate that Wendy Madigan is my biological mother. I guess we both come from psychopaths. And for all I know, I come from two of them."

"Focus on the good memories of your father, Ryan," I said.

I didn't have any good memories of my own father, but when I needed some solace, I thought about my mother, Diamond Thornbush. Yes, that was really her name. She might not have won mother of the year, but she had done the best she could, and I never doubted her love for me.

"He called me."

"Who?"

"My father."

I jolted, nearly spilling the Styrofoam container of spaghetti all over my lap. "What?"

"I know. He's supposed to be dead. But Wendy said he's alive."

"Wendy's crazy."

"True enough. Still, someone claiming to be my father called me."

"Did you tell your brothers?"

"Yeah. They think it was a hoax. But they also don't know that Wendy told me he's alive."

"Did you check out the number?"

"I couldn't. My cell phone went over a cliff, along with my car."

Melanie had told me as much as she knew. None of us were exactly sure what happened, and Ryan couldn't tell us because of a few minutes of retrograde amnesia. I stared at him, and gratitude warmed my body. He could have easily gone over the cliff with his car and phone, but he hadn't. Whatever had happened, I was beyond thankful that he was here. Alive.

"My brothers didn't ask much about it," Ryan continued. "They started asking why I had answered the phone when I was going so fast—"

"Excuse me? Exactly how fast were you going, Ryan?"

"About one sixty when I picked up the phone. One twenty when I looked again."

My heart nearly stopped. What if... Nope. Couldn't go there. He was here. Safe. Concussed, but safe. I wouldn't be a nag. That wasn't what he needed right now.

"Okay." I breathed out slowly, calming my urge to give him hell. "What happened?"

"I got a phone call. A voice said, 'Ryan, this is your father.'"

My blood turned to ice in my veins.

Ruby, this is your father.

How had our fathers—if it was actually Ryan's father who called him—said the exact same thing at nearly the exact same time? This was too eerie. For a moment, my mind hurtled to the impossible. Perhaps my father and Ryan's had been together somehow, both deciding to make a phone call...

No. That was too outrageous.

Though they *were* both members of the future lawmakers club at the private preparatory high school they attended, and Brad Steel had backed my father's "business," for lack of a better word. I had no evidence that he'd continued backing it when my father, along with Tom Simpson and Larry Wade, turned to crime, though.

"Ryan," I said, "I think we need to go on the assumption that Wendy was telling the truth, and that your father may be alive."

"But so much that has come out of her mouth has been complete fabrication."

"Not the most important thing. You *are* her son." I hated sounding so blasé about it, but why beat around the bush at this point? We both knew the truth. We both knew my part in finding the truth. Ryan would eventually have to deal with all of that.

"Don't remind me."

"It doesn't change who you are, Ryan. You're *still* Ryan Steel."

"Only because my father is still my father."

"Yes. You have the same father as Joe, Talon, and Marj. You all share that. That's huge."

He grunted.

"And something else."

"Now what?"

"Wendy might be completely off her rocker, but two things are crystal clear. One, she loves you. In her warped mind, everything she's done has been for you."

He scoffed. "Whatever. What's the other thing?"

"She also loves your father. She'd do anything for him. Including helping him fake his death if he asked her to."

CHAPTER FOUR

Ryan

Ruby was talking like a cop. Well, she *was* a cop. What did I expect? My head no longer hurt, thanks to the drugs pumping into me, but it was still fuzzy, and I wasn't sure I was ready to face what might be my new reality.

My father might be alive.

My father might be involved in some truly heinous stuff.

My father might have faked his own death.

Or...my father might have been *forced* to fake his own death.

That made more sense to me. Everything I knew about Brad Steel negated him faking his own death unless someone or something had made him do it.

I closed my eyes, urging my mind to work. Things were still hazy, but I thought about what Joe had told me from his time being held prisoner by Wendy when she delusionally thought he was our father.

Mathias had shown up, and he'd seemed annoyed with Wendy and her antics, yet he hadn't harmed her even though he'd threatened to. He had demanded what was due him—our father's money. He'd claimed that the Steels had ruined his life, and then he'd said something about our father's will. Simpson had shown up, said their beef was never with us. It was with our father. Then *he* mentioned the will, said they'd made sure there were no loopholes...and one of them said they knew the consequences if they harmed Joe...

That's all I could recall. I'd have to pick Joe's brain when my own was working better.

We'd have to search for my father's will. None of us had actually seen it. It had been read to us by an attorney after our father's death.

Our father's death...

Had Wendy been telling the truth? Was my father alive? And had she helped him fake his death?

Why would he fake his death? Unless...

He did it to protect his children.

"What's churning in that mind of yours?" Ruby asked. "You've been quiet for a while."

The pulse in my throat thumped. "Wendy. My...mother." God, that was still so hard to say.

"What about her?"

"You said she'd do anything for my father, including helping him fake his own death if he asked her to."

"Yeah. Do you think that might have happened?"

"A couple months ago, I'd have said 'no way.' But now..." I breathed out. "Now, I just don't know. I don't know who the hell the man who fathered me actually *was*."

"Consider yourself lucky," she said.

True. She knew who her father was and what he was capable of. He was a monster. But at least she *knew*.

"I'm not discounting what you're saying, Ruby," I said seriously. "I get what your father is. Oh, hell." I raked my fingers through my hair. "I don't even know who *I* am anymore."

"You're Ryan Steel."

"But who *is* Ryan Steel?"

"He's the man he's always been. The man I..." She smiled. "Knowledge—and that's all this is, knowledge about your mother and your father—doesn't change your soul."

I looked at Ruby, her pretty red lips, her rosy cheeks.

All this was big. Huge. And in the midst of it, all I wanted was to lick the smudge of spaghetti sauce off of Ruby's chin.

She was dressed in her normal uniform of white cotton shirt and khaki Dockers. Her hair was pulled back in its tight bun. No makeup graced her face. Classic Ruby.

But I'd seen her in all her glory—walking down the aisle in a light blue sundress with an orchid in her hair, barefoot on the beach in a miniskirt and tank top, and—the best—naked, moonlight streaming over her tight body, her rosy breasts bouncing as we made love.

Made love.

I loved this woman—this woman who had no idea how beautiful she was. Or who did...and hid it for self-protection.

"Take your hair down, baby," I said.

She widened her eyes. "I was in the middle of a sentence."

Had she been? Right, we were talking about my father possibly being alive. Then I'd started thinking about Ruby naked.

"I'm sorry."

"Once you're feeling better, we'll check your phone records and get the number of whoever called you. We'll get to the bottom of this, Ryan. I promise you."

Ruby didn't make promises on a whim. I knew that much about her. She meant to solve this puzzle. After all, she was as involved in it as the rest of us were.

"You want to know something really weird?"

I smiled. "Always."

"My father called me yesterday too."

CHAPTER FIVE

Ruby

He bumped his tray, nearly upending the glass of water he was drinking with the spaghetti. "What? Are you okay?"

"I'm fine. You'll never guess what he wanted."

"What's that?"

"He told me to 'call off the Steels.'"

Ryan scoffed. "Or what?"

I knew one thing. My father didn't make warnings for the hell of it. He wouldn't harm me. He'd consider it offensive. It was okay to rape me, but now that I was grown and a cop? He had a strange desire to see me succeed, which was directly contradictory to him succeeding. That was my theory, at least. With the power he seemed to possess, he could have taken me out long ago.

However, he *could* harm the Steels. He'd have no qualms about that.

That wasn't happening on my watch.

"My father doesn't make empty threats."

"Joe said something about when Wendy was holding him captive—that either Mathias or Simpson, I can't remember which, said they knew the consequences if they harmed Joe. That could have been a lie of course. Are you telling me we should back off?"

"I would never tell you that. Even if I did, you and your brothers would never back off."

His shoulders slumped slightly. "Ruby, *I* might."

I stared at him, my eyes wide. Had I heard him right? That didn't sound at all like the Ryan Steel I knew. And loved. "What?"

He sighed. "I might. I love my brothers and my sister, but they lied to me." He cleared his throat. "*You* lied to me too."

I had known that would come up eventually. "I didn't lie, Ryan."

"Fine. Semantics. You omitted. Then you gave my hair to my sister for a DNA test."

"We've been through that."

He sighed again. "I know. The least you could have done is fought me on it. But no. You did the cop thing. You admitted your wrongdoing and stepped up to take the consequences."

I braced myself. "So what are the consequences?"

"I don't know. I just don't know." He looked me straight in the eyes. "I don't know if I can trust you."

I gulped, my heart pounding. "You can trust me, Ryan. I swear it."

"I'd like to be able to."

"Then do. I won't let you down." I put the container of food on a nearby table and went to him, cupping his cheeks, staring into his sad but beautiful brown eyes.

"I want to. I want...a lot of things from you."

I had no idea what he was getting at. I loved him with all my heart, but I wasn't sure someone as amazing as Ryan Steel could ever love me.

"Anything. What do you need?"

He smiled. "First, you can tell your psycho father that the

Steels aren't going anywhere."

Good sign. I hadn't bought it when he said he might back off. He still considered himself a Steel. Of course he *was* one. He had the same father as the others. "He hung up before I could say anything, but my father isn't stupid. He knows I won't call you off, even if I could."

"Good." He winked. "I've got one hell of a boner right now, so next, you can climb on top of me."

I chilled. We were in the hospital where anyone could walk in. "Ryan, that's not going to happen."

"Why not?"

"You're recovering from a concussion, for one. And we're in a public place."

"No more public than when we were on a nude beach."

"Oh my God..."

"And this is a private room. I'll bet there's a lock on the door."

I looked toward the door. There *was* a lock. Still...this wasn't happening.

Was it?

I was turned on already, just thinking about having Ryan again. "Why would you want to fuck someone you're not sure you trust?"

"Christ, Ruby. I can't help what you do to me. I can't help what I feel."

What do you feel? The question was on the tip of my tongue, but I couldn't bring forth the words. In all likelihood, he only meant that he was feeling something physical.

In truth, so was I.

I couldn't tell Ryan I loved him—I was too insecure, too frightened, to do that—but maybe I could *show* him. Besides, I had to make some use of the pink string flossing my butt. What had I been thinking, trying to wear a thong? It was so not me.

A seductress I was not, but Ryan had asked me earlier to take my hair down, so I slowly raised my hand to the knot at the back of my head and pulled out the two barrettes holding it in place. My nearly black hair tumbled in a sleek mass down my back and over my shoulders.

"Your hair is so beautiful," he said.

I warmed at his approval, turned, and walked to the door. It was already closed, so I simply pushed in the locking mechanism. Then I walked back to the bed.

Ryan's cock was tenting the sheet covering him.

I drew in a deep breath and touched the top button of my shirt.

CHAPTER SIX

Ryan

I was ready to cream myself. Ruby Lee, even in her masculine garb, brought me to my knees. I hadn't expected a striptease, but she seemed willing to give me one. Who was I to complain? Even in my still fuzzy mind, I wanted her beyond any desire I'd yet known.

Her fingers shook slightly. This wasn't something she was used to. Hell, she'd been a virgin before me. Yet just yesterday, she'd ripped the buttons off of her shirt. That had made me fucking crazy.

This time she was taking it slow, and as sexy as it was, I longed for her to rush through it, get naked, and sink down on me.

With each new inch of creamy skin she exposed, my cock grew bigger, harder.

How could I fight what I felt for her?

I loved her. I loved her devotion to her career, her determination to bring her own father—and one of my brother's tormenters—to justice. I loved her self-deprecation, her beauty that everyone but she herself could see.

But how could I feel love without trust?

The shirt went to the floor in a ripple of white cotton. Her full creamy breasts were bulging out of her bra, her nipples protruding through the lace.

Fuck. Trust was overrated.

At least it was in this moment. I wanted her, and I would have her. Now.

With one flick of her wrists, she tossed her bra to the floor with the shirt. Her toned abdomen was gorgeous. Her belly button so sexy. She'd be beautiful with a jewel hanging from it. Maybe I could talk her into one sometime... I wanted to lick that sweet dimple and then keep sliding downward to that succulent place between her legs.

She'd be wet for me. She always was.

Slowly she unbuckled her belt, unbuttoned her pants, slid them gently over her perfect hips.

Lace. Pink lace.

Ruby was wearing a thong.

I'd have bet my fortune she didn't own one. But fuck, I was glad she did.

She looked good enough to eat.

Eating probably wasn't going to happen. I was so fucking hard I needed her on me now.

When her pants fell around her ankles, she turned pink. "Oh."

Adorable. She'd forgotten her sensible shoes. She bent over, untied them, and then flipped them off. She'd screwed up her striptease, but I wasn't going to say anything. She was still beautiful and sexy, and this was no doubt her first striptease ever. Last time I checked, most virgins didn't do stripteases.

Once the shoes and pants were out of the way, she turned around and bent over.

Oh. My. God.

Her ass was so beautiful, red like her cheeks. She inserted

her thumbs in the waistband of the pink lace thong and slowly eased it over her hips.

I grabbed my cock through the sheet and tightened my fist around the base to keep from shooting. She turned around and kicked the thong to the side with the rest of her clothes, standing before me, her long hair curtaining the swell of her breasts, her hard red nipples poking through.

I ached to take my time with her. Kiss her, tug on her raspberry nipples, eat the sweet cream out of her pussy until she was begging me to stop... But not right now. Right now, I needed my cock inside of her hot cunt.

"Come here," I said, low and raspy.

She bent toward me, whisking the sheet away. Then she pushed the light blue hospital gown upward, baring me to her view.

She inhaled.

She'd seen me naked plenty of times. "What is it?"

"You're just so..." She sighed. "You're beautiful, Ryan."

I stared into her sparkling blue eyes. "Baby, you're what's beautiful in this room. Come here."

She looked toward the door timidly.

"No one will interrupt us," I assured her.

"How do you know?"

I didn't, but I'd be damned if we were stopping now. "Trust me."

Big words from someone who wasn't sure he trusted the person he was saying them to, let alone someone who couldn't guarantee a nurse wouldn't knock on the door. But right now, I was thinking with my other head. Big time.

"Please, baby. Sit on me. I need you."

She smiled timidly. "I...want to."

"Nothing stopping you," I groaned through clenched teeth.

She climbed onto the bed, straddling me. She grabbed my cock and rubbed the tip against the wet folds of her pussy. I closed my eyes and concentrated to keep from prematurely ending our escapade.

When she sank down on me, a soft moan escaping her throat, every nerve in my body screamed at me to plunge up into her, but I held still, let her get comfortable. I wanted her to take the lead. I wanted her to fuck me.

She pulled herself off of me, the beautiful muscles in her thighs tensing, stopping right before I was completely withdrawn. The suction of her opening and her silky, wet folds teased my cock head.

"Damn, baby."

She sank down upon me again. I reached forward, grabbing her hips, pulling her off of me again and then pushing her back down. I couldn't help but take charge. I wanted her so badly, and today, although I longed for her to lead, I needed her too badly to wait.

"Your breasts. Play with your nipples for me."

She closed her eyes, obeying, her alabaster hands cupping her round breasts, her thumbs drifting over her hard nipples. Her soft sigh met my ears.

"Does that feel good, baby?"

"Mmm hmm."

I pulled her off my cock again and then pushed her back down. My entire body shuddered, as if I were one big penis and nothing else. My balls tightened, and the base of my cock started sizzling. I was going to come.

I was going to come now.

I lifted her up once more and pushed her down hard upon my cock, gritting my teeth.

The tiny spasms started at the base, flowing out of my cock and into Ruby.

At the same time, her pussy clamped around me, and she bit her bottom lip.

"Ruby, God." The orgasm erupted through me. It was a different sensation, perhaps because I was recovering from a concussion. I didn't know. I knew only that it was rapturous, complete nirvana coming inside this woman.

I held her onto my cock as long as I could, until both of our orgasms quieted. I didn't want to let her go. I looked up at her, into her beautiful blue eyes, her bottom lip now swollen from when she bit down, probably to keep from screaming. At her lovely breasts now flushed pink, her nipples red from her own attention.

I didn't ever want to let her go.

I opened my mouth to speak, not knowing what I was going to say, when a knock interrupted me.

Ruby gasped, quickly moving off of me and off the bed. She grabbed her clothes and then ran to the bathroom.

I covered myself quickly. "Yeah? Come on in."

"The door's locked."

Shit. "Okay. Sorry." Ruby was in the bathroom, so I got up, trying to keep my gown closed in the back, walked to the door, and opened it.

My neurologist stood there. "Just here for my evening rounds, Mr. Steel."

"Yeah, of course. Come on in." I wasn't about to explain to him why the door had been locked. I got back into my bed.

"So how are you feeling?" the doctor asked.

"Good."

"Been eating, I see." He eyed the takeout bag from Papa Tony's. "That's good. Any nausea?"

"Nope. It's all staying down."

"Good. Good sign. I don't see why you can't get out of here tomorrow morning."

"Any possibility of getting out of here tonight, Doc?"

"Sorry. I'd rather have you stay. After all, you were out cold for about twelve hours overnight last night. You're lucky you don't have any signs of hypothermia."

Ruby walked out of the bathroom fully dressed, her cheeks blazing red. She looked to the doctor. "Oh, hello."

"Dr. Anderson, this is my friend Ruby Lee."

"Nice to meet you," Ruby said shyly. "How is he doing?"

"He's doing great," Dr. Anderson said.

"Glad to hear that," Ruby said. "Ryan, I should get going. I know your brothers wanted me to stay but..."

I eyed her feet clad only in socks. "I understand. You probably don't want to leave your shoes."

If possible, she became even more scarlet. I had to stop myself from chuckling. She had put on her androgynous clothing, but her hair still fell around her face and shoulders like a sheet of smooth ebony silk. She wore a beautiful "just fucked" look.

She hastily put on her shoes and grabbed her small handbag. "I'm glad you're doing well, Ryan."

"I'm getting out of here tomorrow. I'll call you."

She nodded and left the room.

"She looks familiar to me," Dr. Anderson said. "I wonder where I've seen her before."

"She's a detective with the Grand Junction PD. She's

probably been in here questioning people."

"That could be." He stroked his cheek thoughtfully. "Yes, that's probably it." He made a few notations on my chart. "The nurse will be in to check your vitals in a few minutes. Be sure to keep that door unlocked, Mr. Steel." He smirked.

No reason to lock it now. Ruby wouldn't be back.

★ ★ ★

Dr. Anderson had given me my walking papers early, during his morning rounds. Talon was due to drive me home in an hour. I didn't feel like sitting around the hospital, so I walked over to a little dive café.

An old man in a flannel shirt sat a few stools down, nursing a cup of coffee. He turned and looked at me strangely.

"You have a problem?" I said.

He shook his head and took the seat next to me. "No problem. You just look familiar to me. Have we met?"

"I don't think so."

He put out his hand. "Name's Mike."

"Ryan Steel."

"Steel. That's why you look so familiar. You're one of them Steel brothers, aren't you?"

"Guilty." Sort of. We were *almost* brothers.

"I've met your brothers. Nice guys."

"Yeah." I had to stop myself from rolling my eyes. "Nice guys."

A bleached-blond waitress in a pink uniform sidled up. "What'll it be?"

"What he's having." I pointed to Mike's coffee. "And two eggs over easy, slice of bacon."

The waitress filled a coffee cup and set it in front of me.

"How are your brothers doing?" Mike asked.

"They're good. Both married now."

"You don't say!" A grin split Mike's wrinkled face. "That's great! They deserve happiness."

Just how much did this guy know about my brothers? I took a swig of coffee—might as well have been water with brown food coloring—and raised my eyebrows. "Do they?"

"I'd think you'd be happy for them."

I sighed. "I am. And you're right. They deserve it. They've been through a lot." I took another drink.

"So why don't you seem all that happy for them?"

I wasn't about to tell a perfect stranger the details of my DNA. "Just got a lot on my mind."

Mike rubbed at his chin. "You may not believe this, but I talked to both of your brothers when they were kind of down in the mouth."

"How the hell is that possible?"

"They both stumbled in to a little dive where I hang out sometimes. Makes this place look like the Ritz."

I looked around. If it made this shithole look like the Ritz, it must be something akin to an old latrine. "You don't say."

"I do say."

"Why the hell would my brothers go into a dive?"

"I asked them that. First thing I noticed was their expensive ostrich cowboy boots."

I looked down at my own feet...shod in expensive ostrich cowboy boots. "I suppose we seem pretty pretentious to a guy like you."

"A guy like me?"

I sighed. "Sorry. I didn't mean any offense."

"None taken. I've worked hard all my life. Never took a handout. And I make ends meet now, in retirement. I just miss my wife. She passed on some time ago."

"Oh. I'm sorry to hear that."

"Yeah. But we all got to go sometime, I guess." He motioned to the waitress. "More coffee please."

"It's on me," I said.

"Thanks. You Steels are generous."

Generous? A shitty cup of coffee might set me back a couple of bucks. That was hardly generous.

"By the way," he continued. "I don't consider you pretentious. I don't judge people. Hell, I'd wear boots like that if I could afford them."

I looked down at my boots once more. These were my work boots. They were nearly trashed. I'd hate for him to see the six other pairs sitting in my walk-in closet.

"You live around here?" I asked.

"Not too far. The place I used to go—where I met your brothers—closed up last week. Some problem with their liquor license. It was a nice little bar and grill when I was younger, though that was some thirty years ago. Things change. Places change."

"And people change," I added.

"Yep, they do." He took a drink from the steaming coffee the waitress had just filled. "Thanks for this, by the way."

"No problem. What brings you to this place?"

"I'm seeing my doc over at the hospital for some routine stuff this morning, so I stumbled in here to wait. The bus only runs up here early in the morning, so I've got some time before my appointment."

"Everything all right?"

"Yeah. Just routine stuff, like I said." He took a drink and smiled. "Your brother with the funny name—Talon, I think—sent me a case of amazing bourbon called Peach Street."

That piqued my interest. "Yeah? That's his favorite." If Talon had sent this old man a case of Peach Street, the guy had done something spectacular to earn it.

"It's great stuff. So smooth. And the aroma." Mike closed his eyes and inhaled. "Something special. I'm saving it. I only have a jigger every couple of days, as a treat." He sighed. "I'm going to miss that old dive bar. Truth is, I get lonely. I like to get out, see people. Now that I'm retired and Melanie is gone, I don't have a lot of human contact."

"Melanie? Joe's wife's name is Melanie."

"No kidding? He mentioned he knew a woman named Melanie, but I didn't know she was someone special to him."

"Yeah. She's a psychotherapist. They just got married in Jamaica."

"Good for him. And Talon?"

"He got married at the same time. Her name is Jade."

"He told me he had a special lady in his life."

Again, I wondered who the hell this man was and how he somehow had my brothers' confidence.

"What about you?" Mike asked. "Any special lady in your life?"

Yeah. One I wasn't sure I could trust anymore. Just like I wasn't sure I could trust my brothers. I didn't respond.

"What's her name?" Mike asked.

"I didn't say there was one."

He laughed. "You didn't. But you would have said 'no' if there wasn't. I've been around the block enough times to know that. What's her name, son?"

I smiled. I was beginning to see why my brothers had talked to this man. "Ruby. Ruby Lee."

"That's a pretty name."

"Yeah. It is."

"You're a good-looking fellow, even better looking than your brothers, I'd say, though don't tell them I said that."

I'd heard that so many times it went in one ear and out the other. Ryan Steel was the handsomest Steel with the best personality. Who'd have thought that Brad Steel and Wendy Madigan could create a more handsome person than Brad and Daphne Steel? Genetics made no sense sometimes.

Mike continued, "So I bet she's tall, blond, and beautiful."

I chuckled. "Well, she's beautiful."

"I got the other two wrong?"

"She's not short, but my sister is six feet, so most women don't seem tall to me. As for the blond? She's about as far away from blond as you can get. Her hair is nearly black."

"Still, she's probably a model, right?"

Again, I chuckled. "She's a cop. A detective, actually."

"A working girl, huh? My Melanie never worked. But we were from a different time."

Actually, I couldn't imagine Ruby—or Jade or Melanie, for that matter—ever staying home. "True."

"Glad your brothers are happy."

I smiled tersely.

"What's your beef with your brothers, son?" Mike asked.

"No beef."

"Bullshit. You've tensed up every time I've mentioned them."

Damn. Did this man know everything about my life?

"No beef," I said again. "Except that they're not my

brothers."

"You'll never convince me of that. There's a huge resemblance."

"Yeah, we all look like our father."

"Must have been a good-looking man."

I took a sip of bad coffee. Thankfully he didn't push the "they're not my brothers" comment.

"I had a brother once," Mike went on. "We had a falling out a couple decades ago. Never spoke again. Mort died a month after Melanie. She always wanted me to make up with him, but I was too stubborn. I'll always regret that. We were really close as kids."

"I'm sorry." My heart went out to the guy.

"Thing is, we weren't even brothers in the biological sense. He was my stepbrother. My real father died in the war when my mother was pregnant with me. I wasn't yet two when she married my father. My true father. The man who raised me. Mort was *his* son. His first wife had died in childbirth. Mort and I were nearly the same age, and people always thought we were twins." He gazed wistfully at the ketchup bottle in front of him. "I miss him."

A brick hit my gut. "You considered him your brother?"

"Well, he *was*. My father adopted me, and my mother adopted Mort. We were brothers in the legal sense."

"But you didn't share a bloodline."

"Hell, what's blood got to do with it? I don't have any childhood memories that don't include my father and Mort. We *were* brothers. I wish..." He stared into space again.

"Mike, I don't want to pry, but what was the fight about? When you and Mort stopped speaking?"

"I can't talk about it. I'm sorry. It just hurts too much."

My phone buzzed. Talon was waiting outside. I laid two hundreds on the bar and pushed them toward Mike. "That's all right. Thanks, Mike. Eat my breakfast, will you? Give the waitress a nice tip, and keep the rest."

"You Steels are generous," he said. "God bless."

"Back at you." I left the bar and spied Talon's truck across the street. I ambled over and got in the passenger side.

I looked at my brother. Same old Tal. Wavy dark hair that he wore too long, a slight crook in his nose from where he had broken it long ago. Talon was my hero.

I closed my eyes.

★ ★ ★

Talon and I had been walking for about an hour, looking for clues. Talon wanted to find out what had happened to his friend Luke Walker, Bryce's cousin. I wasn't that concerned about Luke. I just wanted to tag along with Talon. I always followed him. Joe thought I was a pest and didn't want me around much. But Talon... Talon always made time for me.

Our tummies were full. Mrs. Walker had given us oatmeal cookies and watermelon when we showed up at her door. "Y'all can look around if you want to," she'd said. Her eyes were recessed and sad. "Just come back before dark. Do your mom and dad know you're here?"

Talon had nodded and nudged me so I wouldn't talk. It was a lie. Mom and Dad didn't know where we were, but Joe did. He'd tell them when he got home from school.

"This is where they found the mask," Talon said, looking around.

I wasn't sure how he knew, but he was a lot older than I was.

I was only seven, but Talon was ten. Almost a grown-up.

Nothing was visible. Even the Walkers' house had faded from view this far out. The cattle must not have grazed in this area, because the grass was tall. It brushed our knees.

In the distance stood a little shack.

"Let's go check out that building," Talon said.

I nodded. I'd do whatever he said. We traipsed forward.

The wood was gray and splintered, old. Talon reached out to touch the knotty surface, when—

Something grabbed me. "Talon! Auuuughh!" A large gloved hand clamped over my mouth.

A man dressed all in black, even his face, stood between me and Talon. My heart tried to pound out of my chest. I had to pee so bad.

But Talon was there. He wouldn't let anyone hurt me.

"You leave my brother alone!" Talon shouted.

The other pair of hands lunged toward Talon, but before they could grab him, Talon ran into the man holding me, kicking at his shins. "Let go! Let go! Let go!"

The other man had grabbed the back of Talon's shirt. Still, Talon kicked.

I closed my eyes, brittle fear taking over my body. A kick. Then a fist. Pain lanced through my body. I struggled against the hands gripping me, but I was too little, too weak. Couldn't get away.

Talon gasped and grunted, until a cry of "Motherfucker!" came from behind me and I fell to my knees in the dirt. Somehow Talon had gotten the hands to let go of me.

"Run!" Talon yelled. "Run back to the house! Get Dad! Run, run, run!"

I stood, dazed, immobile. I wasn't going to leave my big

brother.

"Damn it, I said run!"

One of the men shoved Talon to the ground.

"Run!" he kept yelling. "Damn it, Ryan. Run!"

I turned.

I ran.

★ ★ ★

My brother had saved my life that day. Saved me from the torturous fate he'd endured for two months, a fate I was certain I wouldn't have survived. Talon had been three years older, three years tougher. He'd been starved, beaten, raped...and he'd gotten out alive.

I owed him my life.

I had since I was seven years old.

Now I wondered if I knew my brother—*half* brother—at all.

We drove up to the guesthouse where I lived, and I got out of his truck. "You can go," I said to him.

"Nah. I'm coming in. I want to make sure you're all right. You sure you don't want to stay at the house with Jade and me tonight?"

He'd already asked me that three times, and I'd said no three times. I was sick and tired of repeating myself.

"Ry, you're just not yourself," he said as I opened the door.

My golden retriever, Ricky, greeted me with licks and pants. I tousled the soft hair on his neck. "Hey, boy. I missed you."

Talon followed me in. Clearly he wasn't ready to leave quite yet, even though I'd made it clear I wanted to be alone.

"How about a drink?" he said. Then, "Never mind. You probably shouldn't have any alcohol. We'll just have some iced tea." He headed to the kitchen and opened my refrigerator.

Normally that wouldn't have bothered me. We brothers always helped ourselves to each other's food and booze. Today, though, I found it irksome.

I no longer thought of him as my brother. My full blood brother. And I wanted to be alone.

Talon poured two glasses of iced tea and carried them into my family room where he set them on the coffee table and then sat down in one of my leather recliners. "It's time to talk this out, Ry."

CHAPTER SEVEN

Ruby

I walked into work with my hair in a high ponytail. I still wore the same white button-down shirt and Dockers, black today, but I'd never gone to work with my hair any way except up in the tight bun that sometimes hurt my head.

Wearing my hair down had occurred to me, but my hair was so long, and it would get in my way as I did my work. Besides...baby steps. A ponytail was the next logical step after a tight bun. No one would notice anyway.

Boy, had I been wrong. Eight people—yes, I counted—mentioned my hairstyle change before ten in the morning. I might as well have gone into work wearing a hula skirt for all the fuss they made.

Ruby, your hair looks great!

Nice change, Detective Lee.

You look amazing with a ponytail!

Could have knocked me over with a feather.

By ten I hadn't heard from Ryan, so I called the hospital and found out he had been discharged earlier. He'd said he would call me...

No. I was not going to be that woman—that woman who waits on the edge of her seat for her man to call.

I had work to do.

My phone buzzed, and I picked it up. "Detective Lee."

"Ms. Lee?"

The voice was female...and familiar.

My pulse quickened. "Shayna?"

"Yeah. It's me. I'm sorry about the other day."

"Shayna, it's fine. Don't worry about it. Did someone threaten you?"

"I'm at a pay phone. I can't talk long."

"I understand. Can you answer my question?"

"I got a phone call." Her voice shook. "A man said I shouldn't talk to you. To anyone, really, but specifically to you."

I wouldn't bother asking her who the man was. She wouldn't know, and I had my own suspicions. "Has there been any news on Lisa and Juliet?" I asked.

"Nothing. It's so terrible. Their parents are beside themselves. I'm so worried that they're...*dead.*"

I had the same worry, and in a way, if they weren't dead, their fate might be worse. "I know. I'm so sorry. I'm going to do all I can to find them."

I hoped I hadn't just made an empty promise. Juliet and Lisa had been taken from a resort in Jamaica, most likely to be sold into slavery. I had no ties to the Jamaican authorities and no way to get information. I only knew what my intuition and instinct told me.

My father was somehow involved in this.

"You don't have to call me again if you don't think it's safe," I told Shayna. "I understand."

"No. I want to communicate with you. I had to block you on my cell phone. I think"—she cleared her throat—"my phone is tapped."

"That wouldn't surprise me. What kind of evidence do

you have?"

"Just a...feeling."

Shayna had just lost her two best friends, and her mind could be playing tricks on her. But I knew better than to tell her not to trust her intuition. "If you truly think someone is following you, tapping your phone, you need to call the police. Screw that. Go straight to the FBI. Call me from a pay phone if you need to until we figure out a better way to communicate. I'm here for you. And Shayna..."

"Yeah?"

"Take care of yourself. This isn't your fault."

"I know. I mean, yeah. I know."

I knew exactly what she meant. It wasn't her fault, but she still felt responsible. She hadn't been able to talk her friends out of going with their kidnappers, just like I hadn't been able to talk them out of going.

"Thanks, Ms. Lee."

"Call me Ruby. I'll be in touch. Somehow."

"Okay. Bye." She ended the call.

Shayna had reluctantly gone along with her two friends in Jamaica and then jumped off her Jet Ski and nearly drowned. She'd been rescued by some other locals who returned her safely to the resort.

My phone buzzed again.

"Detective Lee."

"Don't talk to that girl again."

The same voice from two days ago. My father's voice. I'd recognize its ooze anywhere. I knew my phone wasn't tapped, which could mean only one thing. My father—or someone who worked for him—had witnessed Shayna's call to me.

"Two calls in a few days?" I said. "To what do I owe this

pleasure?" My father racked my nerves, but I was determined to play it cool with him. I had to if I was going to make him trip up.

"You heard me, Ruby."

"Listen, Theo. I don't hear from you in ages, and then all of a sudden you appear with your girlfriend a few months ago and want to see me. And now you call me. Twice. Seems like you're getting a little nervous. Now that Simpson and Wade are out of the picture, are you starting to feel a little worried about getting caught yourself?"

"I'm not falling into any of your amateur traps, girl," he said. "Just watch your step."

The line went dead.

Nausea crept up my throat. For all my confident words, I was still a wreck when it came to my father. Damned if I would let him know that, though. I initiated a trace on the number he'd called from, knowing it was futile. But...procedure. Then, just in case, I ran a check on my own phone. I was right. It hadn't been tapped.

My father was good. I'd give him that. I'd have brought him down a long time ago if he hadn't been. But he was getting nervous. He'd just made an irreversible error.

He'd proved that my hunch was correct.

He *was* involved in the disappearance of Juliet and Lisa. Why else would he care if I talked to Shayna? The capture of Wade and suicide of Simpson were getting to him. He was in this alone now, and sooner or later, he'd trip up.

Now, more than ever, I was all in.

I made a quick call to the LAPD and filled them in, hoping they'd give Shayna some protection. Then, knowing Shayna wouldn't, I called the FBI. They promised to look into the possibly illegal phone tapping, but I wasn't optimistic. This was small potatoes to them.

I longed to call Ryan and tell him I'd talked to Shayna and to my father, to tell him about my theories. But no. I'd leave him alone for now. He was still recovering from a concussion, after all, and even more than that, his entire world had recently been turned upside down. I had to let him deal with everything. Plus, I had a buttload of work to get done. The PD was of course overworked and understaffed, and I was still catching up from my vacation time in Jamaica.

Come tonight, though, if I hadn't heard from Ryan, I was driving to the ranch.

CHAPTER EIGHT

Ryan

"We've got nothing to talk about, Tal."

My brother—*half* bro— Oh, hell.

Talon shook his head. "The hell we don't. We've come this far. Two of those degenerates who raped me have been taken care of."

I couldn't help but notice how much easier the word "rape" left Talon's lips. He was truly healing. I was so proud of him, of his strength. And I felt like a self-absorbed little shit. Talon had been through so much—way more than finding out his mother wasn't who he thought she was. I closed my eyes as he continued.

"One's behind bars and the other is dead and buried. Only one is at large. We've come so far, Ry, but damn it, none of it is worth shit if it costs me my little brother."

There he sat, sipping iced tea—my strong, determined half brother.

And as long as I still considered him my *half* brother, I wasn't ready to talk.

Was it even my parentage I was grieving? Or was it the loss of trust in my siblings? In my woman? If she even was my woman.

"You should have told me about the DNA test."

He sighed and put his glass of tea back down on the table. "You're right. Jade and Melanie warned us."

"Why didn't you listen to them?"

"Because we truly thought the test would be negative. I did, at least. Joe wasn't so sure. But we figured if it did turn out to be negative, you'd never have to know and you wouldn't be hurt by it at all. We could spare you the worry."

"Spare me the worry? I'm a big boy. You think I've never dealt with worry? I've known worry since I was seven, the day you were taken."

I regretted the words as soon as they'd left my mouth. Again, Talon had been through so much more than I ever had, and he'd been the one who spared me the same fate. I owed him everything. I owed him my life.

Then it dawned on me what was so horrible about this whole thing. I was no longer the full brother of my hero, and that cut into me like a hunting blade slicing my innards into hash.

Nothing could be done. It was what it was. I was the son of Bradford Steel and Wendy Madigan. I was half brother to my siblings. Nothing more, nothing less.

They'd made it clear that they still thought of me as their full brother. I didn't doubt their sincerity. So why did I feel like less of a Steel?

I still had the right father to be a Steel. I just wasn't a *legitimate* Steel.

Yet I was, in the eyes of the law. Daphne Steel's name was on my birth certificate.

"It's all so twisted, Tal."

He nodded. "Agreed. But this doesn't have to be a big deal, Ry."

I widened my eyes, clenching my hands into fists. "Did you really just say that? I find out I have the DNA of a complete loony tune, and it's not a big deal?"

"You're right," he said. "I shouldn't belittle it. But you're in your thirties with no signs of mental illness. You're okay, Ryan. I promise."

"Easy for you to say."

"My mother wasn't exactly mentally fit either."

He had the truth of that. Both he and Jonah had inherited Daphne Steel's depression. I'd never been depressed a day in my life. "I understand that. I just don't want to wake up one day and find I've lost my grip on reality."

"You won't." He looked me straight in the eye. "I won't let you. I promise."

"You have no control over what my brain does. How can you make that promise?"

"How can I not? It's the same promise you made to me countless times when I was heading into darkness. You and Joe were the ones who convinced me to get help. You never turned your back on me, Ry, and I promise I'll never turn my back on you."

And again, what my brother had been through stabbed me in the heart. "Talon, I'm sorry."

"For what?"

"For everything. For what you went through."

"It's water under the bridge. I'm married to the love of my life, and I have the best therapist in the world as my sister-in-law. I'm doing okay. I also have the best little brother on the planet, and I don't want to lose him. You were always there for me. Now it's time for me to be here for you."

"I just wish..."

"We all do, Ry. We all do. But it honestly doesn't matter to Joe, Marj, and me. You're still our brother, just as you always have been. The only person this matters to is you."

"Of course it matters to me! It would matter to you if the situation were reversed."

"Yes, it would. I can't begin to know how you're feeling. But I'm still your brother. So is Joe. And Marj is still your sister. We're sorry that we violated your trust. We thought we were doing what was best. I wish we could take it back, but we can't. I understand you won't forgive us right away, but we're here for you, no matter what."

I can't begin to know how you're feeling.

Talon's words lanced through me.

No, he couldn't know how I was feeling, but I sure as hell couldn't even imagine the hell he'd been through and how it made him feel.

I sighed. Time to grow up. Time to forgive. "I do forgive you, Tal. I'm just not sure I can forget so easily."

"Bro, I get it. Forgetting is the hard part. It doesn't happen. But day by day, remembering gets a little easier."

He was talking about his abduction, the torture, the rapes. Again, I felt like a whiny-assed, snot-nosed kid. "You didn't have to forgive them."

"You're right. And I didn't. They don't deserve my forgiveness."

But my siblings *did* deserve mine. That's what he wasn't saying but what he meant. And he was right.

"No, they don't. But you deserve mine. I already said it. I forgive you for not telling me about the DNA test."

"And Joe and Marj?"

I nodded. "Yeah."

"And Ruby?"

That was a horse of a different color. "I don't know."

"You've got a good thing going, Ry. She kept it from you for the same reasons we did. To try to keep you from being hurt."

"I know. She's told me the whole story."

"I won't tell you what to do, and I don't expect you to forget all this overnight. But think about it. She's good for you, and you're good for her."

"We're both the progeny of nutcases. We at least have that in common." I let out a chuckle. Hell, I could laugh or I could cry.

"We all are, bro," Talon said. "This thing with Dad gets weirder by the minute. I still can't wrap my head around him financing those three. I've been over and over it in my mind, and something doesn't add up. He must have known who took me. He must have fucking *let* them."

"Not according to Larry. He still claims you were never meant to be taken."

"But according to Wendy..." Talon rubbed his chin.

"Which one is more mentally stable?" I laughed out loud. "Now that's a million-dollar question. But seriously, as far as we've been able to tell, Larry has never lost his grip on reality. Wendy has."

"True, but Larry also wasn't always in the confidence of Simpson and Mathias. He was more of a yes man, a follower. I'm not sure he always knew what was going on."

"Could be. He knew the truth about me, though. The one time I went to see him, he kept telling me I had my mother's nose. I didn't know what the hell he was talking about, since only Marj looks like Mom. Then, when I went to see Wendy, I saw it. I have her nose."

"But you'd seen Wendy many times before when we were kids, when Dad died."

"I know. But I wasn't looking for anything then. None of us were."

"True."

"I can't believe Dad—" *Dad. My father.* "Tal, do you think that call I got actually came from Dad?"

"No. I don't. I think it's Wendy playing with your head."

I nodded. "You're probably right. She's already proven that she can get her hands on cell phones while she's in psych lockup. But it wasn't her voice."

"So she got some male patient to make the call. She's smart, cunning. That's been apparent since we've known her."

"She gave me up."

"She did. For Dad. The one thing we know about Wendy is that she would have done anything for Dad. And I think that makes one thing abundantly clear."

"What's that?"

"Dad wanted you. He wanted you raised here, with us. And he paid Wendy handsomely to make sure that happened."

"Yeah. Doesn't make me feel any better, though."

"Why not?"

"Because apparently Dad is just as screwed up as the rest of these people." The grainy image of the future lawmakers club popped into my mind. I'd used a magnifying glass the last time I'd looked at it, and I'd noticed Dad and some of the others were wearing matching rings. I hadn't been able to make out the design on the ring, though.

"Yeah, he might have been." Talon stood. "Hey. Why don't we head over to my place and take a look through that shit in the crawl space? You know, the boxes where Jade and Marj found

Mom's real birth certificate. Maybe we'll find something. Like that ring."

"Dad never wore a ring. He probably got rid of it a long time ago."

"Then we'll have Bryce search for his father's. Come on. Maybe we'll find something else. It can't hurt."

I wasn't much in the mood to go riffling through my father's old shit, but sitting here feeling sorry for myself wasn't cutting it. Plus, I wanted to get a look at my father's will, if possible. "Okay. Let's go."

★ ★ ★

The boxes Jade and Marjorie had gone through months earlier were still sitting in the room. They were full of old documents and yielded nothing new. Talon and I crept into the crawl space and lugged out several more old cartons.

Upon opening them, we found more old documents. Chattel mortgages, deeds of trust... Man, our father never threw anything away.

"This isn't getting us anywhere," I said.

"Well, I'm not stopping until we get through every fucking box," Talon said.

I sighed. "All right. Let's keep digging." I opened another box and took out the first file folder.

And gasped.

"Tal!"

"What is it?"

I held up a document. "It's a quitclaim deed signing over the Shane ranch to the Steel Family Trust."

The Shane ranch was a small operation adjacent to

ours. I'd had a relationship with the owners' daughter, Anna Shane. They'd sold out quickly a couple years ago and moved to Hawaii. Though I'd attempted to get in touch with Anna a few times, she had never responded. We'd already ended our relationship amicably, so I figured she just didn't want to stay in touch.

When I first told Ruby about Anna and how she and her family had moved to Hawaii, Ruby had been skeptical about the whole thing. Now I wasn't sure what to think.

"We bought the Shane ranch?" Talon said.

"It appears so. Why would they transfer it with a quitclaim deed? Seems someone should have insisted on a warranty deed."

"Dad *would* have insisted on a warranty deed," Talon said. "How could we not know about this?"

"Quitclaim deeds are more often used for gifts," I said. "The Shanes wouldn't have just *given* us the ranch."

"No."

"Our accountants must have paid them off. With big money. That's why they went to Hawaii. I don't get it. Why would we buy this? The Shane property wasn't even worth that much."

"I have no clue. I'm beginning to think..." He shook his head. "Honestly, I don't know what to think."

That was the truth. We had a team of accountants and financial advisors who handled our fortune, which we kept in the Steel Trust. My siblings and I didn't bother ourselves too much with the day-to-day management of our money. We each took a sizeable draw and had more than enough to spend on whatever we wanted. Twice a year, we met with the team, and we'd never asked for an audit. This team had been highly respected and trusted by our father, so none of us had thought an audit necessary. But—

"The ranch was deeded to the Steel *Family* Trust. Not the Steel Trust. What the hell is the Steel Family Trust?"

Talon exhaled audibly. "I don't have a fucking clue. Apparently Dad created a separate trust for...something."

"We need to get an independent audit, Tal," I said. "This is ridiculous."

"Agreed. Our father obviously created a trust and never bothered telling any of us about it."

Our father...

Who the hell was he?

I began digging through the file.

And my heart nearly stopped when I found a handwritten note.

Brad, do whatever you have to do to keep that trailer trash away from my son.

CHAPTER NINE

Ruby

Well, Ryan, your time is up.

I pulled up to Ryan's house on Steel Acres Ranch. He hadn't called, and I was determined to make sure he was okay. I'd called his cell first, but he hadn't answered, so here I was, going after him like a bitch in heat.

That wasn't true, of course, but that's what this situation would look like from his angle. In truth, I was simply concerned. The last thing on my mind was sex.

I walked to his door and knocked.

Ricky ran to the window next to the door, wagging his tail.

"Hey, Rick," I said through the door.

When no one answered, I knocked again and rang the doorbell. After a few minutes, I tried the doorknob, and to my astonishment, it opened. It wasn't like Ryan to be so careless. My nerves lurched, and I drew my gun, just in case.

"Hey, there. Where's Ryan?" I petted Ricky's soft head and then let him out the back door to do his business.

I checked the bedroom and all the other rooms. Nothing suspicious. Unfortunately, Ryan was nowhere to be found either.

I jerked when my phone rang. "Detective Lee."

"Ruby, hi."

Ryan! "Where are you? I didn't recognize the number."

"I'm calling from Talon's landline. I left my phone at home."

"You also left your door unlocked."

"I did?"

"Yeah, you did. I'm here now. I let the dog out."

"Oh, thanks. What are you doing there?"

"Looking for you. I was worried. You said you'd call me today, and when you didn't, I feared the worst."

"I'm sorry, baby. I've been kind of stuck in my own head. Things are still a little fuzzy."

I could understand that, given recent events. "It's okay. I'm just glad you're all right."

"I'm fine. Talon and I have been doing some research, and I wanted to tell you that you were right about your hunch. About Anna Shane."

Anna Shane? I searched my memory. Right. Ryan's ex-girlfriend. "Oh?"

"We found some documents. Apparently my deranged mother didn't think Anna was good enough for me and got my father—or rather, the Steel Family Trust, which none of us knew existed—to purchase their ranch. I had no idea we owned the Shane ranch. None of us did."

"Wow. Interesting." My mind reeled. He'd said the Shanes moved only recently, which would have been after Brad Steel's death. Was Wendy Madigan somehow involved with the Steels' money?

"That's not all. It was conveyed by quitclaim deed so there wasn't any record of money exchanging hands. But they obviously got enough to relocate to Hawaii and live happily ever after."

If they were still alive. I hated the words as soon as I thought them.

And then I recalled some other words.

Stay the fuck away from my son, bitch.

Wendy's words to me, more than once.

Was I in danger from Wendy Madigan?

Not going there. She might be crazy, but she was locked up. She was no danger to me or to anyone. If I could believe anything in this mess, I could believe that.

"I'm thinking your mother doesn't think anyone is good enough for you, Ryan."

"You are."

"Not according to her."

"Has she said something to you?"

I was done lying to—or rather, keeping information from—him. "She texted me from the number of a female orderly at lockup. Told me to stay away from you. Then, when Melanie and I went to see her, she told me again. Of course, that was after she denied sending me the text and told me how happy she was for us."

"She's nuts."

"For sure."

"You want to come over? Help us keep looking through this stuff? I'm not going to be home for a while."

"Uh...yeah. I guess."

"Great. Grab my phone, will you? It's in the kitchen."

I let Ricky back in and fed him, grabbed Ryan's phone, and was on my way.

★ ★ ★

When I got to Talon's home, Jade and Marjorie were also there. The five of us were in the basement going through old boxes. Ryan had hardly said hello to me, let alone hugged or kissed me. I chalked it up to how involved he was in this process. Sounded good, anyway.

I was at a disadvantage in that I didn't know what I was looking for, but when I voiced the concern, the others told me not to worry.

"None of us know exactly what we're looking for," Marjorie said. "Just tell us if you find anything that might be suspicious."

"What might that be?" I asked.

"You're a cop. You'll know when you find it," Ryan said.

"As a cop, I approach everything as suspicious. But I'll do my best." I leafed through the documents on my lap.

Nothing, nothing, nothing,

Until...

It was a death certificate. That alone wouldn't raise my suspicions if it belonged to someone in the Steel family. But it didn't. The name on the certificate was John Cunningham. How the hell did all these documents—from after Ryan's father's supposed death—get in the house?

I looked at the date. He'd been born around the same time as my father.

The same time as Bradford Steel...

"Ryan, when did your father die?" I asked.

"About seven years ago," he said. "Why?"

So had this poor schmuck. "Was he about six feet three, two hundred pounds, by any chance?"

"About. Why?"

I handed him the death certificate.

He scanned it. "Ruby, what is... Oh, shit." He handed it to Talon.

"Have any of you seen your father's death certificate?"

"Yeah, of course. It's around here somewhere," Marjorie said. "What's going on?"

Talon handed the certificate to Jade. "What do you make of this?"

She scanned the document.

"Did you ever check the number?" I asked Ryan. "The one your father supposedly called you from?"

"No. Mills and Johnson have been off the map, and that's who we'd have do it."

"Your new phone won't show the call. All I need is permission to access your records, and I can do it through the department."

"You've got permission," Ryan said. "But I don't want to take advantage."

"Besides," Talon said, "our father is not alive. We had him cremated, for God's sake."

"Are you sure?" Jade asked.

"Of course I'm sure. What kind of a question is that?" Talon said.

"Easy, babe. I'll check this document against the database tomorrow. It may be nothing."

"Just out of curiosity," I asked, after texting the requisite department to get Ryan's cell phone records, "who identified the body after your father died?"

"He was taken away in an ambulance," Ryan said. "He had a heart attack and was dead on arrival."

"Still, someone would have had to identify the body for the coroner," I said.

"I don't know," Talon said. "Did either of you?"

Ryan and Marjorie both shook their heads.

"It must have been Joe then," Talon said. "Oldest brother and all. He probably volunteered."

"Call him," I said. "Let's get to the bottom of this."

"For Christ's sake," Talon said.

He got up and left the room, Ryan and Marjorie following.

"This is a lot for them to take," I said to Jade. "I'm sorry about that."

"It's not your fault," Jade said. "You're asking the kind of questions a cop asks. As for me, I'm going to do the lawyer thing and check this out." She fingered the death certificate of John Cunningham. "If I were a betting person, I'd bet this isn't anywhere in the requisite database. Scratch that. I'll bet it *is*, right down to the number on the cert. But I'll bet it bears Brad Steel's name, and that John Cunningham never existed, according to records."

CHAPTER TEN

R y a n

"This is ridiculous," I said, as Talon punched in Joe's number.

"Do you trust Ruby?" Marj asked.

What a loaded question. A week ago, the answer would have been yes. Now I wasn't sure. But I did trust her cop instincts. "Yes."

"Jesus." She swallowed. "This is all so..."

"Twisted?" I said.

"Yeah. That's the word, all right."

Talon laid his phone down on the table in the kitchen. "You're never going to believe this."

"What?" Marjorie and I said in unison.

"Joe *didn't* identify Dad's body. He was going to, but someone else volunteered to do it for him, and he allowed it. He didn't want to see our father's dead body."

"Who?" I asked.

"Wendy Madigan."

I had to stop myself from doubling over. Swallowing down nausea, I fell into a chair at the table. "My mother."

"We'll figure this out, Ry," Marj said, touching my arm.

But I didn't want a sisterly touch. Or a brotherly touch. That wasn't going to cut it right now.

I craved something more. *Someone* more. And she was still downstairs.

I got up, saying nothing to my brother and sister.

"Ry," Talon said. "Joe's on his way over. Where are you going?"

"I'm leaving."

"No. You can't."

"The hell I can't." I walked to the basement door and down the stairs.

Ruby and Jade were talking, Jade holding the death certificate of John Cunningham.

"We're leaving," I said to Ruby.

"We are?"

"Yeah. It's important. Come with me."

She didn't hesitate. Didn't ask any questions. She simply got up and followed me.

★ ★ ★

In my bedroom, she undressed for me when I asked her to.

When she was naked, I undid my jeans and pushed them and my boxers to my knees. "Suck my cock, Ruby."

She knelt before me and timidly touched her lips to my cock head, giving it tiny kisses.

I closed my eyes.

This was Ruby Lee, who had been through so much. Who was a cop, used to taking care of herself. Now she was willing to take care of me. To do whatever I asked of her.

I flashed back to the time in her apartment. I'd just found out about my maternity, and I'd gone to her. She'd submitted to everything I wanted, needed, no questions asked.

She was doing the same now.

It seemed unlike what I knew of her, yet here she was, kneeling before me, taking my cock between her gorgeous red lips.

Her hair was in a ponytail today rather than the tight bun she usually wore. She looked like a goddess—a nude goddess, so beautiful.

My cock was hard as a rock, and I wanted to pick her up, throw her on my bed, and shove it into her.

But first, I'd see how far she was willing to go with obeying my commands.

"That's it, baby," I said. "Lick me. Take me." I resisted the urge—for now—to grab her by that ponytail and fuck her mouth. But God, I wanted to do it. Wanted to make her take all of me down her sweet little throat.

She swirled her tongue around my cock head and then licked my length, stopping to flick her tongue against my tightened balls. I couldn't take it any longer.

I seized her ponytail and met her sparkling blue gaze. "Suck me. All the way, Ruby. Suck me." I pushed her mouth onto my cock.

She opened her lips and took all I gave her. I stopped when I felt my tip nudge the back of her throat. She was still very inexperienced, and I didn't want to choke her. One day, though... One day I'd fuck her gorgeous mouth the way I wanted to at this moment.

She didn't gag. Or if she did, she did a great job of hiding it. This time I was gentler as I pushed her mouth down upon my cock. For a moment, I imagined her mouth in an O, opened with a spider gag. I'd never been much for toys in the bedroom. From what little I knew, my brothers' tastes were darker than my own. But the image of Ruby, those scarlet lips being held open and ready for my cock...

Damn! I nearly came right there.

I continued moving her back and forth along my cock. She added her hand, and who was I to complain? This way she got farther down, almost to the base with each thrust.

"Baby, baby," I said. "God!"

I opened my eyes and met her blue gaze. She was looking directly at me, her mouth full of my cock.

So trusting.

So trusting for someone who'd only lost her virginity weeks ago.

As much as I wanted to come in her mouth, I wanted her pussy more. I pulled her off of my cock and drew her up against my still-clothed body. I took her mouth in a crushing kiss. She opened instantly, our tongues dueling. When I needed a breath, I broke the kiss, panting, and lifted her in my arms and onto my waiting erection.

"Ah, God!" Such sweet suction.

She wrapped around me so completely, hugging me with an intense grip that was almost painful in its pleasure. I worked her on and off my cock, her breasts jiggling and colliding with my cotton shirt. How I wished I'd taken the time to undress so I could feel her soft flesh against my chest. Too late to stop now, though. I was nearly—

"Ahh!" I groaned as I climaxed, filling Ruby's pussy.

As I came down, I set her gently on the bed. Her skin was pink all over, but I wasn't sure if she'd climaxed.

"Did you come, baby?"

She shook her head shyly. "Not this time."

I smiled, unbuttoning my shirt. "Not a problem. I can take care of that."

CHAPTER ELEVEN

Ruby

I lay, floating on the silk of Ryan's comforter. I felt...good. Really good. This was the second time he'd taken me pretty forcefully, and I found that I liked it.

That scared me a little bit.

I'd never been one to give up without a fight. It wasn't in my nature. I'd been fighting my whole life to get ahead, get away from my past, to bring my father to justice.

Submitting wasn't me. So why did I submit to Ryan Steel?

He was gentler with me now as he spread my legs, kissing my thighs. Shivers ran through me at the touch of his fingers, his lips. How had I gone my entire life up until the past few weeks without any of this? How had I ever thought I could live without it?

Now, a life without this very essence of existence seemed empty.

And it hit me.

I could never go back.

I was in love with Ryan Steel. If he didn't return my love? I'd stay anyway. I'd stay until he no longer wanted me because I couldn't live without his touch.

"So beautiful," he said gruffly. "Such a pretty pussy."

He stroked his tongue over my slit and then licked and

tugged on my labia. My nerves sizzled under my skin. He swirled his tongue over my clit, making me crazy, and then he played with my swollen labia once more. Finally, before I nearly cried out for penetration, he thrust two fingers inside my channel.

That along with his hot tongue on my hard clit was enough to shoot me over the edge and into oblivion.

"That's right. Come for me, baby. Come all over me." The deep timbre of his voice vibrated against my slick thighs.

When I finally stopped quaking, I opened my eyes. He was smiling between my legs, his stubbled chin glistening.

"Get ready to roll, baby. We're not even close to done."

He flipped me over onto my hands and knees. A second later, his warm tongue slithered in my crease, touching my...

I went rigid.

"Relax, baby." He kissed one cheek of my ass. "I'm not going in there. Just kissing you." He slid his tongue over my anus once more. "Just let it feel good. Let it take you away."

Take you away... Ryan was the one who needed to be taken away right now, with all that he was dealing with. Then again, I wouldn't mind a pilgrimage to another place either, a few minutes not to think about my father and the horrible things he'd done, was still doing. I'd never in my life considered that a rim job might take me away, but with Ryan, I was willing to try anything.

So I closed my eyes, melted into the covers, and let him do what he wanted to do.

The sensation was warm, slippery. A little jabby. And... kind of improper. I couldn't help wriggling a bit.

He grabbed my hips, steadying me. "Hold still." His tone was commanding.

Something in his voice made me obey.

He continued to tongue me, and again, I sank into the comforter, determined to find the pleasure in what he clearly was enjoying himself.

Still warm, still slippery, and then...

I sighed, moaning softly. Dirty. Taboo. Kink.

And I was enjoying it.

His tongue snaked below, and he massaged my perineum, streaked across my pussy folds, and then he was back at my ass, circling, probing.

Goose bumps erupted all over my body, and again I wriggled, but he kept me in place. I clutched at the covers, moaning, sighing.

So bad. So good. The ultimate contradiction.

Such a fucking turn-on.

I had no idea how sensitive that area was, and I was on the verge of another climax. When he pushed his fingers inside my pussy, I imploded.

I sank into the bed, pleasure surrounding me, my body quivering as he still worked me with his tongue. The covers muffled my cries, and a foggy haze took over my mind.

All I wanted was more of Ryan's tongue on me. Every part of me. Especially *that* part.

He flipped me over and sank his cock into my pussy.

"You're so hot, Ruby," he said. "Such a hot little ass."

The warmth of embarrassment flushed through me, but his dick inside me felt so amazing I didn't care. I wanted to get lost in Ryan Steel, become part of him. As he thrust into me again and again, I imagined us joined forever, our bodies one, our souls united.

In love.

Our souls united in love.

I was so in love with this man, and he didn't even know it. Might never know it.

But I'd relish this time, this joining...and another climax took me higher.

"That's right. Come. God, Ruby. I'm going to—" He plunged into me harder and farther than he ever had, taking me with him into yet one more orgasm.

I looked deep into his smoking dark eyes, and for a moment, I thought I glimpsed his soul.

He collapsed atop me, brushing his lips against mine.

"Thank you," was all he said.

★ ★ ★

When I got to the office the next morning, I already had a message from Jade to call right away.

"Hey," I said when she answered. "It's Ruby."

"You'll never guess what I found."

"The death certificate."

"Yup. And my hunch was right. It's the same certificate except instead of John Cunningham it says Bradford Steel. The birth date and social have been changed to Brad's too, but everything else is the same, right down to the number. No record of John Cunningham. He was probably an indigent that no one missed."

"You're good," I said.

"No better than you. I think the two of us together might be able to solve this thing."

"I sure hope so. I've got to get my father put away."

"You will. *We* will. We're all in this together now, and

we've got some serious brainpower among all of us. The four Steels, you, me, and Melanie—we'll figure this out."

I let out a sigh. "We will." I said it more to convince myself than Jade.

"So...there's another thing."

"What?"

"The quitclaim deed for the Shane ranch. We all looked it over quickly, and none of us noticed the date."

"Uh-oh."

"Yeah. It's several weeks *after* Brad Steel's death."

"Wow. I didn't actually look at the deed."

"Yeah, and there's the fact that the Shanes didn't actually leave until a couple of years ago."

"Ryan said he and Anna broke up two years ago."

"Exactly."

"So the Steels owned the ranch *before* the Shanes left?"

"Apparently."

"That doesn't make any sense."

"I know. The Shanes were paid off somehow, and if Brad was dead, who would have paid them off?"

"Wendy."

"That's my guess as well," Jade agreed.

"But where would Wendy get that kind of money?" My mind was barreling through every possible scenario. "From Brad. Which means..." I shivered.

"Which means," Jade continued, "it's possible that Brad's not dead. It's all adding up. Wendy identified the body. The death certificate of a guy matching Brad's description. The quitclaim deed."

"So Brad *could* have called Ryan." My mind churned. "He could have found out that Ryan now knows he's Wendy's son, and he wanted to talk to him."

"Probably."

"God, Jade. What does this all mean? Why would Brad have faked his own death? What if he's into all this horrid stuff with my father? What's that going to do to Ryan and his brothers and sister?" I didn't even want to go there.

She sighed across the phone line. "I don't know. But they'll deal. They've dealt with worse."

"I guess they'll have to."

"They'll want to know these findings. Do you want to come over tonight? We can tell them together."

"I'm not sure I should be there. The rest of you are all... family."

"You're Ryan's girlfriend, and this involves you as much as it does us."

The thrill of being referred to as "Ryan's girlfriend" was superseded by the knowledge that this did indeed involve me. How I *didn't* want to be reminded of all that. My esteemed father was the reason they were all in this mess. "I'm not sure," I said. "My father—"

"None of us hold you responsible for your father."

"I know that." And I did. Objectively. "All right. If you want me there, I'll be there."

"I do. Come at dinnertime. I'll phone Marj and have her cook up something good. Seven, okay?"

CHAPTER TWELVE

Ryan

My father was alive.

At least, evidence seemed to point to that conclusion.

After a dinner of Marj's famous beef Stroganoff, Ruby and Jade had presented their findings. Truly presented them, as only a cop and an attorney could. By the time they were done, I was convinced beyond a reasonable doubt that my father was alive somewhere, and that he had attempted to call me several days ago.

"So where do we go from here?" I asked.

Joe took charge. "We find Dad."

I cleared my throat. "I guess that means a visit to my— Er...Wendy." Calling her my mother out loud didn't feel right.

"Yeah," Joe said, "and I need to go with you."

"Why you?" Talon asked.

"Because she has a soft spot for me. She thinks I look like Dad. And Ry, of course, because she's his..."

Apparently I wasn't the only one who had a problem saying those words out loud.

"Do you want me to go with you?" Ruby asked, touching my arm.

It was a sweet gesture, but I had to do this with Joe. "No. But thanks for offering."

She smiled shyly.

I startled as Talon's doorbell rang. His mutt, Roger, scampered to the front door, and Talon followed.

He came back a few seconds later with Joe's best friend, Bryce Simpson, who was carrying his nearly one-year-old son, Henry.

"Hey, bud," Joe said. "What are you doing here?"

"I have some news," Bryce said. "Remember you told me to look through my dad's stuff for a ring? Well, I found one."

Marjorie stepped forward and took Henry from Bryce's arms. "How are you, cutie?"

Bryce fished in his pocket and pulled out a man's ring. "It's eighteen-karat gold. All those years we lived a modest existence in Snow Creek, and my father had this stashed away."

Tom Simpson had had a lot more than that stashed away if he was into human trafficking. I wasn't sure how much Joe had shared with Bryce, so I kept mum.

Joe took the ring from Bryce and handed it to me. "You identified the rings in the photo, Ry. You take the first look."

The large stone was black, probably onyx, but we'd have to get a jeweler to identify it. On one side were the initials T and S. But on the other side...

A strange symbol. An oval and an X, one corner of the X touching the elongated part of the oval. Nothing I'd ever seen before. "I'm not sure what to make of this image." I handed it back to Joe.

"I couldn't figure it out either," Bryce said, "But my Uncle Chase is a Mason. He might be able to shed some light on it."

"Is it a Masonic symbol?" Talon asked.

"I have no idea," Bryce replied. "But the Masons know a lot about symbolry, and symbols are a particular hobby of his.

He might know what it is, or he might be able to point us in the right direction. I'll give him a call."

"Great," Joe said. "See if he can come over here tomorrow night and take a look at this. We'll feed him dinner."

"I'd rather see him myself," Bryce said. "This is still all too real for him. The loss of his son and all. This brood will be too much for him. Why don't you come with me tomorrow, Joe?"

"Can't." Joe cleared his throat. "I've got a full day with contractors. The next day?"

"I'll go," I said, standing. "Let's get this taken care of." And while I was in the city, I'd go visit Wendy. Alone.

"That's fine with me. I think at least one of you should be there. You want me to pick you up, Ry?"

"I'll drive myself," I said. "I have some things to do in the city."

"Okay. I'll get in touch with Uncle Chase and text you with the time and place."

"Sounds good." I looked toward Marjorie, who was cooing to a laughing Henry. "Good luck getting your baby back."

Bryce pulled his son out of Marj's arms. "Time to go, big guy."

"Bring him around anytime," Marj said. "I miss him."

Bryce smiled at her. "Will do. See you tomorrow, Ryan."

I handed the ring back to Bryce and then thought better of it. "Do you mind if I keep this? I want to study it a little more carefully."

"Sure. Just bring it with you tomorrow. See you guys." Bryce left.

"What are you thinking, Ry?" Talon asked.

"I just want to look at it with a magnifying glass. I'll take it home, if you guys don't mind."

"Go ahead," Joe said. "You're the one who's going to see Bryce's uncle tomorrow. Figure out everything you can. I sure as hell wouldn't know where to start."

Ruby had gone into the family room with Jade and Melanie.

I wanted her to look more closely at the ring with me. I walked to the family room and touched her shoulder. "Ready to go?"

"Sure. I guess."

We hadn't come together, and she seemed surprised.

She stood. "Thanks for dinner," she said to Jade.

I turned when I heard a shuffling. Jade's mother, Brooke Bailey, came limping down the stairs on Talon's arm.

"Jade," she said, "I have the best news."

"What is it?" Jade asked.

"Nico called! He's coming to see me!"

CHAPTER THIRTEEN

Ruby

Nico.

Nico Kostas was one of my father's many aliases, the one he'd used most recently when romancing Jade's mother.

I had met Brooke Bailey several months ago when she came to town with my father. She was still a beauty, a former supermodel who'd chosen career over motherhood. Her blond hair was cut short now, but I could tell even through her robe that she still had her signature body. Her eyes were a striking light blue, just like Jade's. Ryan had told me about her automobile accident with my father. We were pretty sure he had orchestrated it to collect on a million-dollar insurance policy—

Wait! Was my father in financial trouble? It was certainly possible, now that the Steels were on to him and his two cohorts were out of the picture. Most likely, he was just greedy and figured he could make an easy mill.

With my father, anything was possible.

This was some kind of disturbing setup. No way would my father come to see Brooke when he knew we were all trying to sniff him out. My first guess? He was using Brooke as a pawn, as leverage. But my first inclination was rarely correct when it came to my father. He never did the obvious.

"Mother, I don't want you to see him," Jade said.

Apparently Jade hadn't shared any information about my father with her mother. I knew from Melanie that they weren't close. Still, she wouldn't want her mother in harm's way, and neither did I.

"I agree, Ms. Bailey," I said. "It's not a good idea."

She looked me over, from my ponytail to the jeans and tank top I'd changed into before coming over. "Just what would you know about any of it?"

Clearly she hadn't recognized me. "Nico Kostas is my father."

She eyed me again. "No. His daughter is a mannish policewoman. I met her once."

I let out a huff. "Look again."

She squinted her eyes. "It *is* you. Goodness, you're so pretty. What happened to you?"

"Mother," Jade said, "stop being rude. Ruby is a friend of ours. And she's right. Don't see him."

"But I've missed him so much."

"Ms. Bailey," I said, "my father is—"

Jade eyed me, pleading.

I cleared my throat. "I didn't know he was coming to town."

"He's not. He's sending me a plane ticket."

A chill swept through me. "A ticket where?"

"I don't know. He said it's a surprise."

"You know you can't travel yet," Jade said.

"My doctors say I'm progressing very well. I'm walking without crutches now."

"So? You're still limping."

I opened my mouth to mention that he had probably

orchestrated the car accident to collect insurance money, but then I clamped it shut. That was only a theory, and I had no idea whether Talon and Jade had talked to Brooke about that possibility.

"Please," I said. "Don't go. It's not safe."

"Ruby," Jade said, her eyes resigned. "Go ahead and go with Ryan. I'll tell my mother. *Everything.*"

I nodded. This wouldn't be easy for Jade and Talon. But it was necessary.

Ryan took my arm and looked to Jade. "You sure you guys will be okay?"

"Yes. It had to happen sometime."

Brooke sat down in a recliner, sighing. "Would someone mind telling me exactly what's going on?"

That was our cue to leave. I followed Ryan through the hallway to the front door.

* * *

Ryan had several grades of magnifying glasses, and I was astounded at how much we could actually see on Tom Simpson's ring. It was fashioned from eighteen-karat gold, and it was quite heavy. This ring had been expensive. Business clearly had been good early on, when these men were still in high school.

"How could they have afforded these rings?" I asked.

"I suppose my father might have bought them."

That seemed unlikely, but what did I know about Ryan's father? "Would he have done something like that?"

Ryan sighed. "A few months ago, I'd have bet not. My father was a big believer in earning what you had. Yeah, we were all born rich, thanks to the hard work of our ancestors, but he never let us forget where we came from, and he made sure he instilled the value of hard work in us. He also taught us how to keep track of our own finances, never to trust others."

"And now?"

He shook his head. "Now? I don't have a clue. He obviously created a separate trust and didn't tell us about it. I'd also have bet my father would have never cheated on my mother. But I'm proof that he did."

"Maybe..."

"What do you mean, maybe?"

"Wendy was—*is*—obsessed with your father. Maybe she had herself artificially inseminated?"

"And just how would she have gotten hold of my father's sperm?"

I let out a chuckle. "I haven't thought this *all* the way through yet."

He smiled at me. "I appreciate you trying to make me feel a little better about my father's character, baby. But the truth of the matter is that he fucked Wendy Madigan at least once, and I'm the result."

My heart went out to Ryan. Here he was, struggling with his father's character and his link to my father and the others. I'd long since accepted my own father's character. I'd had to at age fifteen. But I well remembered how I felt at the time.

"So maybe he's not who you thought he was. I get that. I do. But you're still here, Ryan. You're still who you've always been, and knowing you have a different mother than you thought you had doesn't change that. You're still *you*."

"I suppose." He picked up a magnifying glass and stared at the ring again, clearly done with this subject.

I couldn't blame him.

"Do you want to go with me to see Bryce's uncle tomorrow?" he asked.

"I wish I could, but I can't. Too much work. But I will go with you to see someone else after I get off work. Someone who knows exactly what this ring means."

"Yeah? Who's that?"

"Larry Wade."

CHAPTER FOURTEEN

Ryan

I stared at Ruby, a few strands of hair loosening from her sleek ponytail, her blue eyes sparkling.

"You're brilliant," I said. "Why the hell didn't the rest of us think of that?"

"Oh, I'm thinking you all probably had a lot more on your minds. Like whether your father is actually alive and what his role is in all of this."

"Still." I pulled her to me. "Leave it to you to see what should have been right in front of our eyes."

"Don't get too excited. It may not lead to anything. Larry hasn't been very talkative up until this point. Plus, he may claim not to know."

"True. But it can't hurt. After all, he had one of the rings too. I'll be in the city tomorrow to talk to Bryce's uncle. Can I pick you up after work?" I hesitated. "Oh. Will we even be able to get in to see him in the evening?"

Ruby smiled. "I'm a police detective. I can get in to see whoever I want."

"I don't want you to get into any trouble. This isn't your case."

"You let me worry about that."

I touched her cheek, her skin like satin against my rough

fingertips. "Sometimes I can't believe you're in my life."

She looked away shyly. "You've had women before. This is hardly a first for you."

"It's the first time—"

I stopped abruptly. I'd been about to confess my love for her, and I couldn't do that. At least not yet. I had no idea how she felt about me, but that wasn't the real reason for my hesitation. Before I could love her or anyone else, I had to be sure of who *I* was. My world had been turned upside down with the new information regarding my maternity. I wasn't ready to have it turned upside down by a woman.

"The first time what?" she asked.

"Nothing. You're right." The thought of my previous girlfriend, Anna Shane, reminded me of the quitclaim deed we'd found among my father's things. Yet another tentacle in this mystery that was my life.

Her cheeks reddened. "I know you have."

"Ruby, I know what you're thinking. Believe me, you're... different. And I don't mean because you're inexperienced. You're...great in bed, baby."

She reddened even further.

"That's a compliment." I pushed my groin into her. "See? I'm hard for you right now, and we haven't even kissed."

I was crazy hard for her most of the time. It wasn't her hot-as-hell body, her gorgeous face and hair, the fact that she'd tried so hard for so long to be invisible...

No. It was because she was Ruby. The woman I loved.

Still, I was afraid to go there. She *knew* who she was.

I did not know who I was.

Not anymore.

The only thing I knew for sure was that right now, as of

this very moment, I craved her. Needed her. Ached for her.

I crushed my lips to hers.

She opened for me at once, our tongues swirling together. She tasted as she always did, of sweetness, freshness, berries and cream.

I had never thought of myself as a natural dominant before, but with Ruby, who in her daily life was about as far from submissive as anything, I was finding my dominant desires.

I broke the kiss.

"We need to talk," I said.

"Now?" Her nipples protruded through her tank top.

I had to physically stop myself from reaching for them.

"You're still so innocent, baby. I'm not sure where I can go with you."

She laughed. "Ryan, you are six-three and your muscles have muscles. But trust me. I can stop you if I want to."

I didn't doubt it. With her background and her training as a cop, not to mention that killer body that she kept through working out hard, she didn't have much to fear from another person without a weapon. Still, I felt the need to say, "All you have to do to stop me is to tell me no."

She sobered. "Yes, I know that. You would stop if I asked you to. I trust that completely. But I've told you before. I don't do anything I don't want to do."

"Then..."

"What?"

"What would you say about..." God, I'd had no idea how hard it would be to actually give voice to these desires.

"Spit it out, Steel."

I'd known for a while that both of my brothers—as well as

my father, according to Wendy—enjoyed the darker, baser side of their dominant personalities. Not that we talked about that shit. We never had. But Jonah had a dungeon in his house. I'd come across it once while I was house- and dogsitting for him. I hadn't said anything to him. He'd probably be mortified if I knew.

I had never tried anything like that, but now, with Ruby, her sweet submission so intoxicating, I wanted to.

But how to bring it up? Ruby had two sides. Her tough cop side, who wasn't afraid of anything and knew how to take care of herself. But she also had a vulnerable side. The side who'd been nearly raped by her own father and who'd left home at fifteen. Who'd spent her whole adult life, until now, as a virgin, afraid of getting close to a man.

The two times I'd gotten a little rough and forceful with her, she'd taken it. Had seemed to enjoy it, even.

And as she said, she didn't do anything she didn't want to do.

"Would you be willing to try some...new things in the bedroom?"

She closed her eyes for a few seconds. Then, "Like what?"

I opened my mouth to respond, when I suddenly realized I didn't know exactly what to ask her for. I burst out laughing.

"Ryan. You're freaking me out here."

"I'm sorry, baby. I really am. I'm just trying to say that I like taking the dominant role in bed, more than I imagined I would. And I'm not sure whether it's because I'm naturally dominant, or because you seem to be naturally submissive, which, frankly, surprised me a little bit."

She arched her eyebrows. "Ryan, honestly, it surprised me a little bit too."

"But you're okay, right?"

"Yeah. I'm fine. Like I said—"

"You don't do anything you don't want to do," I finished for her.

Now *she* burst out laughing.

And I realized how absurd this whole thing was. "How about this? We continue doing what we're doing, and if you don't want to do something, you just tell me no."

"Sounds reasonable," she said. "Since that's pretty much what we just said."

"Oh, for God's sake." I grabbed her. "Just kiss me."

CHAPTER FIFTEEN

Ruby

His kiss nearly paralyzed me. It was so passionate, so full of fire, and my whole body throbbed, the sensation culminating between my legs. He wanted to get more dominant in the bedroom, and he wanted me to be more submissive...

The whole idea was making me shake with desire.

For someone like me to submit in the bedroom...

It seemed unreal. I'd ask Melanie about it sometime...

Sometime...later.

For now, I was kissing Ryan Steel, our mouths fused together, sighs and groans leaving both our throats and vibrating into each other.

After several amazing moments of the most passionate kiss I'd yet experienced, he broke away from me, panting.

"Bedroom," he grunted, and then scooped me up in his arms.

Had anyone suggested to me a month ago that I'd enjoy being given the caveman treatment, I'd have laughed. But being in the arms of Ryan Steel, easily the best-looking man on the planet, being carried into his bedroom where he would fuck me wildly...

I couldn't wait.

When we arrived, he set me down gently and then eased

the band out of my ponytail, letting my long hair fall over my shoulders and down my back. I'd secretly been hoping that he'd pull on it again, but clearly that wasn't his plan tonight.

His plan...

His plan.

I wanted it to be *his* plan. I wanted him to take the lead, to dominate me, to push me into submission.

My juices trickled just thinking about it.

Ruby Lee. Assertive police detective by day. Submissive by night.

My mind whirled with the concept and then kaleidoscoped with only images, feelings, as Ryan literally tore the tank top from my body.

The lavender tatters landed on his dark hardwood floor. I met his gaze. He wasn't sorry that he'd ruined one of my only shirts that wasn't a white button-down. No, his eyes were not in the least remorseful. They were full of fire, of desire, of unrelenting passion.

My nipples hardened further against the fabric of my bra.

Within seconds, that same bra had joined the cotton tatters of my tank on the floor, and I stood before him topless, my nipples aching.

"Fucking beautiful," he said, pinching one.

I gasped.

"Too much?" he asked.

"No. Not too much. Please. Do whatever you want to me."

I truly meant those words, not even knowing what they might entail. I hadn't experienced everything that was possible in the bedroom. Not even close. Acts might exist that had never even entered my mind.

I didn't care.

At this moment, I wanted whatever he wanted, whatever he longed for. I'd give him what he needed when he needed it. Always.

Because this was who I ultimately was and I hadn't known it?

Or because I was in love with Ryan Steel?

Probably a mixture of both.

Whatever. I'd figure it out later. Right now, I wanted to please him more than I wanted my next breath. If he wanted to shred every piece of clothing I owned, I'd let him.

He pushed me down so I was sitting on the bed and then removed my shoes and socks, my jeans and panties.

"No thong?" he grunted.

"I only own one," I said, breathless.

"Let's remedy that." He spread my legs and inhaled. "God, you smell so good. So ripe."

Ripe I was. Ripe enough that if I were a tomato, I'd have fallen off the vine a while ago.

He ran his fingers through my slick folds, and I tensed. I wanted more. So much more. He knelt by the side of the bed and swiped his tongue across my slit. And God almighty, I nearly flew into an orgasm just from that one small touch of his tongue to my pussy.

Pussy. Funny how I could think the word now without feeling embarrassed.

"You taste so good, baby. Sweetest pussy on earth."

For a few seconds, I wondered how many pussies he could actually compare the taste of mine to, but then I fell backward, melting into the bed as he tugged on my labia and then on my clit. He ate at me, sucking me, licking me, and I reveled in it. He shoved his tongue into my channel, and though I wished it were his cock, I shuddered anyway. So good.

Melting... Slowly melting into the softness of the bed, my pussy being pleasured so completely by this amazing man. Ryan Steel.

My fingers found my nipples, and I started toying with them, first gently, and then not so gently. They were hard as berries, aching for the pleasure I was giving them, aching even more for Ryan's touch.

"So hot when you touch yourself like that, baby," he said, his voice muffled between my legs.

That made me even hotter. Not only was I pleasing myself, I was pleasing *him*. My new goal in life. To please Ryan Steel.

"Here, let me." He reached upward, his mouth still between my legs, and covered my hands with his own. Then he pushed my hands away and twisted both of my nipples while he sank his tongue into my heat.

I moaned, closing my eyes, floating among the silk of his covers. My hips began moving of their own volition, my feet still on the ground. I grated against his face, sliding my slit up to his nose and then down to his chin, his tongue hitting every part of my pussy.

"Ryan. My God. Ryan!"

I shattered into his face, his tongue. He lapped at me as I rose in orgasm, my body shaking, my mind whirling.

"You're so hot, Ruby." He sucked on my clit, igniting more fire within me. "So fucking hot."

All cognitive thought left me, fractured images replacing it as my mind raced with the sensations flowing through my quivering body. His mouth never left mine, even when my clit became so sensitive I wasn't sure I could take it. Still he kept at it, torturing me with pleasure.

"Come again, baby."

And with his command, I did, flying high this time, the convulsions traveling through my arms, my legs, into my fingers and toes, and then catapulting back between my legs, to the very core of me. That private place known only to Ryan Steel.

My mind left my body, floating above me, watching him pleasure me but still feeling every ounce of sensation.

The clink of a belt buckle. The zing of a zipper. And then his cock filling me as still I pulsed around him.

So full. Never empty again. Never empty with Ryan Steel in my life.

"Ryan!" I cried out with each thrust.

"Ruby," he gritted out in response. "My God."

He pushed into me harder, again and again, until he thrust so deeply I was sure he'd touched my heart. As I spasmed around him once more, he groaned, his weight atop me, and I never, ever wanted this feeling to end.

When we both returned to earth, panting, he moved from me and lay next to me on the bed, our legs hanging off.

"God," he said. "It's never been like this before. Never with anyone but you."

Warmth spread through me, and I waited for those three little words.

But they didn't come.

CHAPTER SIXTEEN

Ryan

Ruby hadn't spent the night. I'd driven her back to Talon's to pick up her car, and then she went home. She had work early this morning. Now, I was pulling up to Bryce's aunt and uncle's house in the city. Chase and Victoria Walker had lost their son, Luke, to the same three men who'd abducted and tortured Talon.

Bryce's car was already there, so I walked to the door and rang the bell.

Bryce answered, holding Henry. "Hey, Ry. Come on in."

I walked in as Bryce's mother, Evelyn Simpson, came up and took Henry. This was Tom Simpson's widow. I opened my mouth to say something—I had no idea what—but she turned quickly and took Henry to another room.

"Sorry about that," Bryce said.

"No problem. I wasn't sure what to say anyway." I handed him his father's ring.

"She's still trying to cope. Being around Henry helps, and being here with her sister, who's also trying to heal, helps a little too. But honestly they're both still a mess."

"And your uncle?"

"He's better. I mean, at least now he knows what happened to his son. Closure, he says."

I cleared my throat. Chase Walker was the Freemason we were going to talk to today about the future lawmakers ring. "So...I don't mean to sound stupid, but should I mention Luke?"

Bryce shook his head. "No. Like I said. It's closure to him. He'd rather not dwell on it. Not like he's in denial or anything. He's just trying to move on. He doesn't want to hold my mother responsible for her husband's actions. Neither does my aunt. But it's hard."

"I can imagine."

"He's in his study. We're supposed to go on in."

I nodded. Here went nothing. I followed Bryce to the study. Chase Walker sat behind a large oak desk. He was a big man, bearded and burly, nothing like his son Luke had been. Then again, Luke had only been ten when he was killed. He could have grown into anything.

I shook my head to clear it. I couldn't go there right now. Couldn't think of the life that might have been for Luke Walker and so many others. I had to move forward, not backward. If we could unravel the mystery of the ring, maybe we could finally nail Theodore Mathias and avenge his victims.

"Uncle Chase," Bryce said, handing him the ring. "This is Ryan Steel."

"Ryan," Chase Walker said. "I haven't seen you in forever."

The Walkers had left Snow Creek shortly after Luke had disappeared. I hadn't come into contact with them since. This man had last seen me when I was seven years old.

"How have you been?" I asked. And then wanted to strangle myself. How did I think he had been?

"We're dealing with everything as well as we can." He held up Tom Simpson's ring, eyeing it. "Give me a few minutes to take a look here." He grabbed a jeweler's loupe and started taking notes.

I held my breath. Seconds seemed like hours.

Then Chase cleared his throat. "There are some markings on the inside of the band that I'm going to need a stronger magnifier to see, but this symbol is enigmatic."

"How so?" Bryce asked.

"It's nothing I recognize, but it has similarities to several symbols that I *am* familiar with. Hmm." He typed on his computer. "Let me try something."

We waited a few minutes while he continued.

"I've been using this new program developed by archaeologists to interpret oddly shaped symbols. I'm going to input a few things here."

More tapping on the keys.

After a few more minutes, Bryce asked, "Finding anything?"

Chase's brow was furrowed. "Yeah, as a matter of fact." He turned the computer screen toward us. "Can you see the screen okay? Any glare?"

On the screen was the symbol from the ring, an elongated oval with an X next to it, one of the ends of the X touching the oval, enlarged.

"No glare," I said.

"Good," Chase said. "Now watch. I'm going to twist the ellipse into a circle."

Slowly the oval rounded into a perfect circle, the X still attached.

"Does that make sense to you?" Bryce asked.

"Not yet. Not like this. But if I take the other part of the symbol and twist it the other way, look what we get."

The X slowly maneuvered until it emerged as a cross at the bottom of the circle. The female symbol.

"Now you recognize it?"

We both nodded.

"Why would they put the symbol for female on their ring?" Bryce asked.

"We don't know that they did," Chase said. "All I can tell you for sure is I moved each part of the symbol in opposite ways to the same degree, and this is what I got."

"How did you think to change it in that way?" I asked.

"The ellipse is simply a circle seen from a different slant," Chase replied. "But I noticed the X was comprised of right angles. It's not a stretch from the X to a cross if you know what you're looking at. The ancient Romans used both for crucifixion."

"I can't believe my father would have come up with that," Bryce said.

I didn't believe it either. But Theodore Mathias? I wouldn't put it past him. Everything about him was twisted.

"Whether he did or not, there's something else you should know about this symbol," Chase said.

"What's that?" I asked.

"It's known as the symbol for female, but it's also a planetary symbol. It represents Venus."

"So?" Bryce said.

"That's not all," Chase continued. "The symbol has another meaning."

I held my breath, not sure I wanted to know where this was heading.

Chase's low voice emerged. "Lucifer."

Satan. The devil. Nausea crawled up my throat.

"Before you think your father was a devil worshipper, Bryce," Chase said, "some scholars believe that Lucifer has nothing to do with Satan. It literally means 'light bringer,' which coincides with the planet Venus being the morning star."

My nausea didn't subside.

"Still," Bryce said, "Lucifer is associated with the concept of evil, the devil."

"That's true," Chase agreed. "But there are many symbols that occultists believe are more associated with the devil than this one. There's the sigil of Lucifer, the double-horned pentagram, and that mythological bird, whose name escapes me at the moment. You know. The one that erupts in flames and then rises from the ashes?"

I had to swallow to keep from heaving before I spoke my next words.

"A phoenix."

CHAPTER SEVENTEEN

Ruby

What a day! I gulped down some cheese and crackers from the vending machine for a quick lunch when my phone rang with a number I couldn't identify. Southern California area code.

"Detective Lee."

"It's...Shayna. Shayna Thomas."

"Shayna!" I said too loudly. I lowered my voice. "Are you all right?"

"I'm okay." Her voice shook. "I'm at a pay phone at a gas station. I don't think I was followed."

"Shayna, if you think you're being followed, you need to notify the police."

"I don't know. I'm not sure. It might be all in my mind."

Though I still had no concrete proof that my father was involved in any way with Juliet and Lisa's disappearance, my intuition was on overdrive. After the phone call I'd received from my father after the last time Shayna called me, I knew he was at the helm. Proving it was another story. I'd been on his tail so many times, only to have him elude me. He never left any evidence that was enough to lead to his arrest.

But he would. With Larry Wade and Tom Simpson now gone, my father was getting nervous. I could feel it in the marrow of my bones.

"Just be careful. Don't put yourself in danger to call me. Promise me, okay?"

"I won't. But I had to talk to you."

"What's going on?"

"I got a text. All it said was 'help.' I can't help thinking it was Juliet or Lisa."

"Was it from a number outside the US?" I asked.

"I don't know. It said 'private.'"

"Damn." I bit my lip. "Sorry. It could be a hoax. Someone trying to play with you."

"I know. I thought of that. I just have a feeling it was one of them. I got chills when I read it."

I had always trusted my own intuition, so I again resisted telling Shayna to discount her own. Still, I didn't want her walking into trouble either. "I know you can't forward me the text, but someone needs to get a look at your phone. Your local PD can unblock the number."

"Yeah, I know. But..."

She was scared. I could hear it in her voice as it trembled across the line.

"Look. Never mind the phone. I can access your cell records and get the information for you. My office can run the check. Okay?"

"But what if they find you looking?"

"Don't worry about me. I can take care of myself. Just keep yourself safe. That's the primary objective here. Tell me you understand that."

"I understand. I'm just afraid..."

Of course. Shayna *wasn't* worried about me. She was worried about herself. I had to protect her at all costs, even if it meant not looking into the number.

But what if it *had* come from Juliet or Lisa?

I closed my eyes and exhaled. It didn't matter. I had to put Shayna's safety first. I couldn't go chasing dragons when another's security depended on me leaving them alone. I'd make another call to the LAPD when I got off the phone.

"I won't look into it right now," I assured her. "Please don't worry. It will be okay."

"Thanks for listening to me. Really. I'm so freaked out."

"I'm here for you."

"I have to go. Bye." The phone clicked dead.

I let out a breath of air. Now what? Before I could think what to do, my phone buzzed.

Of course. Dear old Dad. He'd called the last time Shayna had contacted me. I answered without looking at the number. "What is it?" I said through gritted teeth.

"Ruby?"

Shit. It was my boss. "Sorry. I thought you were someone else. What's up?" I tried to sound nonchalant.

"Come down to my office. We have a lead in the Jordan Hayes case."

★ ★ ★

Jordan Hayes had been a young woman working as a receptionist at Tejon Preparatory High School, where my father and the others had been students. She was the one who had gotten Jonah and Melanie access to the yearbooks they needed. Those books had allowed the Steels to uncover their father's involvement with the future lawmakers club. The books in question had been deleted from the online archives and stolen from the school library. Jordan Hayes had gotten them from an off-site facility and given them to Jonah Steel. She had paid for that indiscretion with her life.

I couldn't help but think of all the people who had paid with their lives for coming into contact with my father. As I sat across from my boss, Mark Wilson, several faces emerged in my mind's eye. Luke Walker, a blur because I hadn't known him personally. Gina Cates, my beautiful cousin. Talon Steel. At least my father hadn't taken *his* life.

"So you see what I mean?" Mark said.

I widened my eyes. "Sorry?"

"You're a million miles away, Ruby."

"I apologize. What have you got?"

"A business card. Tucked under the carpeting in Jordan Hayes's apartment."

Tucked under the carpet? Why did that sound so familiar to me?

"And you'll never guess whose business card it is. Jonah Steel's."

I fought the tightening in my throat. "Jonah Steel?"

"Yeah."

My mind raced. "I remember. Jonah Steel's wife, Melanie, said he gave Jordan his business card when they first went to the school looking for information."

"It could be the same card," Mark said. "But I don't buy it."

"Why not?" My blood chilled. Surely Mark wasn't thinking Jonah had anything to do with Jordan's death.

"Number one, it was lodged under the carpeting. It's doubtful Ms. Hayes would have taken the time to hide the card under her carpeting."

"Right. I know that." And that's why it sounded so familiar

to me. I remembered now. The Steels' private investigators, Trevor Mills and Johnny Johnson, had found a business card lodged under the carpeting in one of Talon's guest rooms. This couldn't be a coincidence.

"Number two, you say Steel handed Ms. Hayes the card?"

"As far as I know. That's what Melanie told me, anyway."

"Funny thing, then. The card we found has no fingerprints on it. Not a one."

"See then? Jonah Steel didn't have anything to do with this."

"Of course not. First of all, he most likely wasn't wearing gloves when he handed Ms. Hayes the card. Second, what kind of a moron would go into a woman's apartment, murder her, and then leave a calling card lodged under the carpet?"

Thank God. "For a minute I was sure you were going to go after— Oh, never mind."

"You know me better than that, Ruby, but this card was left by someone for a reason. We need to figure out what that reason is."

I wasn't sure whether I could talk to Mark about the card found in Talon's home. The Steels hadn't gone to the police about the break-in and the rose left on Jade's pillow. It turned out that it hadn't been a break-in at all. Someone, most likely my father, had threatened Talon's housekeeper, Felicia, and forced her to leave the rose for Jade. Why? We could all only guess. I had given up long ago trying to figure out why my father did anything. Until I had the Steels' okay, I had to keep quiet about the similarities in the placement of the cards.

"So there are no prints," I said.

"That's right. So what's the next step?"

"Figuring out who would want to frame Jonah Steel, I

guess."

"Yeah. You have any idea?"

If he only knew. "I do have a few ideas, Mark. Why don't you let me handle this?"

He pushed the file toward me. "It's all yours, kid."

Though being called kid would probably bother some detectives, I let it roll off my back. I had grown up at fifteen. I had never really had the chance to be a kid, so I kind of liked the term. "Thanks, Mark." I took the folder. "Anything else?"

"Yeah. Go home. You look like shit."

I chuckled. "Thanks. I've just been burning the candle on both ends."

"That vacation didn't do you a lot of good, did it?" he said. "And then you came back early too."

I hadn't explained to Mark the reason I had come back from Jamaica early—because of the kidnapping of Juliet and Lisa. Though the resort hadn't closed down, they'd offered refunds and allowed people to leave if they wanted to. Our party had stayed for the wedding and left the next day.

"You know me. Workaholic."

"This can wait till tomorrow, Ruby. Go home and have some 'you' time."

"I'll think about it." I left his office.

But there would be no thinking about it. Once the workday was over, I was meeting Ryan at the prison to see Larry Wade. He was already in the city now, presumably talking with Bryce Simpson's uncle about the future lawmakers ring. I hoped he was getting some good information.

I plopped the new file down on my desk. My phone, which I had left on my desk when I went to see Mark, blinked with a missed call.

A number I didn't recognize.

CHAPTER EIGHTEEN

Ryan

"That's right," Chase said. "The phoenix."

"The phoenix is a symbol of Lucifer? The devil?" Bryce asked. "I've never heard that."

"My guess is that you never studied the occult," his uncle said.

"Not in this lifetime, no," Bryce said.

A vise tightened around my abdomen. The phoenix was an image I was well acquainted with. Ruby's father, Theodore Mathias, had a phoenix tattooed on his forearm. Talon had told me about how he remembered the image from his captivity, how it had been both heaven and hell—the symbol of those who menaced him, yet also a symbol of escape. Of course he hadn't realized all of that until he went through therapy with Melanie. He had been very open with me about what he had learned about himself and those two torturous months he had endured.

He had treated me like a brother.

Again the knife sliced through my gut. My hero. My brother. Talon.

He, Jonah, and Marj had all assured me time and time again that I was still their brother in all the ways that counted. We did, after all, share the same father.

"...can never know for sure."

I wasn't sure whether Bryce or Chase had spoken. Here I was, learning about a ring my father wore, the symbol upon which could mean anything, and I was stuck having a little pity party, feeling sorry for the fact that I had a different mother from my siblings.

Get over yourself, Ryan. There are more important things here.

"Can never know for sure what?" I asked.

"We can never know for sure whether the symbol was meant to be twisted the way I've twisted it," Chase said. "It could simply be a symbol they created themselves that had its own meaning. There's just no way to know."

But I knew.

In my gut, where the dagger was still twisting, I knew.

I doubted that my father and the others worshipped the devil. No, they wouldn't have wasted their time on worship of anything. Simpson, Wade, and Mathias had worshipped only the almighty dollar. Greed was their motivating factor, and when they had figured out that more money could be made by breaking the law than following it, they had gone to the dark side.

The evil side.

That was what those symbols meant. The symbol of Lucifer. The phoenix.

Evil.

★ ★ ★

Ruby and I sat in the visitors area at the prison, waiting for a guard to escort Larry Wade to see us. I hadn't yet told Ruby about what Bryce and I had learned from Chase Walker. I hadn't been able to form the words yet. But I had to tell Larry, and Ruby would hear it then. Larry would know whether we were right.

The guard escorted him to the table, and Larry Wade plunked down. Both of his eyes were blackened today, and he had a cut on his upper lip.

"Seems your fellow inmates aren't treating you very well, Uncle Larry," I said.

"I'm not your uncle, boy."

Another brick in my gut. He was right. He was the half brother of Daphne Steel, so he was half uncle to my siblings, but not to me.

"I'd say that's a good thing," I said. "One less psychopath I'm related to."

Ruby touched my forearm, the warmth of her fingertips seeping into me. She was showing me her presence, trying to soothe me. Problem was, I was currently unsootheable.

"You're not related to me," he said. "But that mother of yours is the queen of the psychos."

He didn't have to tell me. "I didn't come here to talk about my mother."

"Who's this?" He gestured to Ruby.

Ruby flashed a badge. "Detective Ruby Lee, Grand Junction PD. We've met."

"She's with me," I said. "Obviously."

"I'm not here on police business," Ruby reiterated.

"Then why *are* you here? Cops make me nervous."

"She's here because she's a friend of mine," I said. "How did you know I was aware of my true maternity, anyway? You'd have just shocked the hell out of me if I wasn't."

"I keep my ears to the ground," he said.

"You do?"

"People talk. I listen."

"Who the hell is talking about my maternity? Why would anyone in here care?"

"I didn't say it was anyone here."

"Are you saying you have other visitors? Who the hell would want to see you?"

He scoffed. "Kid, you have no idea."

"I have a pretty good idea," Ruby said. "You know I can easily get access to the visitors log, don't you?"

"You think anyone who visited me left a trace of who he might really be?" Larry laughed, wincing. Then he eyed Ruby, narrowing his eyes. "Shit."

"What?" I said.

"You're *her*, aren't you?"

"Who?" Ruby asked. "Who do you think I am?"

"No one." Larry motioned to the guard.

"Not so fast," I said, grabbing his cuffed arms. "You're not going anywhere."

"I have rights, you know. I don't have to talk to you."

"The guards may think you have rights, but as far as I'm concerned, your rights ended the day you took my bro—"

"Damn it!" Larry whisked his arms away. "I had nothing to do with that."

"We know that's a lie," I said. "You tortured and raped him just like the others."

"I had nothing to do with taking him. Ask him yourself. *Two* men took him. I wasn't one of them. I fed him, for God's sake. And I'm the one who fucking helped him to escape."

"And that absolves you from the crimes of rape and false

imprisonment?" I said. "I don't think so."

"Look, kid, you know who your mother is now, but I still have other secrets to keep."

I had to stop myself from standing up and punching him in the fucking nose. "What are the secrets worth to you, Larry? Because I've got all the money in the world."

"You think your brother hasn't already offered me money?"

"I know he has. He offered to pay for the best defense lawyer in the state. You turned him down. I'm going to offer you something else."

Larry eyed Ruby again. "I won't say a word with her here."

"She stays," I said.

Ruby grabbed my arm. "It's okay. I can go."

"No, I want you here. You have every right to be here. There are cops swarming all over this place."

"I don't think the fact that I'm a cop is the issue"—she turned her gaze on Larry—"is it, Mr. Wade?"

Larry said nothing.

He knew who Ruby was. She'd told us that she'd visited him before. So far, Larry had refused to roll over on Theodore Mathias. Surely he must know that Ruby had no loyalty to her father.

Or did he?

I had no idea. I had never faced Larry Wade on my own, but maybe I could get some information.

"All right," I said to Ruby. "Don't go too far."

"I won't. I'll be outside when you're done." She got up and left the visitors area.

"All right, Larry," I said. "Do your damnedest. What can you tell me?"

"Nothing."

"Come on. I got rid of her. You can talk now."

"I know who she is."

"Yeah, I figured that out. You didn't seem to recognize her at first, but she's visited you before."

"He speaks highly of her, you know."

"Who does?"

"You know who."

Damn, this man was a pain in the ass. He still wouldn't say the motherfucker's name. It didn't matter. We already had proof that he was the one we were looking for. And he obviously had something on Larry Wade.

"Does he?"

"Yes. Says she's smart as a whip. Said he's had to work twice as hard the past eleven years to stay off her radar."

"She'll get him," I said. "Don't ever doubt that."

"She won't," he said, wincing. "He wins. He *always* fucking wins. Never gets caught. Never slips up. Simpson got lazy. But not him. He'll never surface."

"I can assure you, his days of winning are numbered. You're locked up. Simpson is dead. My father is dead."

He arched his eyebrows slightly.

"Or am I incorrect about that? Is my father *not* dead?"

CHAPTER NINETEEN

Ruby

I was just as glad to be out of Larry Wade's presence. This was far from the first time I had spoken with him, and he never remembered who I was. At least that was what he claimed. He made my skin crawl more each time. Clearly he feared my father. He had seemed to fear Simpson too, when he was alive. He had systematically refused to roll over on the two of them to either me or the Steels, no matter what we offered.

Maybe Ryan would be able to get the information out of him while I was gone.

No. Why delude myself? That wouldn't happen. Larry was a game player first and foremost. He would never roll over.

But there was something he *did* do. He gave hints. I had heard the whole story, about how Melanie had figured out where to find the information about the future lawmakers club. His mind didn't work like a normal human's. He dealt more in riddles.

And what if...?

What if that was why he'd hired Jade to be the assistant city attorney? What if that was why he had given her the assignment to research the Steels?

Maybe that had been his way of finally bringing the two worst offenders, Simpson and my father, to justice. He thought

Jade would uncover things and start thinking.

And she had.

Of course he must've known that would culminate in his own demise as well. So maybe that *wasn't* how it had happened.

Then again, according to Larry, he had let Talon go, and he'd paid dearly for that, almost with his life.

It was all just too coincidental, otherwise. Damn it. Larry Wade had been feeding us clues this whole time.

I had to go back in and tell Ryan what I figured out.

No, I couldn't do that. What if Larry was finally talking? One look at me and he'd clam up like a mute. I had to stay out here.

I whipped out my cell phone to check my messages. I had turned off my ringer while we were talking to Larry. No new calls. Then I went to my e-mail. How was it possible that I had fifty-seven new e-mails since I had left the office only an hour before?

All work and no play...

I answered a few, until I got to one from an address I didn't recognize. It was a government address, similar to the one I used. I just didn't know the name.

It contained only one sentence.

Tell my son I need to see him.

Wendy Madigan. She'd gotten hold of a cell phone again, obviously. She knew my number. She had texted me before. So why had she e-mailed me this time? Why not e-mail Ryan, if she wanted to see him?

How was she getting our contact information, anyway?

She knew I was a detective, so my e-mail address wouldn't

have been hard to figure out. A standard government e-mail for the city. All she had to figure out was the name. R.Lee probably hadn't taken her too long.

I wouldn't e-mail her back. Besides, whatever phone she had stolen this time was probably back with its original owner by now. Or maybe she had found a contraband phone somewhere in the ward and had hidden it. The woman was cunning. I'd give her that. Still, I wasn't going to respond.

Instead, I logged in to work and traced the e-mail address. It belonged to one of the psychiatrists she was seeing for medication and therapy. Christ! How could a doctor be so negligent as to let a patient hijack his cell phone? She had graduated from orderlies to physicians.

Something niggled in the back of my mind. Something Ryan had told me about his first meeting with Wade.

Mathias isn't dead, and even he isn't the most dangerous.

Not too long after that visit, we'd become embroiled in Ryan's DNA test. None of us had given that statement a second thought.

But according to Larry, someone else was even more dangerous than my father.

I smiled to myself, not because I was happy, but because I had come up with something that I knew the Steel brothers wouldn't.

They would never suspect a woman. Not that they were sexist, or even chauvinist. They were just gentlemen. And now, because the woman I was thinking about was Ryan's mother, they probably didn't want to suspect her at all.

Wendy.

Larry had been talking about Wendy.

And if he was telling the truth...

Ryan was in no danger from Wendy. I felt that in the depths of my bones. She was, first and foremost, a mother.

I didn't think for a minute that Wendy would hurt any of the other Steels, either. She was so obsessed over Bradford Steel, she probably wouldn't harm any of his children.

Or would she?

Had she been the mastermind behind Talon's abduction? She had all but admitted that at one point, but she'd denied it several times over as well.

I'm on to you, Wendy.

She wasn't as crazy as the Steels thought.

No. She played her cards in a very calculating manner. When it benefited her to be crazy, she acted crazy. I had the sick feeling that, despite all evidence to the contrary, Wendy Madigan had never lost her grasp on reality. To the contrary, she *used* reality. She twisted it to suit her purposes. But she never did anything without having a damned good reason for her actions.

Even he isn't the most dangerous.

My God. Ryan's mother was the true mastermind behind everything.

CHAPTER TWENTY

Ryan

"What is death anyway?" Larry asked. "Do any of us really know?"

"Don't try to wax philosophical with me. Just tell me the goddamned truth. Is my father dead, or isn't he?"

"Death is in the eye of the beholder."

I was sick to hell of this. "I think you mean beauty."

"Do I? As far as I'm concerned, I'm dead. I might as well be, stuck in this place."

"You're stuck in this place because of your own actions. You of all people know that. It has nothing to do with death."

"Does it matter? Does it matter whether the person is truly dead, as long as they are dead to you?"

"For the love of God, I just want an answer. We have reason to believe my father is still alive. That he faked his own death, or had it faked for him. What we *don't* know is why. He's our father, for God's sake. You have children, Larry."

"Children I'll never see again, because I'm here. See what I mean? I'm dead to them."

"Your children are better off."

He wiped sweat off his forehead. "I won't disagree with you."

Interesting. Larry actually thought his children were

better off without him. "Do you miss your kids?"

"Of course I do."

"They don't come to visit you?"

"Would you come to visit me if I were *your* father?"

I truthfully had no answer. I had visited my newly found mother, and from what I could tell, she had participated in the abduction of my brother, although not in quite the same way Larry had.

"I'm waiting, Steel."

Did he really want me to respond to that question? "I don't know."

"Bullshit."

I honestly wasn't bullshitting. "It would depend. I know you'll never admit it, but Theodore Mathias is the last of Talon's abductors. That beautiful cop who was sitting beside me earlier is his daughter. You know that. That's why you wanted her to leave. I could tell you that you have nothing to fear from her, but you wouldn't believe it. She wants to see her father pay for all he's done as much as I do. As much as my brothers and sister do. But still..." I had been about to tell Larry that Ruby had opted to see her father when he had to come into town months ago with Brooke Bailey. I closed my mouth. That was Ruby's story to tell. Not mine.

"What?"

"I visited my mother."

"You only just found out that she *was* your mother."

"True. And I have a lot of questions."

"Did you get any answers?"

"Some."

"I wouldn't put faith in anything she says."

"I don't."

"Then why did you see her?"

Why indeed? My mother's relationship with the truth was contorted, at best. Mine, however, was not. And it came to me like a bolt of lightning right into my brain. Why I decided to share it with Larry, I didn't know, but I opened my mouth to speak.

"Because I wanted to. Because I wanted to see her."

"Well, my children don't want to see me."

"You have young grandchildren, right?" Jade had told me that.

"I do. And I never hurt them. I never hurt my children either."

"But you can't say the same for Mathias, can you? He didn't stop at hurting children he was related to."

Larry flattened his lips into a thin line. The bastard still wouldn't talk. Still wouldn't give up Mathias. What the hell did Mathias have on him?

Time to try a different tactic.

"What do you know about my father's will?"

"A whole lot of nothing."

Larry never made anything easy. "Simpson and Mathias seem to think my father owed them something. That there was something in his will to that effect. Do you agree with that?"

"Nobody owes me anything."

"That wasn't my question. Why would Simpson and Mathias think my father owed them something?"

No answer.

"All right. Why would *Simpson* think my father owed him anything?"

Still no response.

"Tom Simpson is dead, Larry. You have nothing to fear

from him."

Once again, his lips remained sealed.

I stood. "I guess we're done here. My offer stands. Whatever you want, Larry. My entire fortune for some answers." I motioned to the guard but then shook my head and sat back down. I'd almost forgotten the most important thing—why I'd come in the first place.

"Tell me about the ring the future lawmakers used to wear."

Larry looked over my head for a moment. "I haven't thought about that in years."

"You had one, didn't you?"

"We all did. Your father paid for them, by the way."

That piece of news didn't surprise me. After all, we'd already found out from Ruby's uncle that my father had financed the future lawmakers. Tom Simpson's ring was not a cheap piece of metal, either.

"Did he? Why are you all of a sudden telling me things? Usually you're so close-lipped."

He chuckled. "I have no idea. I just haven't thought of that ring in years."

"Wendy says she didn't have one."

"I'm pretty sure we all had one. Hers was smaller, made for a woman."

My mother wasn't known for her truthfulness, so I'd take Larry at his word. For now, anyway.

"There's a symbol on the ring. Do you know what it signifies?"

He looked thoughtful. "I don't recall a symbol."

"Oh, come on." And then I remembered. I had the ring! I pulled it out of my pocket. "This one belonged to Tom

Simpson. Look here." I gestured. "What does this bizarre symbol mean?"

He took the ring from me and examined it. "Oh, yeah. I don't know. Someone else designed it."

"Who?"

"I can't say."

"You don't remember? Or you won't tell me."

He stayed silent.

"My father?"

Silence.

"Tom Simpson?"

More silence.

"Mathias?"

His lips twitched slightly.

"Okay. Mathias. That figures. Did he tell you what the symbol meant?"

"I didn't say he designed them."

I wished Ruby were still here. She'd be able to read him better than I could with her cop instinct. "Up to this point, you've refused to even say his name. But we all know it was him, that he's the third of your heinous trio. And it doesn't surprise me one bit to know he's the brains behind this symbol."

"You're wrong. I don't know what the symbol is. Or what it means. Or who came up with it. And if I did, I wouldn't tell you."

"We have our own theories," I said. "So you're telling me that you wore a ring that you had no idea what its meaning was?"

"Hey, it was a ring. It was camaraderie, you know? We all had one."

"Where's yours now?"

"I hocked it long ago. I had some lean years in there. They deserted me after I let your brother go. After they tried to kill me, that is. I didn't get back into their good graces until a few years ago."

I'd already heard that part of the story, so I tried to steer back to the ring. "He never told you what the symbol meant?"

"Nope." Larry twisted his lips into a sly smile. "But I can see why you want to know. The devil is in the details. Just ask your mother."

"Ryan!"

I looked up. Ruby was walking swiftly toward our table. I stood. "What is it? Are you okay?"

"Yeah, fine. I need to talk to you."

"Okay. We're almost done here." I looked to Larry. "She's not leaving. Do you have any more information for me?"

"No." Larry motioned to a guard, who came and took him away.

I looked to Ruby. "Why did you come back?"

"I have a new theory," she said. "And I'm not sure you're going to like it."

CHAPTER TWENTY-ONE

Ruby

I drew in a deep breath and gathered my courage. How was I supposed to tell the man I loved that I suspected his newly found mother was the mastermind behind everything?

I couldn't. Not yet. First, I'd tell him about the e-mail I had received from Wendy via one of her doctor's cell phones.

"Just what I don't need right now. I'm beat. I can't deal with her tonight."

"Lights are probably out in the ward by now anyway," I said. "It can wait. You want to get something to eat?"

"Yeah, that'd be good. What's good around here?"

I rarely ate out, but we found a Mexican place that had good reviews. Over dinner of carnitas and refried beans with *pico de gallo*, I told him about the card that had been found in Jordan Hayes's apartment.

"You can't suspect Joe," Ryan said.

"I don't, and neither does my boss. But the MO is familiar."

"Yeah. That's how we found Colin's business card in the guest room at Talon's house. But surely Felicia couldn't have gotten into Jordan's apartment."

"Probably not, though we're going to want to question her," I said. "Most likely it was my father. Remember, Felicia said the guy who threatened her had spooky blue eyes. Same as Joe said, and same as Melanie said. My father has been wearing colored contacts to disguise himself. At least that's what we suspect."

"Yeah, Joe figured that out too."

"So anyway, it was either my father or someone who was told by my father to place the card at Jordan's. By the way, have you heard from those PIs of yours?"

"Mills and Johnson?" Ryan shook his head. "Nope. They seem to have fallen off the face of the earth."

"I don't like the sound of that. I'm going to look into it at work. I wonder..." I swirled beans around on my plate.

"What?"

"What if Mills and Johnson... No, that's too farfetched."

"What?" he said again.

"Mills and Johnson have been working with police departments in Colorado for years. They wouldn't have gone to the bad side."

"Meaning?"

"What if my father got to them? Paid them off to disappear?"

"Would they do that?"

"They're mercenaries. They go with the highest bidder. And I've had the feeling my father's been having financial trouble."

"We can out-pay your father."

"Maybe they don't know that."

"Everyone knows about the Steel money."

"True. But what if he *could* out-pay your family? What if he dried up his coffers to get them off the case?"

"I guess it's possible. Our money is legitimate, from generations of hard work and solid investments. Crime can pay extremely well. Your father probably has billions in tax-free dollars stashed away." He huffed. "And that's what I just don't get. Tom Simpson was obviously up to his eyeballs in this, yet he continued to live his modest life as the mayor of Snow Creek."

"His cover," I said. "It makes perfect sense."

"Has the department dug up his stash?" he asked.

"Not that I know of. I'm technically not on the case. I just follow it very closely. Plus, anything concerning the money will go to the FBI. They're already on it."

"He must have a shitload of money stashed somewhere."

"Yeah, he might," I agreed.

"Bryce could be a rich man one day."

"Only if he's interested in dirty money," Ruby said. "If the Feds find it—if it exists—it will be confiscated."

"Yeah. True." Ryan finished up his plate. "I wonder..."

"What?"

"You don't think any of the Steel money could be dirty, do you?"

I shook my head. "I've considered that, and I don't think so. Your father and his father ran a legitimate business. If your father has any dirty money anywhere, he was smart enough not to comingle funds."

"I hope so," Ryan said. "It's just..."

"What?"

"The Steel Trust is where we keep the bulk of our holdings. But the Shane ranch was deeded to the Steel *Family* Trust, which of course, none of us knew existed. Joe's trying to get hold of the attorneys to figure it all out." Ryan rubbed at his temples. "I just can't wrap my head around it. My father had a trust none of us knew about. Could that be where he kept...?"

I heard the words he couldn't form. *Where he kept the dirty money.* I couldn't say them aloud either.

"Let me tell you," he continued. "The four of us are going to be keeping a better eye on things from now on."

"Why haven't you always done that?"

"Because this was our father's team of advisors, guys he trusted with his money. Consequently, *we* trusted them. And it's not like we're blue bloods or anything. We work our asses off at the ranch. We need the team to oversee the finances because none of us has the time."

He sounded like he was trying to convince himself, and I understood why. He didn't want to admit that any of them had been negligent in letting the team handle everything. But he knew they had. Not negligent so much as overworked and trusting in their father.

A man they no longer knew.

"And another thing," he continued. "Now that Mills and Johnson are nowhere to be found, we need some new PIs. We've *got* to find my father."

"So you really think he's alive?"

"I think he has to be. We found the death certificate that was clearly tampered with, and none of us actually saw his dead body. Plus, my mother says so."

I opened my mouth to blurt out that he couldn't take anything his mother said seriously, but stopped myself. If what I suspected about Wendy was true, we needed to start considering everything she said more critically. We needed to figure out how to separate the lies from the truth and the reasons behind all of them.

Right now, though, we both needed a break.

"Look," I said. "I'm exhausted, and I have work tomorrow.

Let's sleep on this."

He smiled. "Is that an invitation?"

No, it hadn't been. What was I supposed to say? Before I could think of something appropriate, my cell phone buzzed.

It was a text.

Don't go home tonight.

CHAPTER TWENTY-TWO

R y a n

Ruby's rosy cheeks went white as she looked at her phone.

"What is it, babe?"

She cleared her throat. "Nothing."

"Bullshit. Who texted you?"

"I don't know, actually."

I grabbed the phone out of her hands, not caring whether she liked it or not. The text was still on the screen.

Don't go home tonight.

What the fuck?

I motioned to our waiter to get the check. "You're coming home with me," I said.

"Look, I'm sure—"

"Don't even try to tell me this is nothing. Can you get into your office system from anywhere?"

She nodded.

"We're going to trace this number, figure out who sent this and what it means."

"I can do that right now," she said, "if you'll give me my phone."

I handed it back to her. The waiter came by with the

check, and I handed him a credit card while Ruby tapped away at her phone.

"Anything yet?" I asked.

"Nothing in the regular phone database. Which means it isn't Wendy stealing an orderly's phone again, unless someone at psych lockup has a privatized number, which isn't likely. I'll have to do a more in-depth search."

"Which you can do from my office at my place." I scribbled out a tip and my signature on the credit card receipt the waiter had set in front of me. "Let's go."

★ ★ ★

I poured two glasses of wine for Ruby and me and then looked outside. It was a nice night. Early November. Thanksgiving would be here soon. We'd celebrate at Talon's like we always did, his being the biggest house on the ranch, and this year, we'd have two new family members to include.

Thinking of such a nice family time should have made me happy, but my nerves were jumpy. Ruby was in danger, and that didn't sit well with me at all.

"Any news from the department?" I asked her.

"Not yet. They're keeping watch. No one will get in or out of my place tonight."

"I'm just glad you're not there," I said. "If something..."

"What?"

"Nothing." I handed her a glass of wine and then took a sip from my own. "You want to sit in the hot tub? I need to relax."

"Yeah, as a matter of fact. Relaxing sounds great."

After we'd shed our clothes and donned robes, we headed out into the cool night air. I took the cover off the tub, and the steam rose up around us. We took off our robes and got in. I inhaled, remembering our times in Jamaica under the stars. Even though we lived in the country, so many more stars had been visible in the Caribbean. I inhaled the night air.

"Sometimes I wish we were still in Jamaica," I said, "without a care in the world."

"Jamaica had its own issues," Ruby replied.

"Damn!" I stood and sat on the edge of the tub. "Can't we relax? Can't we just remember the good times? I'm so sorry about those two girls. I really am, Ruby. But my life has taken a one-eighty since we got back, and I just want to relax. To remember."

She stood as well, taking my hand. "Get back in the tub, Ryan."

I obeyed, sitting down next to her, her wet skin against mine. "I'm sorry."

"It's okay. I want to relax too. You have to understand, though, that I haven't really relaxed in the last seventeen years. I even fought it in Jamaica, and then, after Juliet and Lisa..."

I turned toward her, cupping her cheeks. "We had some amazing times. Even *after* Juliet and Lisa."

She nodded, though she didn't smile. "We did."

"Can we concentrate on those times this evening? So much has happened, and all I want to think about is you. You. Here. Safe. There was no way I was letting you go to your apartment tonight."

She opened her mouth, but I shushed her.

"Let me finish. I know you can take care of yourself. I get it. You've been doing it forever, and you're a cop, and you're armed, and you know self-defense. I get all that, Ruby. I do. But goddamnit, let me protect you. I need to."

I did. Talon had protected me all those years ago, and though I'd lay down my life for my brothers and my sister, a new surge was rising within me now. The need to keep Ruby safe was stronger than the need I felt toward my siblings.

That scared the hell out of me.

And that trust thing? When she'd given my siblings my hair for the DNA test without telling me? My love was stronger than that. We'd work through that issue. Together.

"I don't need—"

"Christ, Ruby, did you hear anything I just said?"

She sniffled. I didn't think she was crying. It was probably the heat.

"I did hear you, Ryan. I heard every word. I just can't abide the idea of not protecting myself. It seems...unnatural to me."

"Well, get used to it. You're mine now to protect." I grabbed her and smashed our lips together.

She opened immediately, accepting my kiss, though perhaps not my offer of protection. We'd work on that.

I needed to keep her safe. Needed to keep her with me.

I wanted her with me all the time. She'd have to move in. She was no longer safe at her apartment anyway. Someone was clearly after her, and someone else had sent that warning.

She'd have to—

My thoughts jumbled as she swirled her tongue around mine.

No more thoughts. Only emotion. Pure emotion and physical need. I needed this woman. Needed her in more than a physical and emotional sense. It had transcended beyond that.

This was what my brothers had found, and now I knew why they would never let it go.

I'd never let this woman go.

I groaned into Ruby's mouth, trying to express all the feelings jumbling in my head with this one kiss. I ached for her, longed for her, needed her in the most visceral way.

Damn it, I would have her. I stood and lifted her, turning her so her back was to me. "Hold on to the edge of the tub," I demanded.

With a swift thrust, I entered her, filling her balls deep. "Ah!" A groan of satisfaction left my lips.

This was what it felt like to be home. Home within the body of my love.

I had to tell her. Had to tell her I'd fallen in love with her. Had to tell her she was moving in with me, and I wasn't taking no for an answer.

I demanded everything from her. Right now, and I demanded it as I pounded into her body, taking what was mine. For that's what she was now.

Mine.

I plunged as deeply as I could, taking refuge in her tight little pussy, in her beautiful body. Away from the mess my life had become. Away...

And I came into her, making her mine as I filled her with my semen.

When the orgasm finally subsided and my flaccid penis slipped from her slick channel, I sat down into the water, bringing her with me onto my lap.

"I needed that," I said.

She nodded, saying nothing.

"I'm sorry. I didn't give you a climax."

"That's okay." She let out what sounded like a nervous laugh.

My heart was pounding so hard against my sternum. I had so much to tell her. So much to give her. So much...and I feared she wouldn't be ready to receive it.

She'd have to.

There was no going back for me now.

I was all in.

I looked deeply into her blue eyes.

"Ruby. I'm in love with you."

CHAPTER TWENTY-THREE

Ruby

I'm in love with you.

I played the words over and over in my mind, the steam swirling around us, our skin slick from the combination of warm water and perspiration.

Those words I'd never expected to hear in my life...and they'd come from Ryan Steel. One of the Steel brothers, the best catches in Colorado.

This was surreal.

Had he really uttered them? Or had it been my imagination as we sat under the stars, steam enveloping us, warm water drifting over us? Fantasy churned in the air. Surely I could have created the words in my mind.

"Don't say anything yet," he said. "Come to bed with me. I owe you an orgasm. Or three or four."

It hadn't been fantasy.

He led me out of the tub, helped me put on my robe, and then escorted me back into the house, Ricky frolicking at our heels.

I'm in love with you.

And then, more of his words haunted my mind.

You're mine to protect.

No. I wasn't his. I would never belong to him or anyone

else.

My independence screamed at me to tell him that, to say I wasn't going anywhere with him, and I was certainly not his possession.

But the desire within me overruled my independence, and I continued following him to the bedroom where he laid me gently on his bed.

I'm in love with you.

I was in love with him too. I'd known it for a while, and I wanted to say the words—wanted to so much—but something held me back.

All this time, I'd never dreamed he could actually feel the same way I did. Never dreamed any man could feel that way about me, never dreamed I'd *want* any man to.

Ryan Steel was not *any* man.

He peeled the damp robe from my body, my skin still glistening with moisture. He stood above me, his dark hair wet and slicked back, his eyes smoldering, his pink lips so plump and full. His body... Those broad shoulders, perfect chest and abs, coppery nipples, and black hair smattered over his flesh.

And his cock. He was already hard again. It sprang from his black curls as beautiful as it always did. I took a moment to look at it, to truly examine it. It was a shade darker than his tan skin, and two purple veins marbled around and under the shaft. The tip of his head glistened with a drop of moisture.

I wanted to lick it off, but at the moment, I didn't move. Even though part of me screamed to do what I wanted, to exert my independence, that other part of me, that part I'd kept hidden for so long, yearned to submit.

He leaned over me and brushed his lips against mine. Just a soft, sweet kiss. Then he moved over to my cheek, my neck, sending shivers throughout every cell in my body. He trailed his full lips over my chest, the tops of my breasts, until finally he reached a nipple.

My areolas were already wrinkled and taut, my nipples so hard they strained forward, searching for fingers, lips, a stubbled cheek—anything to brush against them and give them the attention they ached for.

Ryan didn't disappoint. He flicked his tongue over one while thumbing the other. I moaned, straining, lifting my hips off the bed, aching for more of his kisses, his tongue, his touch. His everything.

"So beautiful," he murmured against my skin.

I groaned when he tugged on my nipple with his teeth. I was wet for him, could already smell the earthy musk permeating his bedroom. I inhaled, savoring the aroma, letting it slide into the pores in my skin, making me warm all over.

Ryan continued with my nipple, alternating tugs and sucks with soothing licks while he twisted the other one between his fingers. I squirmed beneath him, undulating my hips, searching for his cock to fill me.

"What do you want, baby?" he asked, his breath warm against my breast.

"Mmm...you."

"You've got me." He glided his hand from my breast down my belly to my vulva and then slid his fingers through my labia. "So wet. God." He pushed a finger into me while he thumbed my clit.

"Oh!" I nearly flew off the bed. The climax was swift and voracious. I moved my hips in tandem with the contractions inside my walls as they illuminated my body with fire and ice simultaneously.

"That's it, my love. Come for me."

My love.

Wow.

If possible, his words increased the intensity of my climax, and I soared even higher, grasping fists full of the silk covering Ryan's bed.

As I came down, sinking into the mattress, he let my nipple drop from his lips and kissed me.

A long, sweet kiss. A kiss full of love.

I had to tell him. Had to tell him I was in love with him too. But right now, I wanted to melt into the amazing kiss he was giving me, show him without words what I was feeling. I wrapped my arms around his neck, pulling him closer, as close as I could. Our tongues tangled and dueled, groans humming from our throats and vibrating against each other's mouths.

I love you, Ryan, I said with that kiss. *I love you so much.*

CHAPTER TWENTY-FOUR

R y a n

The kiss went from sweet to primal in what seemed like an instant. Ruby deepened it, thrust her tongue into my mouth, and took from me, and I was only too happy to give. Our mouths were fused together, the energy between us sizzling so much that visible sparks wouldn't have surprised me if I'd opened my eyes. But I kept them closed and melded into Ruby's mouth, her body.

Here lay a woman who mere weeks ago had never been kissed, yet she was kissing me like the goddess of love herself.

I reveled in it, in her, as she exerted her strength and rolled us over so she was on top of me. My cock nudged against her vulva, her soft hairs tickling the head.

I had to have her, had to feel her slick walls suctioned around my cock. Though it pained me, I broke the kiss.

"Ride me, baby. Sit down on my cock and ride me."

She slid upward, her skin sticking to me from the perspiration between us. Her scent hung in the air. That intoxicating mélange of female musk laced with vanilla. I could smell it forever and never tire of it.

She plunged down onto my cock, her plump breasts bouncing lightly against her chest. Her nipples were dark and ruddy from my attentions, still hard as little berries.

How had this happened? How had she come to mean everything to me? At a time when I wasn't even sure who I was anymore, Ruby Lee helped to define me. I needed her. I could only hope she needed me.

She continued to fuck me, her hips alternating between pistoning and a figure eight that slowly drove me crazy. My whole body seemed covered in flames as my nerves raced around me, making me quiver. My nipples were hard as she brushed her fingers over them and then planted her hands on my chest to support herself as she rocked faster, faster.

I brought my hand to her vulva and fingered her clit as she pulled herself up and then sank down upon my hardness once more. I slid my hands to her hips, that beautiful feminine swell, and then cupped the globes of her perfect ass. I caressed her softness, gliding toward the crease. How I itched to finger her tight little asshole...and I would. But not yet. That would scare her.

She was mine. I felt it in the very depths of my soul. One day I would have all of her.

Just the thought of breaching that tight virgin ass, and I was ready to come, but I didn't want to yet. I needed to have her under me, taking me in all the way.

I lifted her by her hips and sprang up, flipping her onto her back. In a flash I was back inside her, pumping my hard cock into her tight little pussy. I maneuvered her legs onto my shoulders—all that yoga made her extremely flexible, apparently—giving me the angle I needed. I looked into her sparkling blue eyes and was surprised to see a tear slide from one.

No, I couldn't be hurting her. Could I?

"Baby?"

"Yeah?"

"You all right?"

She nodded. "Fine. Keep going. Please."

She didn't need to say any more. I continued my thrusting, taking her, making her mine. Protecting her. As long as I lived, no one would hurt her. Never again.

When her walls began to spasm around me and she cried out in climax, I plunged into her to the hilt, my balls slapping the crease of her ass. As I convulsed, as I emptied every last drop of myself into her body, I closed my eyes and said the words again.

"I'm in love with you, Ruby."

Then I collapsed on top of her, a sweaty mess.

We lay there for a few moments, both breathing rapidly. I finally moved to relieve her of my weight. She was gleaming, covered in perspiration, her hair sticking to her forehead and shoulders.

She'd never looked more beautiful.

I waited. And waited.

Waited for her to return my sentiment. To say the words I wanted to hear.

She remained silent.

I wouldn't pressure her. After all, I was her first relationship...ever. But one way or the other, she'd be moving in with me. For her own safety. It had nothing to do with how I felt about her.

That was a bald-faced lie.

These feelings were so new to me. During the few years that Anna and I were together, we'd spent many nights here, in this very bed. But never had I imagined her staying forever, moving in. Of course she'd never needed my protection either.

We still didn't know who had texted Ruby and told her not to go home tonight. Yes, it could have been a hoax, but I wasn't taking any chances.

I was wet with perspiration. "Shower?" I said to her.

She chuckled. "Yeah. Good idea."

I got up and pulled her off the bed and into my embrace. I held her for a moment, enjoying the warmth of our bodies, and then I led her into my bathroom. I got out a couple of clean towels and handed one to her.

Her cheeks had turned red.

"You okay?"

"Yeah. It's just... I've never showered with a guy before." She looked to her feet. "I mean, I know I've *used* your shower before."

She had. She'd awoken in the middle of the night after a bad dream, and I'd found her in my shower, scrubbing herself raw.

"If you want, you can shower first. I'll leave you alone." I smiled.

"No, of course not. I don't know why I even said that." She hung her towel on the shower door and opened it. "Let's do this."

I couldn't help a laugh. She sounded like a cop getting ready to investigate a crime scene. I gave her a few seconds to get used to the water, and then I entered behind her. Her long hair was pasted to her back in an onyx sheath. So gorgeous. I grabbed my Mane 'n Tail—yes, I used horse shampoo. What was good enough for Sergio was good enough for me—and squirted a liberal amount onto my palm, much more than I used for myself. Ruby had a lot more hair than I did.

"Come here." I turned her around to face me and spread

the shampoo into her hair.

"You don't have to do that."

"Are you crazy? I want to. Your hair is a work of art." I lathered it into her scalp and then pulled it through to her ends. "I might not have even used enough."

She smiled. "It's plenty."

I continued to massage her scalp and then pushed her back into the shower stream to rinse her head. The trickles of water rivered down her beautiful body, and I was hard again.

Damn.

Without so much as a thought, I lifted her, turned around so her back was against the shower wall, and shoved my cock into her once more.

Every time was more amazing than the last. Every time I felt something new with this woman. This time, as our wet bodies slid against each other, a new sensation—something foreign and unsettling but deeply arousing—surged through me.

It wasn't love. I already felt that. It wasn't passion or desire. I was well acquainted with those around Ruby. Yet this emotion contained all three of those and more. It was almost an ache. Emotion so pure and strong that it hurt, but in a good way.

I embraced it, thrust myself into her body as she pressed her dripping breasts into my chest.

"Ryan," she moaned, closing her eyes.

Her orgasm took her with more force than I'd yet seen, and I thrust into her deeply, filling her. I closed my eyes as well, letting her clamping walls milk every last drop of cum out of me. And when the convulsions subsided, still embedded inside her, I said again, "I love you."

Again, she didn't respond.

I set her on the shower floor, and we finished up, washing each other and sharing a few kisses.

When I turned the water off and we stepped out and toweled off, it was time to get serious.

"Ruby," I said to her, her blue eyes slightly bloodshot from the shower, "you're moving in with me."

CHAPTER TWENTY-FIVE

Ruby

Huh?

I'd heard him say he loved me three different times, and each time I'd ached to say it back to him, to reaffirm what I knew in my heart to be true.

But move in with him?

So not happening.

I must have had my jaw dropped nearly to the floor, because he pushed my chin upward.

"Aren't you going to say anything?"

While in the shower, when he had me against the wall, our bodies sopping together as he made love to me, I'd decided to tell him my feelings. To tell him I loved him.

Now? I wasn't sure what to say about anything.

"I..."

"What?"

"I can't move in with you."

"Sure you can."

This was so Ryan. This was the Ryan I'd gotten to know in Jamaica. The Ryan who took charge, didn't take no for an answer, always got what he wanted, flipped words around to suit his purpose.

After he found out that Wendy Madigan was his mother,

rather than become distant, he'd come to me, nearly forced himself on me, and surprise of all surprises, I hadn't said no.

I'd wanted it.

I'd wanted *him*. I'd wanted to help him in any way I could. I still wanted that. But moving in with him wouldn't help him, and it wouldn't help me either.

"You're crazy," I said.

"About you."

That got a smile out of me. That was another classic Ryan Steel line, like the ones he'd given me in the Caribbean—the ones I'd tried so hard to resist but couldn't.

"Look, I—"

He placed two fingers over my lips. "You don't have to tell me you love me, Ruby."

"But I—"

He shushed me again. "Whether you do or not—yet— doesn't matter. I need you safe. You'll be safe here."

"I'm perfectly capable of taking care of myself."

"I'm not saying you aren't."

"Well, yeah, you kind of are. I'm not moving in with you just to be safe. That's not what I'm about."

"Then move in with me because you want to."

It would be so easy to say yes. To confess my love for him— and I did love him beyond reason—and shield myself behind his walls. Behind *him*.

But I couldn't. That wasn't who I was. That wasn't who I'd ever be.

I cupped his cheek. "Ryan, are you sure you love me?" I hated the words as soon as they left my lips. This was "insecure-about-men Ruby" coming out. He'd only recently taken my virginity. He was the only man I had any experience with. Why in the world would he want me?

"I don't say things I don't mean," he said, his dark eyes serious.

No, he didn't. I knew that much about him.

"It's just...so much has gone on in the last two weeks. Your mother—"

"My mother isn't who I thought she was. I'm dealing with that. I'm still dealing with your part in it, as well. But I can't deny my feelings any longer. When you got that text..." He raked his fingers through his damp hair. "I couldn't stand the thought of you being in danger. Even potential danger. I've been living the past several months with everyone I love being in potential danger, and I'm damned sick of it, Ruby. So you're moving in here."

"Don't go all caveman on me," I said. "It isn't you."

"Maybe it *is* me. Maybe I want to have some semblance of control over my life."

"You can't control *me*."

"Damn it!" His fingers threaded through his hair once more. "That's not what I meant and you know it."

I knew what he meant. His life had been turned upside down, and now he wanted to take it back. Beginning with me, apparently.

I took his hand and caressed his palm. "Look. I get it. I get what you've been through. But me moving in with you isn't the answer."

"What do I have to do?" His eyes blazed with dark fire. "*Fuck* you into submission?"

I arched my brows, and my pulse beat rapidly in my neck. Goose bumps erupted all over my flesh, and a flaming arrow shot between my legs. My clit began to throb, and before I knew it, the familiar scent of my arousal permeated the bedroom.

Ryan's eyes glazed over, and he inhaled. He smelled it too.

Did I want to be fucked into submission?

Hell, no. At least not the rational, logical part of me.

But part of me did. The part that wanted to surrender to Ryan Steel in all his masculine glory.

And that frightened me. Big time.

He walked toward me, like a wolf stalking his mate. My rational brain screamed at me to push him away, get out of there, run like hell.

But my libido overrode all reason. He was going to try to fuck me into submission, and I wasn't going to stop him.

A simple "no" would do it. I knew that. Ryan Steel wasn't a rapist. He wasn't any kind of criminal. But he *was* domineering. He had been since the beginning, always getting what he wanted in that jovial way of his. He was far from jovial now, though.

My heart nearly thumped out of my chest, and my tummy fluttered with anxiety. Yet I didn't stop him when he grabbed my shoulders. Didn't stop him when he lifted me in his strong arms and carried me to his bed. Didn't stop him when he nearly ripped the terry robe from my body and spread my legs harshly.

No. I didn't stop him.

I didn't want to.

I wanted this, and I didn't do anything I didn't want to do. He knew this about me, so he knew it now. He knew how much I wanted this. Wanted *him*.

He didn't speak. He acted with feral ferocity, thrusting his tongue between my legs. Then he stopped, staring at me, inhaling.

My arousal. He was smelling my arousal like a damned

animal. Such a turn-on. His eyes were closed, and still he said nothing. Just continued inhaling the aroma that hung in the air.

So I inhaled, and I could smell his arousal too. The scent of lust. It was thick around us.

Finally, he opened his eyes, so dark in their intensity, and began licking between my legs.

My nipples pebbled, and I moved one hand toward my breasts to squeeze them, but he brushed it away and began fingering both of my nipples as he licked me.

I closed my eyes again and became a slave to him, to the feelings he evoked within me. I lifted my hips, gliding them up and down, grinding against his lips and face. The stubble on his cheeks and chin scratched me in the most delicious way. I'd have some nasty razor burn, but I didn't care. I needed this. Needed him. I continued grinding into him, his stubble scratching the inside of my thighs now. He kept up with my movements, sucking me, thrusting his tongue inside me and then tugging on my clit.

I skyrocketed and climbed to the precipice. All of my energy pulsing outward and inward to my secret-most core.

When I finally came down, he was still eating me, and although I whimpered when he took one of his hands from my breasts, I was elated when he thrust two fingers in my pussy. I cried out his name—once, twice, three times. He finger fucked me, moving his fingers in such a way that every part of my pussy walls felt him.

I had nothing to compare this to, but I couldn't even begin to fathom that sex with anyone else could ever be this good. Ryan Steel touched something inside me, something I had ignored for far too long.

When I started another climax, he flipped me over and shoved his cock into me from behind.

Slap!

I gripped the covers when his hand came down on my ass.

I squeezed my eyes shut, waiting for his palm to come down on me again.

It didn't.

Part of me was relieved. Part of me, disappointed.

Who was I? I wasn't sure I knew anymore.

He grunted on top of me, continuing to plunge into me. He said nothing, which surprised me. Normally he talked during sex. Dirty talk. Dirty talk I had come to enjoy. But not this time. This time he was in pure animal mode, taking me.

And I was letting him.

With each thrust, I became more his. I lost more of myself inside of his body.

And suddenly, a lance of fear so sharp speared straight into my heart.

"Ryan," I whispered into the covers, knowing he wouldn't hear me.

"Ryan," I whispered again.

He was all body, all physical, as he continued to slam into me. With each thrust, I felt more of what made me Ruby seeping out and melting into the bed. Leaving me.

I no longer whispered his name. Because though my first instinct was to tell him to stop, I didn't want him to stop. Part of me wanted this. Part of me wanted to become part of him, to lose myself in him.

Another orgasm was imminent, but I bit my lip, fighting against it, fearing that if I came, all that was Ruby Lee would become encompassed in all that was Ryan Steel.

I couldn't let that happen. Even though a big part of me wanted to let it happen.

Finally, he pushed into me so deeply and let out a loud groan. His orgasm. By now I was flat on the bed. He had fucked me so hard that I had fallen from my hands and knees.

Though my body was sated, my mind whirled. Ryan loved me. He'd said so three times, even though I hadn't returned his words despite feeling them in the depths of my heart, my soul.

He rolled off of me onto his back so that he was lying beside my prone form. I turned on my side to look at him. His chest was moving up and down rapidly, his body shiny with perspiration, his arm over his forehead, covering his eyes.

What was he thinking? I glanced at his clock on the night table. It was past midnight. Not surprising.

I wanted to go back to my apartment. I was a cop, for God's sake. I couldn't let some anonymous text scare me away from my own home. Yet that other part of me—that part that wanted to lose myself in Ryan Steel—didn't want to leave.

Ryan let out a soft snore. He had fallen asleep.

No way was I going to fall asleep with my mind racing as it was. I would stay here—only because I couldn't stand the idea of Ryan waking up and finding me gone. I couldn't do that to him.

I had to work things out, and this was all so new to me that I knew I couldn't do it on my own.

Tomorrow I would call Melanie and begin therapy. I needed to figure myself out. I needed to be whole for Ryan.

But first, when he woke up, I would tell Ryan Steel that I loved him.

CHAPTER TWENTY-SIX

Ryan

I woke up, the sheet twisted around my body. "Ruby?"

Damn. My clock showed seven a.m. I had forgotten to set my alarm. I was late getting out to the fields. Where was Ruby?

Fear settled in my gut. Had she gone home? No, she wouldn't have. She wouldn't have put herself in danger. I sat up quickly and found my robe. I walked swiftly through the house. "Ruby?"

No answer.

When I got to the kitchen, I noticed Ricky sitting outside the door, on the deck. Then I saw Ruby sitting in the family room. I walked toward the sofa.

"Hey," I said.

"Hey, sleepyhead."

"Why didn't you wake me?"

"I figured I'd let you sleep. We were up pretty late last night."

"I should've gotten up two hours ago," I said.

"I only just got up about fifteen minutes ago. I fed Ricky and let him out, made a pot of coffee. I need to leave pretty soon to get to work on time."

The thought of her leaving sent a spear through my stomach. Somehow, I had to convince her to move in with me.

And that thought brought last night back to the forefront of my mind.

"Baby..."

"What?"

"I'm...sorry."

"About what?"

"About trying to...fuck you into submission."

She laughed. She fucking laughed!

"What's so fucking funny?"

"You didn't fuck me into anything, Ryan. I've told you many times before. I don't do anything I don't want to do."

"Oh. Good. I guess."

"I was actually going to wake you up soon," she said. "We need to talk."

Yes, we did need to talk, and I had to figure out a really quick way to get her to move in with me.

She stood. "Want some coffee?"

I nodded, and we walked back into the kitchen. She poured two cups and set them on the table. Then she sat down. I followed suit.

"Ryan, last night was... There really aren't any words."

"Does that mean it was good or bad?"

She smiled. "It was good. Very good."

"Thank God."

"And I want to tell you..." She bit her lip, looking down. Then she met my gaze, her blue eyes burning. "I love you, Ryan. I really do love you."

Happiness surged through me. And a giant weight floated off my shoulders. Though I had wanted to hear those words last night, I'd had no idea how much they truly meant to me until they left her lips.

"Do you? Really?"

"I do. I have for a while. I just never in a million years dreamed that you could love me."

I took her hand, entwining her fingers with mine. "I do. What I feel for you is something I never imagined. It's almost an ache."

"I'm glad to hear you say that. Since I have no frame of reference, I wasn't sure exactly what I was feeling, but you just described it perfectly."

"Then will you move in with me? Let me protect you?"

She closed her eyes and let out a breath of air. "I'm sorry, Ryan. I can't move in with you."

"Why? If we love each other—"

She held up her hand to stop me. "Because. Because I need to figure some things out about myself first. And quite frankly, you're not ready for this either."

"Ruby, I know exactly what I'm ready for."

"Do you? You admit yourself that your life has just been upended. Don't you need to work through all of that before you start a serious relationship?"

"I'm pretty sure that ship has sailed, Ruby. This relationship is already serious."

"Because we love each other?"

"Yes, because we love each other. Don't you know anything about relationships?" I regretted the words as soon as I said them. Of course she didn't know anything about relationships. I was her first one. "I'm sorry. I shouldn't have said that."

"It's okay. But I think this is new for both of us."

She had the right of that. "So it's new. So what? I want you to move in with me. I want you to be safe."

"Keeping me safe is not the best reason to have me move in

with you," she said. "I may not know much about relationships, but I do know that much."

"Fine," I said. "I love you. Isn't that a good enough reason?"

"It's a wonderful reason. I love you too, and a big part of me really wants to live here with you. But I just can't. Not until I figure a few things out."

"Can't we figure them out together?"

"I wish we could." She massaged the fingers of my right hand. "But there's still a lot of my life that I haven't dealt with, Ryan. I need to work through those things before I live with someone."

I heaved a sigh. "I need to say it, baby. I don't want you going back to your apartment."

"I'll be fine."

"I'm booking a hotel room for you in the city."

"Ryan..."

"No arguments. I'm putting my foot down."

She opened her mouth, and I expected a hell of an argument, but then she closed it.

"Okay." She squeezed my hand. "I need to go to work." She stood and turned, but then turned back almost immediately. "And you need to find out what your mother wants."

Crap. I'd nearly forgotten that my mother had e-mailed Ruby asking to see me. I quickly texted my foreman and told him I wouldn't be in the field until this afternoon. "All right. Do you want to go with me?"

"I would if I could, but I need to get to work."

"All right, but we still need to talk."

"Ryan, I told you—"

"No, not about you moving in. About that theory you said you had. The one you think I'm not going to like."

★ ★ ★

My mother looked more tired than usual. Still, I saw beauty in her. I wasn't sure why. I had seen pictures of her when she was young, and she had been quite beautiful. Now, if I looked at her objectively, I saw a sixty-something-year-old woman with brown greasy hair and gray roots. She did have nice eyes though. They were blue, lighter than Ruby's and not as sparkling, but deep and soulful. When she looked at me, her face lit up, and I could see what my father had seen in her.

"Thank you for coming," she said, smiling.

"Ruby tells me that you hijacked one of your doctor's e-mail accounts."

"I do what I have to do."

"If you keep this up, and you get caught, they're going to take away what few privileges you still have."

"Don't you worry about me, my darling. I have everything under control."

"Do you? Because it seems to me that if you had everything under control, you wouldn't be in here."

She laughed softly. "My dear, your father never understood how my life worked, and I see you don't either."

That was for sure. "Speaking of my father, I have a lot of questions for you."

"Ask away. I keep no secrets from my son."

First lie of the day. She had been keeping a secret from me my entire life until recently, but now was not the time to call her on that. "We found a death certificate in my father's papers. A death certificate in the name of John Cunningham, who just happened to have the same date of death as my father and who happened to have the same physical characteristics.

That same certificate is in the Colorado database under my father's name. Same number and everything. Only the name was changed."

"Yes?"

"So my father is alive, then?"

"Of course he is. Haven't I already told you that?"

"Wendy, you lie as much as you tell the truth. How am I supposed to know the difference?"

"I would never lie about your father, Ryan. You and he are everything to me."

"Then where is he? Why did you let me think he was dead all these years?"

"I don't know where he is, Ryan."

"That's bullshit. Why are you keeping me from my father?"

Her blue eyes misted. "I wish I did know where he is. I do know that he'll come for me one day and get me out of here."

"Can you get in touch with him?"

"I have something for you," she said.

"Don't change the subject on me, Wendy."

"Please. Could you call me mother?"

When hell freezes over. "Fine." I would do whatever it took to get the truth. I had to force the word from my lips. "Mother."

The orderly sitting next to her handed her a jewelry box. She slid it across the table to me. "For you."

I opened the box. Nestled on cotton was a sapphire bracelet set in platinum or white gold. I couldn't tell which.

"What is this? And what am I supposed to do with a woman's bracelet?"

"Your father gave it to me the day you were born. He said it belonged to his mother. I've never worn it. I could never bring myself to. Every time I looked at it, I thought of you and what I had given up. So I want you to have it. Keep it as a way to remember me."

My immediate reaction was that the bracelet was tainted. Tainted with the betrayal of my father, my mothers. Yes, both of them. Daphne Steel had furthered the deception. Nothing good could come from anything Wendy could give me.

But then I looked at my mother. Wendy looked genuinely sad. Her eyes were sunken and glazed over. Without meaning to, I actually felt a sliver of pity for her.

Maybe the way to get her to do something was to treat her as my mother. To feign love for her. I hated the idea of it, but I needed information. So I took the bracelet from the box and fingered it. Had it truly belonged to my grandmother? She'd died before I was born, and Talon and Joe would be too young to remember whether she'd ever worn a sapphire bracelet.

"It's a beautiful piece," I said. "My father must have loved you very much."

I had no idea, but maybe he had. Maybe... I never really knew Bradford Steel. None of us had. Maybe this woman had truly known him, and not just in the biblical sense. Maybe she was the key.

"Thank you for saying that," Wendy said. "We were each other's true loves."

Then why didn't he go to you after our mother died? The question hovered on my lips, but I didn't ask it. Mentioning Daphne Steel wouldn't get me where I needed to be right now.

"This is an expensive bracelet," I said. "Why did you keep it? You could have sold it."

"I couldn't part with it, and I didn't need any money. You know that."

True. She'd said my father had paid her five million dollars to give me up. But the timing didn't quite coincide. The five-million-dollar transfer had left the Steel account twenty-five years ago, around the time Talon was taken. I'd been born thirty-two years ago.

"If you couldn't part with it, why didn't you wear it?"

"I don't expect you to understand."

"Then help me. Help me understand...Mother."

CHAPTER TWENTY-SEVEN

Ruby

"Congratulations," Melanie said to me. "You're the first patient I've seen in this office in weeks." She smiled. "It feels good to be back here."

"I'm glad my uncle dropped the medical malpractice lawsuit against you," I said.

"You and me both. But there's still so much to figure out about Gina and her death and how it all relates to...well, to your father."

My father. Everything always came back to my father.

"But you came here to talk to me professionally. I appreciate your trust in me, Ruby. I truly do."

"Talon and Jonah say you're the best."

She laughed. "They might be a little bit biased."

I hoped she could hear the sincerity in my voice. "I've heard in great detail from Ryan how much Talon has changed for the better since he started seeing you. And I know the whole story of how he suffered at the hands of my father and the others. I wouldn't be here if I didn't think you were the best therapist in the state. I appreciate you seeing me on such short notice."

"Not a problem. I'm not officially back until next week, but I was here getting the office ready. Are you hungry? I know this is your lunch hour. We can order something in."

"No. I'm fine." I gripped the arms of the forest-green leather recliner upon which I sat. Was this where Talon had sat? Where Gina had sat?

"All right. What can I help you with?"

Where to start? I fidgeted a little. "I need to become..." *Shit, Ruby. Just say it.* "I need to become whole, Melanie. I don't know exactly where to start, but that's where I need to end."

"What makes you think you're not whole just as you are?"

I couldn't help a laugh. "Are you kidding? I was a virgin until age thirty-two. I've been dressing down for over a decade to keep men from noticing me. Even that didn't stop some of them, but I was able to scare them off."

"So you're not a virgin anymore then?"

"Surely you've heard all about what happened in Jamaica."

She smiled. "The Steels don't kiss and tell, but of course I had a hunch."

Heat burned my cheeks.

"Don't be embarrassed. I'm proof enough that no one can resist the Steel men."

That got a smile out of me. "So you resisted at first?"

"I did. But we're not here to talk about me."

True. And I *was* paying her. Or rather, my insurance was. "I'm finding out some things about myself that...surprise me. Even disturb me a little."

"What things?"

I inhaled and let my breath out slowly. Here went nothing. "I've been afraid of men for so long. I really took a big chance with Ryan, and I never expected it to turn into something."

"Has it turned into something?"

I nodded. "I love him. And what's even more unbelievable? He loves me."

"That's wonderful! And just to reiterate what I said on the phone, everything you say in our sessions is completely confidential. I won't go running to Jonah with this news."

"I know that." Melanie was a consummate professional.

"So what are you finding out about yourself that troubles you?"

I fidgeted some more. "I've always been attracted to men. I just never let it go anywhere. I didn't want them to be attracted to me."

"That makes perfect sense, considering what you went through with your father."

I'd told Melanie weeks ago that my father had attacked me but that I'd escaped before he could rape me. "I get that. I do. But then I look at people like Talon. Gina. Colin Morse. The people who weren't lucky enough to escape. I don't know how Colin is dealing with things since it was so recent, but Talon and Gina didn't swear off the opposite sex."

"How anyone else handled a similar situation really isn't relevant. People are individuals. We all handle things in our own way."

That didn't make me feel a whole lot better.

"At any rate, you seem to have come out of your shell quite a bit. You've lost your virginity, and you've fallen in love. Those are very special things."

"I know that. And I want to be with Ryan. More than anything, actually. But there are a few things holding me back."

"What?"

"First, my father. I haven't been able to bring him to justice. I feel like a failure."

"You're not a failure, Ruby. Your father has eluded everyone. Not just you."

"I know that. But still... I have to see him behind bars before I can do anything else."

"Says who?"

"Says me."

She smiled. "So before you can have a relationship, you need to make sure your father is captured."

I chuckled. "When you say it like that, it sounds really stupid."

"It's not stupid. But it *is* irrelevant. Why would you want to punish yourself for things your father has done?"

"I don't."

"Sure you do. You said yourself that your father being at large is keeping you from delving into a relationship with Ryan—a relationship you say you want."

"Yes. I want it. I just don't *want* to want it."

"Relationships with other people are what make us human, Ruby. It's no sin to want that."

"I know that. I just mean...I never *thought* I'd want it."

"I never thought I'd be pregnant at forty. Things change." She smiled.

"This is a little different from that."

"I know. But things do change. *People* change. Maybe you've changed. And if you have, that's okay."

Was it? "This was never part of my plan for myself."

"Plans change."

"Yes, I know. Maybe I'm not explaining this right."

"You're explaining it just fine. But there's one thing you need to truly accept."

"What's that?"

"You are not responsible for your father's actions. You never were."

"Of course. I know that."

"Yes, you know that. But part of you is taking the blame, and that's why you feel so personally responsible for all of his victims and personally responsible for getting him put away."

"It's just..."

"You can't be held responsible for your DNA. You and Ryan have that in common."

We did. I'd never actually thought of it in those terms. "He seems to be dealing with it better than I am." Then I shook my head. "I'm sorry I said that. I can't belittle what has happened to his life. He's having a hard time. It's easier for him sometimes than it is for others."

"Sounds like he's reacting normally."

"He is. It gets to him sometimes. He still blames me a little bit, I think."

"Yet he told you he loves you?"

I smiled. "Yeah. He did."

"Then either he doesn't blame you, or even if he does, the love he feels is stronger than any other feeling he has about you. That's a good thing."

"I suppose."

"So tell me, then. Is the love you feel for him stronger than the things holding you back?"

CHAPTER TWENTY-EIGHT

Ryan

Wendy smiled. "That sounds so wonderful, you calling me Mother."

Part of me was glad it sounded good to her, because it was making me cringe and want to blow chunks on the table. I didn't consider this woman my mother. I no longer considered Daphne Steel my mother either. So where exactly did that leave me?

"Are you going to help me understand?"

She closed her eyes, a dreamy smile on her face. "Your father and I met in high school."

I already knew that.

"He was so handsome. So strong. Even at seventeen. He took my virginity. And I took his. We were soul mates, Ryan. That's why you're so important. You're the progeny of two soul mates."

I still didn't understand. This was clearly all part of Wendy's delusions. She might think of my father as her soul mate, but he'd never thought of her as his.

Had he?

"Why were you never together?"

"He got Daphne Wade pregnant."

"I know that story."

"It's why we weren't together."

"What about later? After my mo— Er...Daphne died?"

Her eyes darkened with...anger? "Too much had happened by then. He'd had another child with her, and she was only two or so."

Yes. Marjorie. "Again, I know all that, Mother."

"Your brother had been taken."

Now we were getting somewhere.

"He couldn't forgive you, could he? For the part you played in Talon's abduction?"

She sighed. "I didn't want to do that, Ryan. You must believe me. I would never intentionally contribute to any child's suffering."

I cleared my throat, looked down at my thighs, and desperately tried to contain my rage at the woman who'd borne me. Flying off the deep end would not help. "So it's true, then. You helped with Talon's abduction." My mind whirled. "My—" *Shit*. "Daphne was pregnant with Marjorie when Talon was abducted. That's it, isn't it? This is so sick. You were angry with him because he got her pregnant."

"It's not sick, Ryan. He was supposed to remain faithful to me. He promised me, after you were born, that he'd never sleep with her again."

My blood boiled in my veins. She'd had a child tortured and raped? The child of the man she professed to love? Because, in her warped little mind, she thought my father had cheated on her? I had to stop myself from dry heaving. I carried genes from this monster.

I gripped the table, my knuckles white, and forced myself to keep sitting when what I wanted was to stand and kick the shit out of this woman. My fucking mother.

"You promised me the truth, Mother."

"That is the truth, my darling. All of it."

I cleared my throat. "Larry Wade says Talon was never supposed to be taken."

"Larry Wade knows very little. He wasn't the brains of the bunch."

"He isn't stupid, either. He's a lawyer, for God's sake."

"Yes, he's a lawyer. So was Tom. They were in law school together, actually." She closed her eyes again.

I needed to stop this little jaunt down memory lane. I needed more of the truth, and I needed it now. Larry had always been, according to Talon, a yes man to the other two, Simpson and Mathias.

"Who, then, was the brains of the bunch? Mathias?"

She opened her eyes, settling her gaze on me.

"Who do you think?"

Her look said it all.

Mathias is still out there, and even he isn't the most dangerous.

"It was you. You were the brains...*Mother.*"

She smiled then. A motherly smile. It sickened me.

"You're brilliant. Just like I always knew you'd be."

Still, she hadn't admitted it.

"So tell me, Mother. In what world is it okay to have a little boy abducted and tortured to pay back a man who supposedly cheated on you?"

"In *my* world."

She was sick. So damned sick. Bile crept up my throat, and bitterness coated my tongue. "*Your* world?"

"I promised you the truth, dear. I didn't promise you would understand."

"I asked you to help me understand, but this is so twisted." I stood, rage boiling. "Who in hell could understand this?"

One of the orderlies flanking her stood. "Sir, you need to sit down and calm yourself, or you're going to have to leave."

Get a grip, Ryan. She's talking. Don't stop now.

I sat down.

I clenched my jaw. "Where the hell is my father?" I said through gritted teeth.

"He will come to you when the time is right."

"Did you help him fake his death?"

"I'd do anything for him."

Not an answer. "How can you continue to say that, when you had his son abducted and raped?"

"That was a sad casualty. It was unfortunate. But you should be thanking me, Ryan."

"Thanking you? Are you crazy? What the hell for?"

"They let you go that day. Because you're *my* son."

CHAPTER TWENTY-NINE

Ruby

So tell me, then. Is the love you feel for him stronger than whatever is holding you back?

Melanie's question played over in my mind.

Yes! The word was in my head, where I was shouting it. But instead, I said, "I don't know. These feelings are all so new to me."

"I understand."

"I never thought I'd feel love for a man. Not like this."

"True love can be a little surprising when it creeps up on you. I should know." She smiled.

"It's not just the feeling that's surprising," I said.

"What else?"

"It's..." I swallowed, embarrassment overwhelming me. "It's the sex."

"What about the sex? Are you not enjoying it?"

"Oh, no." God, my cheeks must be red as a fire truck. "I'm definitely enjoying it."

"Then what?"

"I'm... I feel like I'm no longer me when I'm with him. Like I'm losing myself. Like I *want* to lose myself. It scares me."

"Why?"

"Because I've been on my own since I was a kid. I've

depended on no one but myself for seventeen years. And now all of a sudden I'm ready to give all that up? It doesn't make any sense. Like last night..."

"What happened last night?"

"I...forced myself not to have an orgasm. Which I know sounds ridiculous. Orgasms are pretty amazing. Part of me can't believe I went this long without them."

"Why do you think you forced yourself not to have one?"

"I was afraid. It was like I wasn't me anymore. We were becoming this Ruby-Ryan creature. I'm not ready for that."

"I think you need to take a step back here and put this in perspective," she said. "You have very little experience, so you have nothing to compare this to, but true love with the right person can definitely feel like you're becoming one being. That's part of what makes it so special."

"So this is true love, then?"

"Only you and Ryan can answer that."

I closed my eyes for a few seconds. I already knew the answer.

"Let me ask you this," she said. "Did you dislike the feeling you were having? Of becoming part of him?"

"No." I remembered the headiness, the nirvana of melting into his skin, his body. "I loved it. That's what freaks me out. I don't want to lose myself."

"Ruby," Melanie said, edging along the couch so she was closer to me. "I think you might finally be *finding* yourself."

★ ★ ★

I finished the afternoon at work and then headed to the gym to do some kickboxing. I hadn't said anything in my session with Melanie about the eerie text I'd gotten last night or the phone call I'd missed from an unrecognized number. Of course it hadn't been traceable. The blues had been to my apartment and checked it out, assuring me it was safe. Still, Ryan had arranged for me to spend the night at a nearby hotel, and I wanted to go there. I just didn't *want* to want to go there. Story of my life these days. I wanted to retain my independence, go to my apartment, prove that no one could harm me.

But I wasn't invincible. If I knew anything, I knew that.

Melanie had said that maybe I was finding myself, not losing myself. I had gone to her for a reason—to become whole before I took more of a plunge with Ryan. Was it possible that taking such a plunge was part of becoming whole?

What makes you think you're not already whole, Ruby?

I finished my workout and toweled off my face. Time for a quick shower and then...

The hotel.

★ ★ ★

A key had been left for me at the front desk, and I quickly ascended to the fourth floor to find my room. I opened the door and tossed my purse and overnight bag on a nearby table. The blues had been kind enough to pack for me, and God only knew what I'd find inside. Where was the bed? Shit, had he really reserved a whole suite for me?

Steel money. They certainly didn't do things halfway.

I picked up my belongings and headed toward the door near the end of the small living area. I opened it—

I gasped.

Ryan stood there, fully clothed, his hair in disarray and a

primal look of lust in his dark and blazing eyes.

"Get undressed."

"Ry—"

"I said get undressed. I need you. Now."

Something in me forced me to obey his command. That something that scared me. That something that made me feel I was losing myself.

Ruby, I think you might finally be finding yourself.

Was I? Truly?

Did I become any less Ruby Lee just because I wanted to obey Ryan Steel? Give him what he wanted? What he needed?

How did he know I'd come here? Was I that transparent? I'd nearly gone back to my apartment.

But I hadn't.

And he'd known I wouldn't.

How had he known? How?

"I'm waiting," he said.

I shed my jacket. My fingers shaking, I unbuttoned my shirt and shed it as well. Then my bra. I bent down to untie my shoes and then kicked them off, toeing off my socks. I unbuckled my belt, unzipped my pants, and slid them off my hips along with my panties.

I stood before Ryan naked.

Naked and vulnerable.

Ruby, I think you might finally be finding yourself.

It was time to find out.

CHAPTER THIRTY

R y a n

I yanked her toward me and crushed our lips together in a kiss of passion and lust. Her scent was already lingering in the air. I'd smelled it even before she'd taken off her pants.

She was ripe. Ripe for me. Only for me.

I ripped my mouth from hers and inhaled a deep breath. "No one else will ever kiss these lips, Ruby. No one else will fuck your tight little body. Do you understand?"

Her blue eyes were glazed over, her lips ruddy and swollen from the bruising kiss I'd given her.

"Answer me. Do you understand?"

She nodded, shivering.

I clamped my mouth onto hers once more.

She responded to me as no woman ever had. When we kissed, with so much passion and fervor, I could hardly believe no one had kissed this mouth before. But no one had. Only *I* had, and that knowledge made me crazy. Crazy with lust. Crazy with passion. Crazy with desire.

Crazy with love.

What I felt for this woman was something I'd never felt before. It ate at me, consumed me. It was a hunger that demanded to be sated. As I held her against me, her naked flesh against my still-clothed body, I knew I was never letting her go.

Her hair fell down her back in a long ponytail, and I grabbed it and pulled on it, yanking her mouth away from mine with a loud smack.

"I love kissing you," I said. "I love kissing your lips. I love how our tongues feel together. I love everything about what we are together, Ruby."

Before she could answer, I clamped my mouth onto hers once more. We continued our kiss, and I walked her toward the bed, until her knees met the mattress and she sat down.

I knew what I wanted from her. I didn't want to scare her, but I had to ask for what I needed. I unbuckled my belt and unsnapped my jeans, sliding them and my boxers over my hips. My cock sprang out, so fucking hard. As hard as I'd ever been. Her beautiful dark lips were right at the perfect level.

"Suck my cock," I commanded.

Though I expected her to start with tiny little kisses, she instead thrust her mouth upon me, taking me about three-quarters of the way before she backed off, licking my head.

I groaned. So good. Had anything ever felt as heavenly? Maybe. Maybe being inside that tight little twat of hers. And one day, inside that sweet ass.

I grabbed her ponytail and began moving her mouth on and off me. She could have stopped me if she'd wanted to. She was a trained policewoman. But when I looked into her blue eyes, they shone with lust and satisfaction.

She liked what she was doing. She liked what I was doing to her.

God, she was the perfect woman for me.

I was so turned on, so hot, and I knew I wouldn't last long. As much as I wanted to shoot down her throat, I needed to get inside her first.

Shit. I still had all my clothes on. But I couldn't wait. I needed her. Now. As much as it pained me, I pulled my cock out of her mouth. "Lie back, baby."

She obeyed, spreading her legs.

For a moment, I looked at her. At the beautiful swollen pink flesh open for me. I inhaled that scent all around us that seemed to be coming from everywhere, only it wasn't. It was coming from her beautiful body exposed to my view.

I planted my hand on the bed, forcing her thighs closer to her body, her entrance at the perfect angle. And I thrust into her.

Sweet heaven.

Sweet home.

Inside Ruby, I was home.

I stayed locked to the hilt for a few seconds, loving the way her walls hugged my cock. For an instant, I thought my life would be perfect if I could just stay embedded in her body forever.

But my balls ached, my cock throbbed. So I pulled out and pushed back inside her wetness. She cried out, her fingers sliding toward her vulva. She rubbed her own juices over her hard nub, and I lost it.

"Come," I commanded. "Come now."

Her walls spasmed around me, and she cried out my name—an angel's song to my ears.

Could I truly induce orgasm in her just by demanding it? The thought made me hum with power. I pulled back out and slammed home, filling her, taking her, giving myself to her and only her.

When my body stopped shuddering, my cock finally stopped throbbing, I closed my eyes, trying to hold back what

I knew was coming.

But I couldn't.

A tear fell from one eye and trailed down my cheek, and then one from the other.

CHAPTER THIRTY-ONE

Ruby

I was still enraptured from my orgasm when I noticed his tears. He pulled out of me and pulled his pants up around his hips, although he didn't snap or buckle them.

I waited. Waited for him to tell me what to do. As wrong as waiting for a command felt, it also felt so very right.

Instead, he only stared at me. Not at my naked body. He looked into my eyes with a look so tortured that I thought I could see into his soul. Something was bothering him. Something big. So big that it elicited a tear...and then another.

I stopped my mouth from dropping open. I wouldn't mention the tears. That would embarrass him.

He was still fully clothed, and I sat up and took his hands, bringing him down upon the bed beside me.

"Ryan," I said. "What's wrong?"

He let go of one of my hands and trailed his finger up my arm, my shoulder, my cheekbone, around to the band holding my ponytail in place. He pulled it out of my hair and let my tresses fall down my back. "You're so fucking beautiful," he said.

His eyes were still tortured, his lids heavy, his dark irises glassy. He continued touching me, lightly running his fingers over my body.

Then he closed his eyes and inhaled. "I can always smell you. Your scent intoxicates me. Makes me want you so much."

I touched his cheek. "I'm right here. You have me."

He opened his eyes. "Something happened today." Then he tilted his head slightly to the side. "No, that's not right. Nothing happened. I just found out something. Most of my life has been a lie."

"Ryan, your life hasn't been a lie. I know you're still dealing with the fact that you have a different mother than your brothers and sister. But you will—"

He placed two fingers over my lips. "I'm not talking about that. Am I used to it yet? Hell, no. But I will deal with that. What I found out today is, in a strange way, even more important to me. It changes everything I've known as truth for the last twenty-five years."

Twenty-five years? Ryan was thirty-two years old, same as me. What could he have found out that changed the past twenty-five years of his life? He would've been seven years old.

He'd been seven years old when Talon was taken.

I gently removed his hand from my mouth. "What is it, Ryan? What are you talking about?"

"For the last twenty-five years, my brother Talon has been my hero. And now..."

"And now...what?"

"My psychotic mother. I went to see her."

I knew that, of course. I'd told him about the e-mail I got from Wendy.

"What happened?"

"I asked her to tell me the truth. I asked her to help me understand." He threaded his fingers through his unruly hair. "I'll never understand, Ruby. I'll never understand how or why she could've done the things she did."

"That's a good thing," I said. "I'll never understand why my father has done the things he's done either. I don't want to understand. I don't want my mind to work in that warped way."

"I know that. I agree with you. But what I found out today changes everything."

"I can assure you that nothing has changed," I said. Perhaps he found out that Wendy was more than any of us had bargained for. That she was the mastermind behind all of this. But now was not the time to voice my theory.

"But it has." He squeezed my hand. "I got away that day. I got away because Talon freed me from the guy holding me and told me to run. At least that's what I always thought."

I wasn't sure what to say, so I didn't say anything, just continued holding his hand, rubbing my thumb into his palm.

"But my mother told me... God, do you have any idea how much I hate calling her my mother?"

I couldn't help letting out a stilted laugh. "Of course I do."

Finally, a tiny smile twitched at Ryan's lips. "Of course you do. That was a stupid thing for me to say."

"Tell me. You can tell me anything, Ryan. I... I love you."

He sighed. "I love you too, baby."

"Then trust me." Those were loaded words, I knew. In his eyes, I had betrayed him when I gave a strand of his hair to Marjorie to have his DNA tested. We loved each other, but it would still take some time to recover from that.

He closed his eyes. "I'm trying."

"I know."

He opened his eyes. "My mother said Simpson and Mathias let me go that day because I was *her* son. That's why Talon was taken and I wasn't. Because I'm the spawn of that

psychotic bitch who apparently was calling the shots that day."
He paused a moment, swallowing hard. "Do you have any idea
what this does to me, Ruby? Any idea how this changes my
history?"

"Ryan, it doesn't have to change anything."

"All these years... The way I remember it..." He rose from
the bed, holding his pants up. He buckled them and began
pacing around. "Talon. The brother I trusted with my life.
The brother I thought had *saved* my life. Saved me from the
horrible fate that he endured those months." He slammed his
fist against the closet door. "And now? I find out it's been a lie.
Talon didn't save me that day. My fucked-up mother did."

"Look," I said. "The most important thing is that you got
away, isn't it?"

"No. No, it's not, Ruby. I got away solely because of my
parentage. And my poor brother..." He choked back a sob. "My
poor brother went through hell that I was spared because I'm
the son of that fucked-up maniac."

Guilt. More guilt. Ryan had always harbored guilt because
he got away. He loved Talon almost to the point of worship
because his brother had saved him from that fate. Yet still the
guilt ate at him because he had gotten away. And now this... I
rose and went to him. I wrapped my arms around him, but he
did not respond.

"It's not fair," he said.

I caressed his upper arms still covered in his cotton shirt.
I could say many things right now. I could tell him none of
this was his fault. I could tell him there was no reason to feel
guilty. That Talon never wanted him to feel that way. I could
tell him that maybe it did happen the way he remembered it.
That maybe his psycho mother was lying. But I didn't say any

of that. Instead, I nuzzled into his chest.

"No, it's not fair, Ryan."

He sniffled, and I knew he was trying to hold back tears. I wanted to tell him that he didn't have to hold back tears in front of me, that he could cry if he wanted to. But I knew how hard it was for me to cry in front of another person. He needed to believe in his strength right now. I wouldn't take that away from him.

I continued to hold him, still naked, he still fully clothed. We stood together for seconds that turned into minutes.

Finally, I pulled away. "Let me get you something. A glass of water maybe?"

"Yeah. Thanks."

I walked into the bathroom and draped one of the luxury robes around me. Then I filled a glass of water and returned, handing it to Ryan. He had sat back down on the bed.

"Have you ever talked to anyone about what happened that day?" I asked.

He nodded. "I had to tell everyone when I got back. I told my mother—or the woman who I thought was my mother at the time—my father, the police. For a long time I had nightmares. Even after Talon came back. But we never talked about it. My mother and father never wanted to mention it. And then my mother...er...Daphne..."

"She *was* your mother, Ryan, in every way that matters. It's okay to think of her as your mother."

He took a long gulp of the water. "Our father never let us see her body."

"He was probably trying to protect you."

"I'm not sure any of us ever forgave him for that. That was another knife that had twisted in my gut when he died.

Or rather, when he faked his death. I always felt guilty about not forgiving him. And now?" He raked his fingers through his hair. "I find out that woman wasn't even my mother, and that my father is most likely not dead."

I sat quietly beside him, not saying anything. I didn't know what to say anyway. I just wanted him to know I was there. That he could depend on me.

He took another sip of water. "You'll never believe this either. According to Wendy, she was the brains of the whole operation."

This didn't surprise me. I had already come up with that theory on my own. A wisp of gratitude swept through me. Now I didn't have to voice it to Ryan.

"She came around a lot, even before my mother died. She was based in Denver as a journalist for the National News Network. She was smart, a good reporter, as far as any of us knew. She won awards for her work, and all this time she's been a complete sociopath."

"Intelligent criminals know how to cover their tracks." I should know.

"I never thought much about her coming around. Now I know why she did."

"To see you? To see your father?" I asked.

"Both, according to her. And here's the most twisted thing of all. Do you want to know why she orchestrated Talon's abduction?"

My stomach spiraled into knots. I did want to know. Needed to know. "Why?"

"Because my mother was pregnant with Marjorie. According to Wendy, my father had promised never to have sex with my mother again, and in her warped mind, he had cheated on her with his own wife."

He took what was left in the glass of water and splashed it over his face. "Can you believe that? She had a ten-year-old boy tortured and raped because my father had sex with his wife."

My heart dropped to my stomach. My father was just as much to blame for what happened to Talon when he was taken. After all, he actually helped do the deed. But in an obscure way, I was actually relieved that he hadn't been the catalyst for what that poor boy had endured.

"My brother was taken, tortured, raped..." He sniffled, and another tear rolled down his cheek.

I ached to brush it away for him, but I didn't want to draw attention to it. He wouldn't want that.

"On the orders of the woman who is my biological mother. And those same orders were to let me go. All these years, Talon was my hero. He had saved me. Let me get away. And now?" He stood and threw the empty glass against the wall. Shards scattered over the floor. "All these years later, my own mother is the hero? My own mother is the reason I got away? And my own fucking mother is the reason my brother went through hell?" He turned to me, his eyes tortured. "How the fuck am I supposed to live with that?"

CHAPTER THIRTY-TWO

Ryan

Ruby didn't answer me. I didn't expect her to. Though the question wasn't rhetorical, there was no answer she could've given me that would've been satisfactory anyway. She was living with her own demons.

She picked up her purse that she had dropped to the floor when she had first come into the bedroom and walked to the phone on the desk. "I'm just going to call housekeeping to get this cleaned up."

That was Ruby. Always cleaning up. Always taking care of things. That's what cops did.

A few seconds later, she said, "I'm going to get dressed. We're going to go down to the bar and have a drink. To give them a chance to pick up and vacuum, okay?"

I simply nodded.

She gathered all of her clothes and went to the bathroom. I sat back down on the bed.

My brothers and I had always wondered all these years, before we had even told Marjorie the truth, why our father had swept this whole thing under the rug. Why we were never allowed to deal with the shitstorm of that summer. Talon should have been in therapy long ago, along with the rest of us. If we had been able to deal with it, if we had been able to...

Christ. Daphne Steel might still be alive today. Joe, Talon, and Marj had been denied their mother.

I was angry. But no longer at my brothers and sister. No longer with Ruby. I was fucking enraged with my mother. My biological mother.

Oddly, though, someone else bore even more of my anger. My father. Bradford Steel.

He had never let our family heal. I still didn't know what the real relationship was between Wendy and my father. I might never know. And I couldn't bring myself to be angry with my father for having sex with his own wife and giving us our little sister. But I *was* angry. Despite the fact that I wouldn't exist if he hadn't, I was damned angry at him for fucking Wendy when he was married to Daphne. I was even angrier about him not letting us heal from Talon's ordeal. I had watched both my brothers struggle all those years after the abduction. My father could've helped them avoid all of that.

Instead, he'd left us to flounder. Oh, he'd taken care of the family after his wife had taken her life, raised us to understand hard work and the value of money. But he had never let us heal. Then, seven years ago, he left us again, that time physically.

And then something occurred to me. He'd "died" seven years ago, the year Marj had turned eighteen. A legal adult. He'd waited until all of his children were legal adults. There had to be something there.

★ ★ ★

Ruby and I sat in a booth in the hotel bar, a bottle of Steel Cabernet between us.

"I can't believe you just paid for a bottle of your own

wine," she said.

"What can I say? It was the best on the wine list."

She took a sip from her goblet. "I wish I had some words of wisdom for you, Ryan."

"It's okay."

"No, it's far from okay. But what you need to remember is that no one holds you responsible for what happened to Talon."

"I know that." It didn't change how I felt in my mind, though.

"I went to see Melanie," she said.

I widened my eyes. "You mean for therapy?"

She nodded. "It helped. Helped a lot, actually. I'm going to try to see her once a week, as my schedule allows. We talked about a lot of stuff, and one of the things was how I've always felt responsible for my father's crimes. It's why I became a cop, and why I've tried to atone for what he's done by being the best cop I can be. I haven't been able to put him away yet, but I've put away a lot of other shitheads."

"You're not responsible for his actions."

She smiled. "No, I'm not. And neither are you responsible for your mother's actions."

I couldn't help a slight chuckle. I'd walked right into that one. "I know that."

"I know you do. I also know that doesn't make it any easier."

"You know what scares the hell out of me? Having to tell my brothers all of this."

"Why should that scare you? They love you just as much as they ever did."

"How can I tell Talon? How can I tell him that my mother had him tortured to punish our father for getting *his* mother pregnant? That I was let go simply because I was hers?"

"Doesn't he already know? Seems to me you told me that Wendy had pretty much told Joe and Talon as much."

"True. But that was before..."

"Before what?"

"Well, first of all, before they knew the truth about my parentage. And second of all, when we all thought Wendy was just a nutty liar."

"Wendy *is* a nutty liar."

"I'm not so certain of that anymore."

Ruby looked down at her wineglass for a minute.

"What is it?" I asked.

"I've been doing some thinking about Wendy," she said. "I have a theory that I haven't had a chance to discuss with you yet. Part of it you already figured out yourself, that Wendy has been in more of a position of control than any of us ever thought. But there's something else I've been considering."

"And?"

"Don't get me wrong. Wendy is a completely twisted psychopath. And yes, she's a liar. But I've dealt with many psychos in my day, Ryan, and something about Wendy stands out. The woman is smart. Not just run-of-the-mill smart, but genius smart. When she lies, I'm pretty sure she lies on purpose. For a reason. She may play the crazy liar at times, but I think she always knows what she's doing."

I shook my head. "Honestly, baby, nothing would surprise me about the woman."

"I'm sorry I haven't had a chance to discuss this with you before now."

"It's okay. We've all been busy. By the way, were you able to get a trace on the number of the text that warned you not to go home last night?"

"Unfortunately, no. It appears to have come from a disposable phone, which has, of course, disappeared into thin air."

"At least that means it probably wasn't my mother," I said.

"Not necessarily. Your mother seems to know how to get what she wants. She could have easily gotten an orderly to smuggle in a disposable phone for her."

"Shit." I ran my fingers through my hair. "Just when I thought there might be something she *isn't* responsible for."

"The police were at my apartment today. Nothing seemed amiss. It could have been a hoax."

"I don't care. I want you here, where you're safe."

"I understand. One thing I've tried to pride myself on over the years is not doing stupid things." She let out a nervous laugh. "You know, like driving a hundred and fifty miles an hour and then answering the phone."

"Touché," I said. "But I was—"

"It's okay," she interrupted. "I honestly get where you were coming from. Do you think I haven't considered taking off? Just leaving all this shit behind? Believe me. I've been tempted more times than I can tell you."

I forced out a laugh. "When I first became attracted to you, I never dreamed we'd have so much in common."

"You mean DNA we wish we could escape?" She shook her head. "Neither did I."

"You still think your father had something to do with Juliet and Lisa?"

She nodded. "Why else would he have called me and told me not to talk to Shayna? His involvement might be ancillary, but he's in it somehow. And now that Wendy pretty much validated that they were in human trafficking, it makes even more sense."

I guffawed.

"What?" she asked.

"Just the fact that you used the phrase 'makes sense.' As if any of this could actually make sense."

She took a sip of her wine and smiled. "True enough. You deal with something for so long, and it begins to seem normal. I see it all the time in my work. Cops have to fight against that."

I finished my wine and poured a glass. "We have to find your father, Ruby. And we have to find *my* father too."

CHAPTER THIRTY-THREE

Ruby

"Well, we both know where to start," I said.

Ryan nodded, sipping his wine. "Yeah. My mother."

"Or..." My mind whizzed rapidly. "Since your mother hasn't been forthcoming, and we never know whether she's telling the truth..."

"But you said yourself that she always knows what she's saying, whether it's the truth or a lie."

"True, but that doesn't really help us because we don't always know the reasons behind why she says what she says. We can try Larry Wade again, but honestly, I'm not sure he's been privy to some of the stuff that my father, Simpson, and Wendy have cooked up."

"I've gotten that same feeling," Ryan said, "and Talon always maintained that Larry was more of a follower of the other two. Oh my God!"

"What?" I asked.

"I can't believe I forgot about this. Remember the last time we saw Larry, and you came back in, saying you wanted to talk to me?"

"Yeah."

"I had been asking Larry about the symbol on Simpson's ring. On all of their rings. Of course, he refused to talk about it, but then he said something interesting. He said, 'I understand why you would want to know. The devil is in the details. Just ask your mother.'"

I dropped my mouth open. "So maybe Bryce's uncle was right. Maybe it *was* a symbol for evil."

"Melanie always said that Larry talks in riddles. It seems weird that he would use that cliché while we were talking about the ring unless he meant something."

I sighed. "I wish I could say any of this was surprising, but I've known for a long time just how evil my father is."

"But *my* father," Ryan said. "My father also wore that ring."

"We don't know for sure that he even understood what the symbol meant."

He lowered his brows. "My father would have known. Or he would've asked."

"You don't know that, Ryan. And even if he did ask, they might have lied to him."

"A couple of months ago, baby, I might've bought that. But no longer. My father was clearly into this, maybe not as deeply as the others, but he was. Hell, he gave them money."

"Did you have any success uncovering his will?" I asked.

"No. We haven't found it yet. Joe is going to contact the attorney who read it to us. But if my father has paid him off, it may not do any good."

I took his hand across the table. "We *will* figure this out. We've come this far. I promise you I won't quit until my father is behind bars where he deserves to be."

He finished the second glass of wine. "I know you won't quit. I know my brothers won't either. But I..." He sighed. "I don't know how much more I can take of this."

He looked sad and forlorn. I understood why. He had come to me tonight, needing me, and I had given him what he needed. It clearly hadn't been enough. Even *I* knew enough to know that sex couldn't fix someone's problems. It could relieve a little bit of stress, but that was about it. I rubbed the top of his hand. "The glass is probably cleaned up by now. Let's go to the room and go to bed. Things will be brighter in the morning."

He attempted a smile but failed. "I love you, Ruby. I do. But I don't know if things will ever be bright again."

★ ★ ★

After a busy day at the office, I was getting ready to head back to the hotel that Ryan had booked for the week. My cell phone buzzed.

"Detective Lee."

"It's me. Shayna."

I looked around the office. Most of the staff and officers had taken off for the evening. I was alone and could speak freely. "Shayna. Are you all right?"

"I still think I'm being followed sometimes. It could be my imagination."

"It could be." Though I didn't believe it. But I didn't want to alarm her.

"I got another text." She choked back a sob. "It just said 'help.'"

"Did it come from a number?"

"No. It just said private."

"Shayna, this is the second time this has happened. Please, I need your permission to access your phone records. We can figure out what's going on."

"I'm...scared."

"These messages came to your cell phone number, correct? The one you blocked me on?"

"Yes."

Good. I had that number. "Look. If you think this came from Juliet and Lisa, we owe it to them to look into it."

"I know. I know. I'm just so scared. So frightened."

"I understand. Haven't the police been out to talk to you? I've called them."

"They have, but I don't know much, and I'm—"

The line went dead.

Shit. "Shayna? Shayna?"

No use. I quickly traced the number. It was a pay phone at a gas station in East LA. I called the LAPD—*again*—and told them what had happened. I didn't expect them to do anything, but I had to try.

Then my phone buzzed again.

CHAPTER THIRTY-FOUR

Ryan

Again I sat in the place I most didn't want to be. The visitor's room at psych lockup, facing my mother. I didn't expect to be any more successful getting answers, but I had to try.

"Where's my father?"

"I've already told you. I don't know."

"Mother, you promised to be truthful with me, so let me be truthful with you. I don't believe that you don't know where my father is."

"I don't. He calls me when he needs to."

"Then the hospital should have a record of his calls coming in."

"Maybe. I don't know."

"Or does he call you on a cell phone?"

"Maybe. I don't know."

"You're not supposed to have access to cell phones here, but clearly you've been able to find one when you needed."

"But how could I find one to get an incoming call?"

"Exactly." Of course, I wouldn't put anything past her. She might have a contraband cell phone hidden somewhere here. "So I'm sure you have no problem if I ask the hospital to see the record of incoming and outgoing phone calls."

"I certainly wouldn't have any problem with you doing

that, darling. But those are private records. You won't be able to get access." She smiled eerily.

"Maybe. Maybe not." Of course I would be able to. Money talked.

"I do miss him, your father."

So do I. The words were on the tip of my tongue, but I didn't say them. I had spent many years missing my father. Now, I didn't even know him anymore.

"I'm sure you do, he being your soul mate and all." I had to stop myself from rolling my eyes.

"I wish I could make you understand what your father and I mean to each other," she said.

"I've asked you many times, Mother. Please. Help me understand."

"I don't think anyone can understand what it means to be a soul mate unless he or she has experienced that type of connection himself. Tell me, Ryan. Is that the type of connection you have with your police detective?"

No way in hell was I discussing my relationship with Ruby with this woman. "We haven't been together long enough to know yet, Mother. Why don't you tell me what kind of relationship you and my father have?"

She closed her eyes and smiled dreamily. Eerily dreamily. "It was a connection on all levels. Physical. Mental. Emotional. Spiritual. Even transcendental."

"Transcendental? Are you telling me that you and my father existed on some alternate plane in the universe?"

She opened her eyes. "Sometimes it felt that way. Yes."

Again, I had to keep from rolling my eyes.

"All right. What exactly do you mean by that?"

"That it was meaningful. We hungered for each other in a

physical way. But it was so much more than that. We coveted each other."

I had to stop myself from wanting to vomit. Thinking of my father and this woman together, knowing what I knew about her, made me want to be violently ill. And the fact that their union resulted in me...

I swallowed. "Why didn't you get together then?"

"I moved away with my family after my sophomore year in high school. Even though we were separated, we wrote to each other, saw each other when we could. There was always a heat between us. An ache for each other. We couldn't be in the same room together without ripping each other's clothes off."

That was a lie. Growing up, I had seen Wendy and my father together. She had come around occasionally. She'd even come around after my father had allegedly died. She was the one who had helped us keep Talon's heroics overseas out of the mainstream media.

I said only, "Okay."

"We had a love like ones you only read about. Like Romeo and Juliet."

"Romeo and Juliet both ended up committing suicide," I said.

"Still, we were like that. Star-crossed lovers."

"Why did my father marry Daphne then? If he was in love with you, why didn't he just pay her child support and not marry her?"

"Because Bradford Steel is a man of honor. He lived up to his responsibilities."

A man of honor? I'd once thought so. No longer. "Did you ask him to stay with you?"

"I didn't have to. I knew him well enough to know that he

would do what he had to do. We were both seeing other people at that time." She shook her head, rolling her eyes. "Daphne was never Brad's type."

"They always seemed happy enough to me."

"How can you say that? You were only nine when she died. What could a nine-year-old possibly know about love and happiness?"

Enough was enough. "I know more about love and happiness than you possibly could, Mother."

"Do you expect me to get upset? How could I? I only wanted a life of love and happiness for you, my darling son. I wanted only the best for you. Your father was the best."

"Was it truly love you felt for my father?" I asked. "Or was it obsession?"

She smiled, the eerie smile I had come to know. "My dear, is there really any difference? What is love, anyway? What is obsession?"

I sighed, raking my fingers through my hair. "Please, Mother. Please help me find my father."

"Why is that so important to you?"

"How can you ask me that? Because he's my father, for God's sake. Because he owes me a goddamned explanation for what has become my life."

"Ryan," she said seriously. "Please be careful what you wish for. I adore your father. He is everything to me. But he's brought a lot of pain into my life as well. He married someone else. I had to give up my son for him. That's the kind of deep connection your father and I have. I did whatever he asked. All because of the love I felt for him. The obsessive, coveting love." She closed her eyes and sighed. "Sometimes the things we covet are the things that destroy us."

CHAPTER THIRTY-FIVE

Ruby

"Detective Lee."

"Ruby, it's Mark."

"Hey."

"I need you to stay late tonight. Some information has come in, and I need you to take a look."

Crap. I'd been looking forward to dinner with Ryan. He'd promised me an elegant meal at the best restaurant in the city. "Sure. Just let me make a call."

I texted Ryan that I'd be working late at my boss's request and that I was sorry I couldn't make our dinner date. Then I walked to Mark's office, which was at the end of the hallway, somewhat isolated.

The door was closed, which was odd. Mark had a notorious open-door policy. Should I knock or walk in? To be on the safe side, I knocked.

"Come in," he called, his voice a bit...off.

I cocked my head and turned the doorknob. Something niggled at the back of my neck. But this was Mark, who I trusted. Not only was he a great cop, he was a friend. I opened the door.

And I gasped, my heart racing.

A masked man was holding a Glock to Mark's temple.

"I'm sorry, Ruby," Mark said, his voice shaking now.

"Some cop you are," the man said, his voice muffled. "I walked right in here."

Mark wouldn't have fallen for a ruse unless it was exceedingly well thought out. I had yet to meet someone who could deceive my boss.

And then I knew. Nausea climbed up my throat. How the hell had he gotten in here with a weapon? He'd had help. *Inside* help. Was there no one my father couldn't get to?

"Put the gun down, Theo."

He looked at me with intensely odd blue eyes. The colored contacts Jonah and Melanie had talked about. His face was covered in a black mask, his eyes distorted, and he'd tried to disguise his voice, but I would know him anywhere.

"Here's what's going to happen," my father said. "You're going to call off the Steel brothers, and you're going to stop trailing me. Got it? Otherwise, your boss here meets his maker."

"Don't listen to him, Ruby," Mark said. "He's bluffing."

My father pushed the gun farther into Mark's temple, wrinkling the skin. "I don't bluff."

No, my father didn't bluff.

"Let him go," I said.

"Not until you do as I say."

"How stupid are you?" Mark asked, his voice never wavering. The man had nerves of steel. "You walk right into the police station and make demands? How the hell did you get past security? Past the blues on duty? You'll never get out of here alive."

"You'll die before *I* do," my father said.

"You need money, don't you?" I said. "I don't have any, but

I can get some."

"From your Steel boyfriend?"

"What does it matter, as long as I get it?"

"The only money I want is from his father."

I raised one eyebrow. "Then tell me where his father is."

"He's dead."

"That's an old song, Dad. We know he's alive. We know he faked his own death. What we don't know is why."

"I don't know any more than you do."

"You're lying. And now you're going broke, aren't you? How much did it cost you to pay off Mills and Johnson? To get them off the Steels' case?"

"I don't know what you're talking about."

"Ruby," Mark said, his voice still calm. "I can handle this."

My gun was in my shoulder holster. I was fast, but I wouldn't be fast enough. By the time I could get to my weapon and take down my father, Mark would have a bullet in his brain.

Oddly, I didn't fear for my own life. So many years had passed, and my father hadn't taken me out. He could have, but he hadn't. I had every confidence that I wasn't about to lose my life.

I wasn't very confident about Mark's life, though. I had to get him out of here.

This was all surreal. Mark was an outstanding detective and a renowned martial artist as well. How could my father have gotten the best of him?

Unless...

Mark didn't seem frightened at all. Even the best cop in the world freaked out with a gun at his head.

Mark couldn't possibly be in league with my father. Could he?

I didn't have time for this. I had to believe in Mark's integrity. I'd get him out of this mess, even if it meant sacrificing the chance to bring down my father.

"Let him go, Dad," I said. "I'll get you money, if that's what you need. I'll convince Ryan to let this go. I'll do whatever it takes. Mark is a good cop, and he's innocent here."

"No one in the world is innocent."

I couldn't help myself. "Certainly not you. Tell me, what turned you into such a sick bastard?"

My father faltered for a millisecond, and in a flash, Mark executed a perfect knife hand and dislodged my father's sidearm.

But a shot rang out, and Mark went down.

By the time I was armed, my father had run out of the room.

"Go after him," Mark said breathlessly. "I'm okay. You can get him. Take him down."

He was bleeding profusely from his side. He was far from okay.

If I left now, I could get Mathias. Bring the bastard down. Someone had most likely heard the gunshot. Help would come...

But maybe not in time.

I had to stop my feet from taking off after my father. He wasn't worth Mark's life. I applied pressure to try to slow down the bleeding and then tore at Mark's shirt for a makeshift bandage.

"Hang in there, boss. You're going to be okay."

"I'm so sorry, Ruby. He... He threatened my wife. I didn't know what to do. Have to call..." His eyes closed, and he lost consciousness.

Blues swarmed in within seconds, and I called the paramedics. Mark was barely breathing when they arrived minutes later. They bagged him with oxygen and got him on a stretcher. I stayed to answer questions from the cops who'd burst in.

When the officers were satisfied they had all they needed, I stared down at my hands coated in Mark's blood, shivering. Thoughts jumbled in my head, my mind shifting from one bloody image to another. His wife. I had to call his wife, Yvonne. I grabbed my cell phone out of my pocket and dialed Mark's home number.

One ring.

Two.

Three.

And then a breathless, "Hello?"

"Yvonne? It's Ruby Lee from the station."

"Ruby, hi."

On the force for eleven years, and I still hadn't gotten used to giving out bad news. My stomach dropped. "You need to get to the ER. Mark's been shot."

CHAPTER THIRTY-SIX

Ryan

"You're saying your love for my father destroyed you?"

"In some ways."

"Then why would you keep pursuing him? Were you some kind of glutton for punishment?"

A plastic smile formed on her face. "Nothing about your father was ever punishing. Except in the bedroom."

I really wasn't up for hearing about my father's bedroom antics with this woman. Really, there were some things I didn't need to know. But if it would shed some light...

I had to force the words out. "What do you mean by that?"

"He liked bondage, your father. And so did I."

Big TMI. "Is that so?"

"Yes. He loved to tie me up. Didn't like being tied up himself, though."

I cleared my throat. "Oh?"

"No. Not at all. These last several years have been hell for him."

What? I stood. "You have my father tied up somewhere? As a prisoner? You vicious bitch!"

Back to her plastic smile. "Ryan, is that any way to talk to your mother?"

I looked to the orderlies. "We're done here. This bitch

should be in chains somewhere. I won't be back."

I walked out as my phone buzzed. Two texts from Ruby, the first one telling me she wouldn't be able to make dinner tonight. The second one had just come in.

I'm at Valleycrest ER. My boss has been shot. We need to talk.

★ ★ ★

"It crossed my mind at first," Ruby said, after explaining what had happened, "that somehow Mark was in cahoots with my father. Then I took the thought out of my head. I've known him for three years. He's a good cop. I wanted to respect his integrity."

"You might not have been wrong," I said. "If he's as good a martial artist as you say he is, he should have been able to disarm your father. And how did Mathias get into the station with a gun, for God's sake?"

She shook her head. "I can't go there. I can't play the 'what if' game and figure out every scenario. My boss was shot, and it's all my fault."

"Christ, Ruby, haven't we had this talk? How the hell is this *your* fault?"

Ruby stood, pulling at a few locks of hair that had come loose from her ponytail. "Because he's my fucking father! When will this all end, Ryan?"

Wouldn't I like to know? I had no answer to that question, so I said only, "You know it's not your fault."

"He was there. Right within my reach, but I let him go to save my boss, who might have been in on the whole thing. I made the wrong decision."

"You did what you thought was right. No one can fault that."

"But if I let him go to save a man that might be in on it with him?"

"So you believed in your boss. You've known him a while. He's always been a good cop, hasn't he?"

"As far as I know. Not a spot on his record. But obviously that doesn't mean shit."

"You're not clairvoyant, Ruby."

"I should be. When it comes to Theodore Mathias, I should be a fucking mind reader after all this time." She sat back down. "Damn! I should have gone with my first instinct. I had the feeling I was being played, that Mark was somehow in on it. Why didn't I go with that? I've always trusted my intuition before."

"Is his wife here?" I asked.

She nodded. "She's with some family over there." She gestured to a woman flanked by several others in the corner of the large waiting area.

"What's the prognosis?"

"I haven't heard anything yet. He'd better fucking live, though. I have a lot of questions for the bastard."

"You don't know—"

"Oh, yes, I do," she said. "That's the very last time I ignore my intuition. The very fucking last time. How could I have been so stupid?"

I rubbed her forearm. "Don't blame yourself."

"Easy for you to say."

I opened my mouth to argue, but shut it before the words came out. She didn't need to hear all about my visit with my mother. At least not yet.

"I'm sorry," she said. "That wasn't fair."

No, it wasn't. But again, I didn't say it.

A doctor in blue scrubs entered the area and walked straight to Ruby's boss's wife. A few words were exchanged, and then the woman let out a heavy sob.

"Looks like he didn't make it. Well, that's what getting involved with my father gets you." A tear slid down Ruby's cheek, and she wiped it away angrily. "He doesn't deserve any tears. No one involved with my father does."

I took her hand and pulled her back down beside me. "You still don't know exactly what happened."

"And now that he's gone, I never will." She sighed. "I suppose I should say something to his wife."

"No, you don't have to. That can wait. She has her family with her. She'll be okay. You and I need to get out of here."

"And go where?"

"What about our dinner?"

She crossed her arms over her chest. "I couldn't eat."

"All right. To the hotel then."

She attempted a smile. "I'm really not in the mood, Ryan."

I smiled and took her hand. "You leave that to me."

★ ★ ★

I handed Ruby the glass of wine I'd poured for her from the bottle of Steel Merlot that I picked up at the hotel bar.

She took a deep gulp and sighed. "Good," she said.

"I'm sorry about all you've been through," I said.

"Tonight? Or my whole life?" She took another sip of wine.

"Both. You've seen more than a person should have to."

"So have you. And I'm sorry, too."

I brushed my lips across hers, just that small contact igniting my groin. "You want to talk?"

She sighed again. "About what? What else is there to talk about? It is what it is." She smiled. "You know what? I want to fuck."

I widened my eyes. I couldn't believe those words had come from this woman who mere weeks ago had been a virgin, and who mere minutes ago had said she wasn't in the mood.

"You can't escape by fucking," I said. "God knows I've tried, as you know."

"True. But what's wrong with wanting to feel good, if only for a little while?"

I smiled. "Absolutely nothing." I took her glass from her and set it on the table. I looked at her. She looked exhausted, her hair falling out of her high ponytail, her eyes heavy lidded. She wore her regular work uniform of Dockers and a button-down. We still had to work on her wardrobe...

But right now, I wanted only to offer her comfort. And, to be honest, I wanted some comfort in return.

The talk with my mother had left me strangled. I'd been angry at her, calling her a vicious bitch. It was no less than she deserved. Was my father truly being held captive somewhere? I knew better than to take anything my mother said at face value. I'd left angry, saying I wouldn't be back.

But that was a lie.

I'd be back. I'd go back until this whole thing was solved.

My fucking mother...

She'd given me that bracelet. The sapphire bracelet that my father had supposedly given her. I'd been carrying it around in my pocket since. I wasn't sure why. It certainly wasn't to feel closer to Wendy. I couldn't stand the woman who'd given me life. I'd thought it tainted.

But no, it wasn't tainted. It had belonged to my grandmother.

As I looked at Ruby, her eyes a perfect match to the sapphires set in silvery white, I suddenly knew the perfect thing to do with it.

I'd give it to Ruby. It would be beautiful against her milky skin.

Oddly, it hadn't crossed my mind to give it to Ruby at the time, but now, looking at her, so forlorn and empty, I wanted her to have it. The piece had been made for her. It would never have shined upon Wendy—or even my grandmother, according to the photos I'd seen—the way it would illuminate Ruby.

I pulled it out of my pocket, the weight of it heavy in my palm. "I have something for you." I held it out to her.

"What is this?"

"It's a bracelet. It's made for you. I didn't know it until just now, but that is why I have it. To give it to you."

"You didn't buy it?"

I couldn't lie to her. Would she take it if she knew the truth?

"My mother gave it to me. She said it belonged to my grandmother, and that my father gave it to her when I was born." I let out a small huff, shaking my head. "I have no idea if that's the truth or not. Who fucking knows? All I know is I've kept it with me, wondering what the hell I'd do with it, and when I looked at you just now, I knew."

She fingered the bracelet. "It *is* beautiful."

"It was made for my grandmother, and it was made for

you."

"Was it?" She bit her lower lip. "I don't think I can accept it." She held it back to me.

Suddenly, it became more important than anything for her to accept and wear this bracelet—as if it would give me something good to take out of the relationship with the woman who was my mother.

"Please. I want you to have it. Honestly. I had no idea why it fell in my lap, but now I do. Here." I took it from her and clasped it around her right wrist. "It fits perfectly. It truly was made for you. Look at the color against your skin. And it matches your eyes."

"It's not really me." She scoffed. "Look at me. I can't pull something like this off."

"You can." I fingered the jewels around her wrist. "You're beautiful. So much more beautiful than any trinket could ever be."

She shook her wrist. "This is hardly a trinket."

"Maybe not. But it's perfect on you. Please. Keep it. For me."

"It's a lovely gift, but it's not something you bought for me, Ryan. Why is it so important to you that I keep it?"

How could I explain? "Because I'm not sure I could pick anything out that better suits you, baby. And if you keep this and wear it, then in some obscure way, I can feel like having Wendy Madigan for my mother isn't just a curse. Maybe something good came out of it."

She smiled and caressed my cheek, the bracelet sparkling as she moved. "Something very good did come out of it, Ryan. *You.*"

My heart nearly melted. How I loved this woman. I pulled

her to me in a soft embrace. "You're wonderful," I whispered in her ear. "Please keep the bracelet."

She pulled away. "If it means that much to you, I'll keep it. But honestly, when would I wear it? It's certainly not appropriate for work."

"You'll wear it tonight," I said. "You'll wear that bracelet... and nothing else."

CHAPTER THIRTY-SEVEN

Ruby

Oddly, I had gotten used to stripping for Ryan. He seemed to like me naked while he kept his clothes on. Truth be told, I liked it too. Part of me felt vulnerable, yes. Very vulnerable. But laced within that vulnerability was an innate feeling of power.

There was power in being a woman—a power in femininity—and I'd hidden my femininity for so long that I'd never experienced it. I'd spent my life building a strong body and a strong mind, all the while ignoring my femininity. I hadn't missed it. At least I hadn't thought I had.

Until now.

I peeled my clothes from my body until I stood naked, only the sapphire bracelet adorning me. My nipples pebbled as Ryan stared at me, the bulge growing beneath his jeans.

Power.

I had this power over him.

And I liked it. I liked it very much.

Every other time I'd been naked with Ryan fully clothed, he'd attacked me, made me come, and then thrust into me without bothering to disrobe himself. Not this time, though.

He kept his distance, though I hungered for him to come and take me, make me his.

I stayed quiet for a few moments, looking at him, but then had to say something. "What are you doing?"

"You've stripped for me so many times. I figured I owed you the same courtesy."

My breath caught when he tugged open a button of his shirt, and then another. With each new inch of bronze skin exposed, my heart fluttered a little faster. I ached to reach out and touch him, feel his flesh beneath my fingertips, but I held back, mesmerized by his movements, the striations in his muscles, the rustling of his garments as he discarded them.

Ryan Steel was so beautiful. So magnificent. His shirt hit the floor, and he raised one leg and discarded one cowboy boot, and then the other. Slowly he unbuckled his belt and unsnapped his jeans. Over his muscular hips the clothes went until they reached his ankles. He kicked them off, toeing off his socks as well.

Ryan Steel stood before me, naked and glorious, his cock springing forward in its magnificence.

I stood, unmoving, gawking at him, resisting the urge to reach toward him, run my fingers over his taut flesh, grab his hard member and bring it into my body.

I inhaled.

The vanilla musk scent permeated the air, but something else was mixed in. Ryan. His earthy masculine aroma mingled with mine. I inhaled again, letting the odor penetrate the most inner layers of my body.

He came toward me then and lifted my wrist, staring at the expensive bauble I wore.

"You're so beautiful. It's perfect."

I looked down. The sapphires were midnight blue against my pale skin, the platinum shiny and silver.

"I never imagined I could pull off anything like this," I said. "I never imagined owning anything so perfectly beautiful."

"It's not beautiful," he said, caressing my forearm. "*You* are." He pulled me to him.

Our lips met softly at first, sliding over each other's in a smooth caress. I parted for him, and he delved his tongue into my mouth, searching. I met him, returning his kiss, savoring the slowness and the softness. We didn't often kiss like this. Normally we were ferocious with each other. Not this time. This was a gentle kiss. A kiss not of lust but of comfort.

Comfort I craved.

We continued to kiss, our arms around each other, moving slightly as if we were on a dance floor sliding against each other to a slow ballad.

Melodies played in my mind. Music I didn't recognize floated in the air around us as we danced to the slow rhythm. The kiss deepened, though instead of becoming frantic, it became more comforting. Our mouths were fused together, and with my eyes closed, I almost felt like we were floating on a cloud. A soft pink cloud of comfort and love.

Though I sizzled between my legs, I had no desire to break the kiss and demand something more. Ryan's cock was hard, pushing in my belly, and I knew he was aching too. But he made no move to break the kiss either.

Slowly we continued our enchanting dance, until the backs of my knees hit the edge of the bed. Ryan didn't break the kiss but swiftly lifted me in his arms, our mouths still joined, and then we were lying on the bed, still kissing.

He rolled over so that he was on top of me, bracing his weight on one arm so as not to crush me. Still we kissed, pulling back, pressing our lips together in little pecks, and then joining them again, our tongues twirling.

We stayed that way for a long time.

The temperature in my core increased, and I began undulating my hips. Smoothly, so smooth I hardly even noticed at first, Ryan entered me.

Sweet completion. Perfect comfort.

He groaned, pulling out and then pushing back in.

His groan vibrated down my throat.

I wrapped one of my legs around his waist, gliding against him as our bodies met again and again. This was slow, sweet lovemaking—something I hadn't yet experienced.

Ryan was always showing me something new.

All I wanted, all I needed was to be with Ryan. If I could stay with him—if we could become hermits, never leave this room—

I stopped that thought, for I knew it was impossible. I didn't want impossible dreams clawing at me. Not now.

I surrendered to the moment. Locked both my legs around his back and relished the feeling of him inside me. He was still pumping slowly, easing in and out of me, and I felt every hard inch of him inside the walls of my pussy.

I savored it. Welcomed it. The completeness in our joining.

Ryan finally moved his mouth away from mine, trailing kisses to my ear. "I need to come, baby."

I whimpered, and I finally let go of the sweet feeling of comfort and made way for the climax that was imminent.

"Come," I said to him. "Come with me, Ryan."

I brought my lips to his neck, sucking on his smooth flesh, as the orgasm ripped through me. I imagined us flying, hovering over the earth, floating among the clouds, as both of our bodies shook in climax. This orgasm was different. I thought I would give up the comfort when I let go to come, but it was still there. Even as my body shuddered in response to the physical rapture, comfort enveloped me in a soft cloud.

We were both out of breath when the shudders finally stopped. Still, that beautiful feeling of contentment overwhelmed me.

We lay together, silent, for a few moments.

Finally, Ryan rolled over onto his back. "Wow," he said.

"Wow," I agreed.

"I don't know about you, baby, but that was just what I needed."

"Me too. I think we were both looking for comfort."

"I didn't realize that until you just said it." He smiled. "Thank you."

"Thank you? What for?"

"For always giving me what I need. At any given time, Ruby, you either let me give to you or take. Whatever I need."

"I... I guess I never thought about it. But I love you, Ryan. I will give you whatever you need if it's within my power."

"That's what makes you so special."

There was nothing special about me, but I wasn't about to argue with Ryan during our afterglow. The word special belonged to people like Ryan Steel and his brothers.

"You know, I'm going to have to go back to my apartment at some point."

"Why? I have a perfectly good house at the ranch, and there's plenty of room for you there."

We were back to this. I wasn't ready to move in with him, but I didn't want to argue after the beautiful lovemaking we'd just shared. So I simply said, "We'll figure things out."

I giggled when Ryan's stomach growled.

"I guess we forgot to eat," I said. "Everything will be closed by now."

"Maybe room service?" Ryan arched his eyebrows.

"It has to be after midnight."

"Let me see what I can do." Ryan rose and searched for his phone in the pocket of his jeans.

I took advantage of the view and ogled his gorgeous ass. I remembered how, when we were in Jamaica, I had accidentally brushed my fingers over his asshole. It had scared me at the time, but now I found myself wanting to explore every tiny bit of his beautiful body, including the forbidden parts.

I shuddered for a moment. If I felt that way about him... He probably felt the same way about me. He'd already licked me there once. Was anal sex something he wanted?

I still felt so naïve about men. As scared as I was, I itched to bring up the subject with him. If only because I wanted to touch him there, maybe lick him there—something I had never imagined wanting to do to another person. But Ryan... I wanted to experience everything with him. Everything the universe had to offer.

Ryan turned back to me, still naked, and smiling. "How does pizza sound?"

"Sounds perfect," I said.

"It will be here in about half an hour. What on earth could we possibly do until then?"

CHAPTER THIRTY-EIGHT

R y a n

Ruby was still lying on the bed, her head propped up by pillows. Her body was covered in a shiny coat of glistening perspiration. The sapphire bracelet sparkled on her wrist. For a moment, I imagined her body covered in a bikini made of sapphires and platinum. Maybe a few small diamonds for glitter.

But Ruby didn't need that kind of ornamentation. She was at her most beautiful naked, with her hair down. Right now, it was still in the messy ponytail. I pulled her forward and worked the band out of her hair.

"God, Ryan. It's going to be a big tangled mess."

"No. It's beautiful."

She looked down shyly.

I tipped her chin up, forcing her gaze to mine. "Everything about you is beautiful, Ruby. You're the only one who never saw it. You tried hiding away your beauty, covering it up, but I saw it." I smiled. "And you know what? I don't think you've had nearly enough orgasms." I gave her a quick kiss on the lips and then nuzzled her neck, sliding down, giving each nipple a tug with my lips and then spreading her legs. I inhaled her sweet scent.

Then I dived in. I slid my tongue between her wet folds, nipping at her clit. She tasted so good, our juices mingled together. I looked up at her, her eyes glazed over as she watched me. "I think I could eat you forever, baby."

I continued my assault, thrusting my tongue into her wetness and then adding two fingers. That was all it took to send her over the edge. She clamped down on my hand, and I took my mouth from her for a moment and watched her lips quiver with the contractions of her climax.

But only for a moment. Then I sank my tongue back into that beautiful, delicious pussy.

"Ryan!" she cried out. "God, Ryan!"

Her voice spurred me on, and I continued to fuck her with my fingers while I nipped at her clit. She smothered me in her cream and I savored it, licking my lips. When she came again, this time I didn't lean back. I clamped my lips around her clit and sucked, taking her higher and higher.

When her shuddering slowed, I pushed her thighs forward. Her little rose of an asshole beckoned. It shone with the juices that had dripped from her pussy. How I longed to stroke it with my tongue once again, to show her the pleasures it would bring.

Ruby was still so inexperienced. No way would she be ready for real ass play.

One day. And hopefully soon.

"Beautiful," I whispered, looking at the paradise between her legs.

Then I couldn't help myself. I swiped my tongue over her rosy anus.

Before she could object, I went back to her pussy, sucking her labia between my teeth and tugging.

But she grabbed my hair and pulled me forward. "Need you inside me now. Please."

Since she said please. I crawled upward, giving each turgid nipple a tug as I went, and plunged into her heat.

Sweet home.

She hugged me so completely. So effortlessly. As if she'd been created to perfectly cast my cock. I groaned as I pulled out and thrust back in. Heaven. Sweet paradise. Paradise between the legs of the woman I loved.

I closed my eyes and surrendered to the moment, to this woman, as I—

Someone knocked at the door.

I stopped in midthrust.

Ruby chuckled. "Pizza."

As if on cue, my stomach growled.

"Shit," I said.

"You have to answer it, or he'll leave."

"Guess I'll have blue balls for a while." I pulled out—with great effort—and stood, shucking my jeans over my legs, my hard on apparent.

Ruby burst out laughing. "I'll get the door." She got up and yelled, "Just a minute!" Then she put on a robe from the bathroom and left the bedroom.

I willed my cock down to half-mast—that was the best I was going to get—and went into the living area to join her. She had poured two more glasses of the merlot and dished out two slices of pizza onto napkins.

"Come and get it," she said.

I inhaled the spicy tomato aroma. Pizza and wine. Then sleep.

And then...tomorrow.

★ ★ ★

Back at the ranch, I rode through the vineyards to check on things and then went to do my usual tastings of what was aging in the barrels. I needed to hire some help. Jade had helped me in the office when she first came to town but had left to work in the city attorney's office once she passed the bar exam. I hadn't gotten around to hiring anyone else.

Ruby popped into my mind.

She'd be great. She was smart and she learned quickly. Plus, she liked wine and wanted to know more about it. But she'd never leave the police force. I couldn't ask her to. She'd consider it an insult.

She was at work now, most likely answering questions about her boss's death. One more death at the hands of Theodore Mathias. She and I had come from some paragons of parenthood between the two of us.

DNA didn't lie. I wondered if Ruby had ever considered having her DNA tested. My fate was sealed at this point, but maybe hers wasn't. Did she know for sure that she was Theodore Mathias's daughter? She didn't look anything like him, except for her hair color. Of course that didn't mean anything. Talon and Joe didn't look anything like Daphne Steel, except for their hair color.

I wouldn't bring it up, but if she did, I'd support her in getting a test. To do a test, though, we'd need Mathias's DNA. Getting that could be a problem.

I looked at my phone for the time. Nearly lunch. I was meeting Talon and Joe at the main house to discuss the future lawmakers ring. I had a lot to tell them.

★ ★ ★

"Yeah, that's what he said." I took a bite of my juicy hamburger. "'The devil is in the details.'"

"It could mean nothing," Talon said.

"Or it could mean everything," Joe contradicted. "It could be one of his obscure clues, like Melanie said."

"But how likely is it that Bryce's uncle figured the whole thing out just by using a computer program to twist and realign the symbol? It could have come up as anything." Talon sipped his iced tea.

"True," Joe said. "But there's no denying that it's a form of the female symbol. The other meanings may or may not be accurate."

"Mathias has the phoenix tattoo," I interjected. "Another symbol of evil or the devil."

"Look," Talon said, "I'll be the last person to take Mathias's side, but lots of people like the symbolism of the phoenix. Most people probably don't even know that occultists associate it with the devil. Hell, Jade was going to get one herself. Thank God she didn't."

"My mother was no help," I said. "But that's no surprise."

"And she won't budge on Dad?"

I shook my head. "Just says he'll come to us when he's ready to. Oh"—I swallowed—"she seemed to indicate that he was being held captive somewhere."

"What?"

"Don't take anything she says too seriously," I said. "But that's what she seemed to be getting at."

"We have to find him," Joe said.

"How? Larry won't say anything," Talon said. "And Wendy

doesn't even know what the truth is."

"She *might* know," I said. "Ruby has this theory that there are reasons behind all of Wendy's lies. That she's very calculating."

"Larry did say she was a genius," Joe said.

"Larry's a psycho," Talon said. "Don't forget that he took part in everything they did to me. He didn't just stand idly by and watch."

"Tal, they're all psychos. That's a given." Joe cleared his throat. "In fact, there's something we really need to consider."

"What?" I asked.

"We need to consider that Dad might be just as psychotic as the rest of these people."

CHAPTER THIRTY-NINE

Ruby

After I'd gone through what happened with Mark and my father the previous evening for about the nineteenth time, I was finally let go.

I was supposed to go back to the hotel, and I would, but Ryan had texted me that he'd be late getting into town because he was talking to his brothers. I could only imagine what about. So I decided to take advantage of some extra time and go visit my aunt and uncle, Erica and Rodney Cates. Erica was my father's sister and had been in and out of mental hospitals her whole life. Their daughter, Gina, who had been a patient of Melanie's, had supposedly committed suicide because she had never been able to deal with the sexual abuse by my father when she was younger.

My father—a fucking model citizen.

Melanie and I thought she had probably been murdered, most likely also by my father, who'd made it look like a suicide.

I was surprised when Melanie told me my uncle had dropped the lawsuit against her. Did he have new information? That's what I aimed to find out. I drove to the townhome they'd rented in the city, left my car, and knocked.

I didn't expect my uncle to answer, so I was pleasantly—or unpleasantly—surprised when he came to the door.

"Detective," he said.

"I need to talk to you."

He opened the screen door. "What the hell? Come on in."

I entered and followed him into the living room.

"Have a seat," he said.

I sat down on the couch.

"So what do you want?" he asked, sitting in a chair across from me.

"My friend Melanie told me you dropped the lawsuit against her."

"Yeah."

"I'm glad you did, but I want to know why."

He stood and paced nervously before sitting down again. "Do I really have to tell you? You of all people should know what kind of a man your father is."

"You've *always* known that, so I don't buy it. Why did you drop the lawsuit? Do you have new information on Gina's death?"

"Wouldn't the cops get that before I do?"

"As far as the cops are concerned, it was a suicide. No one's probing."

"*You* are."

"Yeah. I'm trying. But you know as well as I do that my father never leaves a trail. He's been getting a little more nervous lately, though, now that Wade and Simpson are out of the picture."

Rodney sighed heavily. "I never would have hurt my little girl in a million years."

"Then why did you let my father hurt her?"

"I didn't."

"Bullshit. You always knew what kind of man he was. How

could you leave her alone with him? How?" I grasped the seat cushion to keep from standing and drawing my gun.

"You don't understand."

"*What* don't I understand? That my father's a maniac? Believe me, I get that. He would have raped me if I hadn't gotten away. I'd probably be a slave to some drug lord right now if I hadn't taken control of my own life when I was fifteen."

"So you *know*, then."

"That my father deals in human beings? Yeah. Your friend Wendy Madigan filled me in, though I had kind of figured it out on my own."

"None of us ever meant it to go this far." He rubbed at his forehead. "I never meant for Erica or Gina to be involved in any of this. It's been hell on them both."

"Since Erica is crazy and Gina's dead, yeah, I agree. That's hell for sure, especially when you could have prevented it."

"No one regrets that more than I do."

"You let this happen under your nose, Rodney. You don't get the privilege of having regrets."

He didn't respond.

"I need to ask. Is Gina truly dead?"

"Of course. Why would you even question that?"

"Because I didn't see the body. And it's come to my attention lately that sometimes dead people aren't actually dead."

"We found her dead in the car in the garage. We cremated her."

"So *you* actually found the body?"

"No. Erica did."

"And you saw it later?"

"No. The coroner had taken it away by then."

My mind whirled. "Let me get this straight. You never saw your daughter's dead body?"

"No. I can see her in my nightmares, though."

I nearly gagged. "Please spare me the sanctimonious sadness. You let my father rape her. She couldn't have meant that much to you."

He shook his head. "You don't understand."

"Believe me, I'm glad I don't. But don't change the subject. You're telling me that you never saw Gina's body? Only Erica did?"

He nodded. "That's right."

I stood this time and paced around the room, my rubber-soled shoes catching on the worn-out carpet. "Are you sure about that? That Erica saw the body? That it was actually Gina?"

"Of course I am! Erica wouldn't lie about something like that."

"Wouldn't she? Or maybe she wouldn't know the difference. Her mental state has never been stellar."

"She loved her child! We both did."

Again, I had to hold back a gag. As much as I wanted to argue the point that no one who let a child be raped loved her, I kept silent on that subject. "How much of a hold does my father have over Erica?"

"Erica knows what he is, but he's still her brother."

"I've seen the death certificate, Rodney. It says you were the reporting party. How could you report it if you never even saw a body?"

"Erica was beside herself. I had to be the one to talk to the authorities."

"You're lying. If the coroner came before you got there,

he'd put down Erica as the reporting party. Don't try to put one over on me."

"I'm not. I swear."

He sounded sincere, but that meant nothing. These future lawmakers had obviously been bred to lie. Whether it was a lie or not really didn't matter. My father had somehow gotten into secured databases before to change records. The Steels had uncovered those doings. Someone could have easily changed the reporting party on Gina's death certificate to Rodney. And in some offbeat way, it made sense that my father would do that to protect his sister from any possible interrogation.

"I need to talk to Erica."

He shook his head. "She doesn't want to see anyone. The nurse is with her now."

"A live-in?"

"No. We can't afford that. Insurance pays for a nurse for four hours in the evening."

"I see. What if I ask the nurse if it's okay if I speak to her?"

"That's not possible."

"Why not?"

He stood, shoving his hands into the pockets of his pants. "Because there's no nurse. I lied. I figured if you thought there was a nurse, you'd leave her alone."

"For Christ's sake, Rodney, I don't want to harm her. I just want to talk to her. Gina was my cousin. And as much as I'd like to forget my bloodlines, this involves my father. She might have information that could help me find him."

"That's just it. She doesn't want you to find him."

"After what he did to Gina? How can that be?"

"She's afraid of him. We both are."

I widened my eyes. I hadn't considered that, though I

probably should have. My father had a warped perception of loyalty to family ties.

"Please. I just want to talk to her. If she gets agitated, I'll leave."

"I'm sorry. No."

Since the woman was crazy as a loon anyway, talking to her was probably futile. I decided not to push it. Maybe Rodney had other information.

"Look, my father was in town last night. He came to the station. He had to have had help. Did he get it from you?"

"No. He wouldn't trust me to help him."

"Who would he trust? Wendy?"

"Not likely, and she's locked up in psych."

"I know. Who else?"

"Simpson."

"Dead. Who else?"

"Only one other, though they had a falling out a long time ago. And he's also dead."

"And who might that be?"

"Steel. Brad Steel."

★ ★ ★

I sat in the hotel room, typing on my laptop. Ryan still hadn't arrived, and I hadn't gotten a text from him in a couple hours. I was starting to worry.

I'd also been worrying about how I was going to tell him about the conversation with my uncle, specifically that, according to him, Brad Steel was one of the people my father trusted...or at least had in the past. That didn't bode well for Ryan's father.

Rodney could very well be lying. I didn't trust any of them as far as I could throw them.

But what if he was telling the truth? What did that say about Ryan's father and his involvement in this mess?

I didn't want to think about it. One thing was certain though. If Bradford Steel was alive, we needed to find him. Without him, there would be no closure for any of us.

I jolted when the door handle turned. *Relax, it's only Ryan.* I smiled as the door opened.

CHAPTER FORTY

Ryan

Ice froze in my veins.

It wasn't a new thought to me, but it was the first time any of us had voiced it.

Our father might be as psychopathic as the rest of these people.

Talon nodded. "Joe's right."

"I know he is," I said. "I just don't want to think about having two biological parents that are so mentally deficient. What the hell kind of DNA is floating around in my cells? I don't get it. What happens to people to make them this way? To do these kinds of things?"

"Ry," Joe said, "if we could identify what makes people do these kinds of things, we'd have fixed it by now."

"Dad had a good life," I continued. "Great parents who loved him. A good work ethic. All the money in the goddamned world." I shook my head. "I just don't get it."

"Be glad you don't get it," Talon said. "That means you didn't inherit whatever nutjob gene he was carrying. I'm thankful none of us did."

"But he was a model citizen," I said. "Everyone knew and respected him and the Steel operation."

"Psychopaths often seem to have great lives to outsiders,"

Joe said. "Look at Wendy. She was a respected newswoman. Tom Simpson was our mayor, for God's sake, and Larry was the city attorney. We now know the secret lives all of them were leading."

I winced. "Are you saying that Dad had a secret life too?"

Joe sighed. "I think that's pretty clear at this point. I've talked to Melanie at length about this. Many psychopaths are never caught because they're smart and they cover up their crimes. One thing about Dad, Tom, Larry, and Wendy. None of them are dummies."

I scraped my fingers through my hair. "I want to know my story. How I came to be."

"You know that," Talon said.

"No, I don't. I don't know for sure if Dad fucked Wendy." Ruby's odd theory hadn't left my mind, and even though I'd discounted it at first, I'd been ruminating on it. "I wouldn't put it past her to get her hands on his sperm and have herself artificially inseminated."

"Exactly how would she get her hands on his sperm? I doubt Dad ever deposited any specimens in a sperm bank. I know you don't want to believe it, Ry, but Dad fucked Wendy."

"You're right. I don't want to believe it."

"None of us do," Talon said. "We all thought more of Dad than that. But he did. You're proof of that."

"Still, I want to look into it. I'm going to call all the sperm banks in Colorado—" I couldn't help a raucous laugh. "Good God, what am I thinking? Dad would never donate sperm, and those records are probably sealed anyway."

"You're thinking you deserve an explanation for what happened," Joe said. "But it's time for you to accept that there isn't one—at least not one that makes sense to rational people."

"Hence us questioning Dad's mental state," Talon agreed.

I couldn't fault my brothers' observations, but I just wasn't ready to accept that I came from not one but two psychopaths. How the hell had all of this happened? Dad had loved Mom... er, Daphne. Yet my mother claimed he loved her and only her. "I don't see any evidence that Dad loved Wendy as much as she claims," I said.

"I don't either," Joe said. "I wondered that from the beginning. If they were so in love, why didn't she come into the picture after Mom died? It doesn't make any sense."

I let out a sigh. "We may never get all the answers. None of these people can be trusted, including our own father."

Talon nodded. "I've had to accept that as well, even though I'd love to know why I had to endure the hell I endured. But the most important thing is to find Mathias and bring him to justice. We got two of them, and Wendy's in psych lockup. Only one to go."

"Yeah, the most elusive one." I regarded Talon—the brother I'd always considered my hero. I didn't want to ask the next question, but I had to. "Tal...what do you remember about the day you were taken? What do you remember about how I got away?"

Talon closed his eyes.

"If you don't want to talk about this, you don't have to."

He opened his eyes. "It's okay. But first, why do you want to know?"

Wendy had already told Tal and Joe that I'd been spared because I was her son, and I didn't want to confirm it. But I had no choice if I wanted Talon to answer my question. I quickly explained my conversation with Wendy.

"I'm overwhelmed with guilt, Tal," I said. "To think that I

was spared because I'm that psycho's son. It should have been me."

"Don't say that," Joe said.

"I can't help it. I have to know. Is that how it happened, Tal? Because I remember a guy holding me and you somehow hitting him in the groin. He let me go, and you yelled at me to run."

"Yes, that's what I remember," he said.

"So it *was* you. You saved me. Wendy is lying."

"As much as I'd love to think it was all me," Talon said, "the reality is that Simpson and Mathias could probably have easily handled two little boys. I was ten. I most likely didn't do that much damage to his groin."

An anvil settled in my gut. Talon had admitted it. He probably wasn't the reason I'd gotten away.

"Don't look so glum, Ry," he said. "I'm glad you got away. I don't hold any resentment toward you."

"Maybe you should."

"Look. I can't change what happened, and if I could, do you think for a minute I'd have you go through that hell instead of me? Hell, no. If I'd had a choice between myself and either of you, I'd have chosen me."

"Me too," Joe said, sighing. "In a minute."

I studied my two brothers. They looked so much alike. Even though all three of us resembled our father, Tal and Joe were so similar in appearance. Now we knew why. Would I have gone in their places if I'd had the choice?

The answer shot straight into my brain with no hesitation. Yes.

I would have done anything to protect my brothers.

"Me too," I agreed.

"That's what brothers do," Talon said.

And I realized it didn't really matter whether Talon was the reason I got away or not. He'd tried to help me get away, and he'd told me to run.

He was still my hero—my true brother in all ways—and he always would be.

★ ★ ★

I was exhausted by the time I got to the hotel. I inserted the keycard and opened the door. Everything was dark. Ruby must have already gone to bed. As much as I would have loved a romp with her, I was also fatigued, so it was just as well she was already asleep. I wouldn't wake her.

I poured myself half a glass of wine to unwind and sat down in the living area for a few minutes, reflecting on the conversation I'd had with my brothers. One thing was clear. We had to locate our father. That was the only way we'd get the answers we needed.

I sighed and downed the wine. Snuggling up to Ruby was the prescription I needed.

I set down the goblet and opened the door to the bedroom. It was dark. I undressed quickly and got into bed.

She wasn't there.

CHAPTER FORTY-ONE

Ruby

Come with me if you want answers.

I knew better than to trust my father. Unfortunately, I had already taken my gun out of my ankle holster and set my phone down when he came through my hotel room door uninvited. But I desperately wanted answers, and even though leaving with him might turn out to be the stupidest thing I'd ever done, my curiosity won out. I didn't stop to think how he'd gotten a key to my room, how he'd come into the hotel unnoticed.

While I didn't trust him—not even a little bit—I didn't think he'd hurt me. It seemed to be a game with him. He'd stay just out of my reach, and he'd also leave me alone.

For once, he wasn't wearing a ski mask or the blue contacts. But he was wearing a Colorado Rockies skullcap, which covered his black hair, and black pants and a hoodie. I guessed he was going for gangsta hood.

We didn't go far. Just to another room in the same hotel. The top floor. I sat, uneasy, on one of the chairs in the room.

"Wine?" he asked.

"No, thanks." No way was I going to risk getting even slightly inebriated.

"Mind if I have some?"

"Suit yourself."

He poured himself a glass and then sat down across from me. "You look good."

"Am I supposed to say thanks?"

"That's up to you. You were always a beautiful girl, Ruby. Why you've been hiding it behind those masculine clothes all these years is beyond me."

Maybe because you tried to rape me and instilled an irrational fear of men in your teenage daughter.

I stayed silent. Then, "You said you had answers."

"I do. But first I need you to guarantee me passage out of the country."

"No can do," I said. "Are you forgetting I'm an officer of the law? I could arrest you right now."

"Without a gun? I don't think so." He unzipped his hoodie to expose a shoulder holster and Glock.

Though my stomach lurched, as it always did when I encountered someone who was armed, I wasn't shocked. "If you wanted to hurt me, you'd have done it long ago." Still, I began devising ways in my mind to disarm him.

"Maybe. Maybe not. Maybe I've been amusing myself watching you try to catch me all these years."

"Seems you've found other ways to amuse yourself, Pops. You know...raping and torturing people? Kids? Then selling them into slavery? Must be really amusing for you or you wouldn't do it."

He laughed. Actually laughed! "I do it for the money, kid."

"Don't give me that bullshit. Maybe you sell them for the money. The raping and torturing is just for fun. Admit it, you shit-eating psychopath."

"Is that any way to talk to your father?"

"It is when he's a shit-eating psychopath."

He didn't respond. And then I saw it. On the ring finger of his right hand. The ring, identical to Tom Simpson's. I couldn't help staring. Was the symbol the same? I couldn't get a good look from the angle where I was.

"You promised me answers," I said again.

"Would you believe anything a shit-eating psychopath told you?" he asked.

As much as I hated to admit it, he had a good point. My heart was beating like a bass drum, but I couldn't show my nervousness. I needed him to see that I was maintaining control, that I didn't fear him.

"Your ring," I said. "May I see it?"

"Of course." He removed it and handed it to me. "It will belong to you someday. You're my only child."

"Thank God. You certainly shouldn't be allowed to reproduce."

"Believe it or not, Ruby, I never meant to reproduce. I told you a long time ago that your mother was a one-night stand gone wrong."

I ignored his heinous remark and fingered the ring. It was identical to Simpson's, right down to the enigmatic symbol. "What does this symbol mean?"

"It represents an old club I belonged to a long time ago."

"Yes, the future lawmakers club in high school. I know all about that."

"You're a good investigator. A good cop, Ruby. I'm proud of you."

Say what? "I haven't brought *you* down yet."

"True. But I'm uncatchable. I'm careful, very cautious."

Delusions of grandeur. I'd have to ask Melanie if that was a symptom of psychopathy. If I ever got out of here, that was.

"Back to the ring," I said. "What does the symbol mean?"

"It symbolizes our commitment to each other and to the club, among other things."

"What was the club about?"

"What do you think? We were future lawmakers."

"And what laws would those be? All you've done is *break* the law."

"Think about it. You're smart. You're my daughter, for God's sake. Oh, and if you're thinking that maybe you're not, that maybe the whole thing is a hellacious mistake, give it up. I had your DNA tested when your mother flew the coop. I figured the whore might have been lying on your birth certificate."

I stood, fear raging through my veins, but I was not going to let him speak badly about my mother. Flew the coop? The woman had died. "Don't ever mention my mother again."

"Fine by me. But you should know this. Your mother gave you to me. She's the reason you were sent to me."

Keep calm, Ruby. He's just trying to distract you from the ring. I breathed in deeply and let the air out slowly. I said nothing.

He continued trying to bait me. "She phoned me and told me she could no longer afford you, and that it was my turn."

"She died. That's why I was sent to you."

"Your mother didn't die, Ruby. When I refused to take you, she abandoned you and you became a ward of the state. When officials called me, I had no choice but to take you. But rest assured, I made sure you were truly mine."

No. My mother loved me. She did the best she could. Grief overwhelmed me. My father's face blurred, and I blinked. Had to stay cool. *Had* to. "You're lying, you son of a bitch."

"I'm not."

"Oh? Where is my mother then?"

"I have no idea. Do you think I give a shit where she is?"

"I do. Where is she, you asshole!"

"She didn't want you. It's no use trying to find her."

"You're lying! My mother loved me. She loved me." I choked back tears. "I'm out of here." I stood and turned toward the door, but he yanked me back.

"You're not going anywhere."

CHAPTER FORTY-TWO

Ryan

My heart pounded. Where the hell was Ruby? I flipped on the lights and looked around. Her purse lay on the night table. I quickly unzipped it and dumped the contents on the bed. Her wallet. And her phone. She wouldn't have left without either.

I turned my gaze toward the dresser.

And a cannonball hit my stomach.

Her gun sat on top of the wooden surface.

Wherever she was, she was unarmed.

I quickly called 9-1-1, but they told me what I already knew. They couldn't do anything until an adult was missing more than twenty-four hours.

I couldn't just sit here. She wouldn't have left willingly without her phone and her gun. So I'd search. I'd begin at her apartment. The number from the text she'd received warning her not to go home hadn't been traceable. Big shock there.

God, I was exhausted, but I had to go after Ruby.

I couldn't imagine a world without her in it.

I traipsed downstairs and drove to Ruby's apartment. Of course, it was locked. I called a locksmith and paid him a shit ton of green to open the door without any evidence that I lived there. Money still talked.

I entered the small apartment that consisted only of a

tiny living room, a galley kitchen, and a small bedroom and bathroom. I turned on all the lights and started looking for something. I wasn't sure what, but I'd know it when I found it.

I ransacked the tiny alcove, pulling up her sheets and stripping the bed. Then I went through her dresser drawers. Nothing except lots of plain cotton underwear. Her closet held more of her sensible clothes and shoes. Time to try the living room.

On one side of the wall stood a large bookshelf. I was determined to leave no stone unturned, so I pulled out each book and leafed through it, looking for anything that might be hidden inside.

Nothing.

I pulled out her sofa cushions and plunged my hands inside the crevices, searching. Some loose change, but that was it.

I looked under her sofa. Nothing except another book. I pulled it out. It was an old copy of Mary Wollstonecraft's *A Vindication of the Rights of Woman*. I'd heard of it. The author was the mother of Mary Shelley, who had penned the original *Frankenstein*. Written in the eighteenth century, it was an early treatise on feminism. I turned it over and let the pages open.

A small piece of paper fluttered to the ground.

I picked it up.

It was a pale pink, almost like the old-fashioned stationery my mother—or the woman I'd thought was my mother at the time—kept on hand for letters and notes. On one side were several drawings. I gulped as I recognized them. One was the female symbol. One was the symbol on Simpson's ring. The others were variations.

On the other side, some words were written—a quote

from the classical playwright Euripides.

There is no worse evil than a bad woman.

★ ★ ★

After going through her kitchen and finding nothing, I cleaned up as best I could and took the Wollstonecraft book and the paper I'd found in it back to the hotel. I texted Ruby, thinking if she was back she'd have her phone, but I didn't expect a response.

I didn't get one.

The book puzzled me. Ruby might well read early feminist literature, but the paper with the image and the quote was an enigma.

Someone had planted it. Perhaps the whole book, but certainly at least the paper hiding within its pages. Someone had been in Ruby's apartment, and someone had warned her not to go there.

The quote rang in my ears.

There is no worse evil than a bad woman.

Why Euripides? Did he have something against women? I wasn't well versed in the classic Greek philosophers. I'd have to do some research. And why the ring design?

And then it hit me like a ton of cement pouring over me and dragging me down.

The quote.

The symbol on the ring.

They both referred to one woman.

My mother.

CHAPTER FORTY-THREE

Ruby

"The hell I'm not. You can't keep me here. I don't care what you're carrying. I'm out of here." I stood and headed toward the door.

He didn't come after me and try to yank me back. No, he was too cool for that. He knew what would get me.

"I know where Brad Steel is."

I stopped and could move no farther, as though my feet were mired in quicksand. "Where?" I asked without turning back to face him.

"He's safe. He's in hiding."

"Why?" I still didn't turn around.

"That's a question with many possible answers. I can only give you mine, and it's speculation."

This time I turned. Usually I could spot a liar a mile away, but my father was good. I'd bet good money he could pass a lie detector test as if he had ice in his veins.

"First, tell me where he is," I said.

"In a compound off the coast of Jamaica."

Jamaica? We'd just been to Jamaica. Juliet and Lisa were taken from a resort in Jamaica. Nausea permeated my throat.

"What kind of compound? Is that where you run your trafficking through? Is that why you don't want me talking to

Shayna?"

"Shayna's a lucky girl. And a smart one."

"I know that. She got away from your goons, thank God. But her friends weren't so lucky."

"Her friends are safe."

"Safe meaning what? That they're not dead? That hardly constitutes safe in your world."

"They're victims of their own stupidity."

I couldn't deny the truth of his words. "So what? A moment of stupidity shouldn't condemn you to a life of slavery and humiliation. Those girls had futures."

"Did they? Aspiring actresses in LA are a dime a dozen. We find women there all the time. They're willing to do almost anything for that one big chance." His voice oozed with sleaziness.

Rage coursed through me. "Goddamnit, they are *people*! What gives you the right to play God with their lives?"

I didn't expect an answer, and I didn't get one. I had to calm down and get a grip. My father had successfully derailed me from the subject at hand. Brad Steel.

"What's Brad Steel doing at a compound somewhere near Jamaica?"

"He's there of his own free will."

"Wendy told Ryan that he was being held captive."

"That's between her and Steel. I don't know what he's doing there, whether he's in captivity or not. I can only tell you no one forced him to go there."

"Is that where Juliet and Lisa are?"

No response.

"What about Gina? Is that where Gina is?"

Again, no response.

My father was difficult to read, but if Gina was truly dead, he would have said so. I was sure of it.

My cousin was alive.

"She didn't kill herself, did she? You forged a death certificate for her and convinced your sister she had committed suicide. There was never any body, was there? You convinced Erica that she'd seen a body, had her tell Rodney. God, no wonder the woman is crazy!"

"You don't know what you're talking about."

"Don't I? I think I'm getting pretty fucking close to the truth, Pops. Is Gina there too? At the compound, being trained for slavery? Or has she already been sold?"

"You're a smart girl. You figure it out."

"I *have* figured it out. If it takes me my entire life, I will expose you and bring you down."

"Maybe you will, and maybe you won't," he said, his brown eyes slitted. "But I can assure you it won't be tonight."

A blast of sound permeated the room.

The fire alarm.

My father had arranged to have the building evacuated so he could make his getaway. And here I was, unarmed, unable to hold him.

I wouldn't even try.

He walked past me, brushing my arm slightly. "Don't take the elevators, Ruby. In case of fire, always take the stairs." He walked out of the room.

I ran after him, but the hallways were already crowding with hotel guests. It was late, and most of them were in bathrobes or pajamas. I watched the purple Rockies skullcap float above the heads until it disappeared in the stairwell.

I'd failed once again.

CHAPTER FORTY-FOUR

Ryan

Damn! A fire alarm at this time of night? I was still up, of course, concerned about Ruby. Where was she? I opened the door to our room. People were congregating in the halls, trying to get to the stairwells. It was a giant clusterfuck.

I sniffed. No smoke. It had to be a hoax. Some kid probably thought it was funny to pull the alarm. High school bullshit. I went back into the room and shut the door. I wasn't leaving.

Quickly I checked my phone. Nothing. I paced the living area, most likely leaving a trail on the thin hotel carpeting. Her apartment hadn't yielded any clues other than the book and the paper, but neither of those gave me any idea where she might be.

I couldn't lose her. Not now. Not ever.

I thought back to our first walk on the beach in Jamaica in the moonlight.

★ ★ ★

Her eyes were the clearest blue. Amazing I could see them in the dark, but they were mesmerizing.

Was this truly the mousy woman I'd sat next to on the plane? God, what would she look like when she was really dressed up for the wedding?

Wow. Just wow.

I grinned. Enter Ryan Steel ultra-flirt mode. "Maybe I wanted to walk with you."

She rolled her blue eyes. "Please," she said sardonically.

"Please walk with me?" I widened my grin.

"Thanks. I'd love to."

I touched her arm again.

Again, she pulled away. "Grabby, aren't you? And you know that's not what I meant."

Man, this wasn't going to be easy. Her lips were still dark, though the meal had probably taken care of most of her red lipstick. This was Ruby's natural lip color, darker than I remembered from the plane, and God, it was a turn-on.

I hadn't dared to think it before, but this woman was beautiful.

Stunning.

"We're both here, and it's an amazing night." I looked up at the night sky aglow with the moon and stars. "What would a walk hurt?" Though I longed to, I didn't touch her again. She obviously didn't appreciate it, though I wasn't sure why. I hadn't done anything to her that I wouldn't do to anyone else. Just touched her forearm pretty innocently. Man, she was jumpy.

She let out a sigh. "Fine."

I held out my arm, thinking it would be no big deal for her to slide hers through it. She shook her head and started walking.

This one was certainly going to be a challenge, but I hadn't yet met a woman I couldn't lure into my bed. The thought surprised me. When had I decided that I wanted Ruby Lee in my bed? But there was no doubt about it.

I did.

She was about Jade's size, probably around five feet seven inches. *Although her boobs weren't quite as big as Jade's, they were close. Bigger than Melanie's, and even bigger than Juliet's. Perky too. Little hard nipples protruded through her blue cotton tank. She was clearly going braless, and if I had it my way, she wouldn't wear a bra this whole trip.*

How to approach her—that was the question. Normally, I'd try taking her hand, especially for a midnight walk on the beach. But Ruby clearly didn't want to be touched. I didn't know why, though it could definitely have to do with her father. He had, after all, raped my brother and his own niece.

And then my jaw clenched.

Oh my God. Had that beast raped his own daughter?

That wasn't something I could ask her, obviously. Maybe Ruby was a woman to stay away from. Maybe I should leave her alone. After all, she hadn't asked for my advances, though I'd hardly even made an advance yet.

I should definitely stay away from her.

"It is a gorgeous night," she said, interrupting my thoughts.

And it was. I looked again at the myriad stars sprinkled across the night sky, at the nearly full moon reflecting light upon the water before us.

And I looked at her.

She was the most beautiful thing in the night.

The thought entered my mind from seemingly nowhere. Had I ever thought that of any woman? More beautiful than a starry night?

No. I hadn't.

★ ★ ★

I couldn't live without her now. Finally, I understood what

my brothers had with their wives, and why they were so determined to keep it at all costs.

I wasn't giving her up.

That goddamned fire alarm was still blaring. Still no scent of smoke anywhere.

I didn't have my laptop with me, but my phone was a minicomputer. I began typing, trying to figure out what to do next, whom to call.

My brothers of course. I started punching in Joe's number when a pounding on my door startled me.

I opened the door to find a burly security guard standing there. "You have to leave, sir. Fire marshal's orders."

"I don't smell any smoke," I said.

"Doesn't matter. It was probably a prank, but we have to check everything out."

"Sorry, I'm not leaving. I've got important things to do here."

"Don't make me take you by force."

You and what army? The words were on the tip of my tongue. But the guy was armed.

"Crap." I pushed my hair off my forehead. "All right then."

Still holding my phone, I followed the guard down the hall to the stairwell. A few stragglers were walking down the stairs. No one seemed the least bit worried about a fire.

Guests in pajamas and robes had congregated outside the hotel in the atrium by the swimming pool, which was closed for the season. I scanned faces in the darkness, not looking for anyone in particular, when the most beautiful pair of blue eyes pierced back at me.

Ruby!

I ran toward her, nearly knocking down an elderly man.

I apologized quickly, steadying him, and then walked swiftly through the throng of people to my love.

"Ryan!" She nearly jumped into my arms.

I kissed her cheeks, the top of her head. "Where have you been? I've been worried sick!"

"You won't believe where I was and who's responsible for this stupid fire alarm." She sighed. "My father was here."

CHAPTER FORTY-FIVE

Ruby

Once the fire marshal was convinced there were no smoldering embers hiding in the hotel, we were ushered back to our rooms for the night. I'd told Ryan about the conversation with my father while we were outside, and when we got back to the hotel room, he handed me a book.

"Is this yours?"

Mary Wollstonecraft. Interesting. "No, but actually, I've always wanted to read it. Where did you get it?"

"At your apartment."

I pulled at my hair. "What?"

"I went there tonight looking for you. I turned the place inside out looking for clues to where you might be. I was scared shitless, Ruby. You left your gun and your phone. I thought someone had taken you."

"Someone sort of had. I'm really sorry you were worried."

"That doesn't matter now that you're okay. But someone planted this in your apartment under the sofa. Maybe that text you got warning you not to go home wasn't a warning as much as a way to keep you away so this could be planted."

"Maybe. But why would someone plant an old feminism book at my place?"

"Because of what was inside." He handed me a piece of

pink paper.

"*There is no worse evil than a bad woman.* Great. A misogynist was in my house."

"I'm not sure that's true. Turn it over."

I did...and gasped. "The symbol."

"Yeah. And it starts out as the traditional female symbol, just like Bryce's uncle predicted."

"So the symbol must have both meanings then. The female, and evil. Hence the quote. A bad woman."

"And who's the worst woman you know?" Ryan's eyes were sad.

I clasped my hand to my mouth. I didn't want to say it.

He said it for me. "My mother."

"Then we were right, and your mother wasn't lying. She is the mastermind of this whole thing."

"That's what this clue seems to indicate. She is truly evil."

"My father and Bryce's aren't any better, so don't feel alone in this, Ryan."

"I hate to say this to you, but I always assumed your father was the worst of the bunch."

"To be honest, so did I."

"And now, to know it's my mother. The woman I grew inside of..." He rubbed the back of his neck. "How can I live with this?"

"First of all, remember that we're still just speculating here. This so-called clue could have been planted to throw us off."

"It's not speculation. I feel it in my bones," he said.

Truthfully, so did I. I cleared my throat. "As to living with it, do it the same way I have. Be the best person you can be, and don't let the fact that you're related to a psycho taint you. It's not easy, but you can do it. Besides, there isn't time to dwell on it anyhow. We need to figure out who planted this in my apartment and why."

"I know," he said.

"I'll take the book and paper into work tomorrow and have fingerprints extracted. Hopefully that will yield some useful information. At least maybe we can find out who planted it." But I knew we wouldn't. Whoever planted it had most likely used gloves, and the only fingerprints we'd find would be mine and Ryan's.

But I had to try.

"Then what?"

"We find your father. I guess we start by sending out some PIs to look at small islands around Jamaica."

"What if your father was lying?"

"He's hard to read," I said, "but I didn't get the feeling he was lying. In fact, I got a strong feeling that he was telling the truth, for once."

"Why would he want to give my father up?"

"I'm not sure he does. I think he wants to lure you and your brothers out to this compound, wherever it is, and take care of all of you once and for all. That's what makes sense to me. Look at it from his perspective. His two partners are out of the picture. Wendy is in psych lockup. His sister is completely nuts, and now my uncle Rodney is starting to talk. Added to that, I think he's running out of funds. Why else would he have tried to have Jade's mother killed for insurance money? He's getting scared, and he's starting to make mistakes. He's called me several times, and he actually came to this hotel tonight, when usually he sticks to the shadows. He knows his time is running out." I sighed. "He's setting a trap. What we have to do is make him think we're falling into it."

Ryan nodded. "Shit. I'll talk to Joe and Tal, see if they can get their foremen to take over for a few weeks. We'll need to be on this full time."

"Perfect. I have a ton of vacation time. Jamaica was the first vacation I took since I've been on the force."

"Hell, no. You're not coming along. I can't have you in danger."

I dropped my mouth open. "Are you kidding me? This is *my* father we're talking about as well as yours. I am sure as hell going along. Besides, I'm a trained police detective. Don't say I won't be an asset, especially since Mills and Johnson have disappeared."

"Ruby, please. You have no idea what I went through tonight. I thought you had disappeared."

"I'm fine. And I'm going."

"Please. Don't do this. I need to know you're safe."

"That's great. You get to know I'm safe, but I'll be worried sick over you while you're out doing God knows what around people who are potentially more dangerous than my father. That's not fair, Ryan."

"Damn it!" He raked his fingers through his disheveled hair and then grabbed me. "You're going to fucking do what I say!"

"You can't—"

His lips came down on mine. He was playing me, dominating me, and though I rebelled against him mentally, physically, my body took over. My lips parted, and my tongue darted out to meet his.

I was powerless in this man's presence. Powerless to resist the passion between us. I melted into the kiss and let him take me away.

No more Theodore Mathias. No more Wendy Madigan.

Just Ryan. Just me. Just the Ryan-Ruby combination we became when we succumbed to our desires and our lovemaking caused the earth to move.

How had I lived without this for so long?

None of that mattered. I could have been with a hundred past lovers and none would have compared to what I had with Ryan Steel. I knew that in the depth of my bones, the core of my soul.

Our kiss was crazed, hot and wet, and just when I thought I might pass out from the beauty of it, he broke it with a loud smack.

"Bed," he said. "Now."

The thought of disobeying him never entered my mind. I walked to the bed, my legs shaking and barely able to hold my weight. Then I turned to meet his blazing eyes.

His gaze seared my flesh.

Normally this was the time he ordered me to strip off my clothes. I thought I might beat him to the punch, so I began unbuttoning my blouse.

He shook his head at me. "This time, you undress me."

This was something new. For once maybe he would be naked before I was. I wasn't sure that had ever happened between us. I turned the corners of my lips up into a sly smile. I would be happy to undress him, to bare, inch by inch, every piece of his magnificent physique. Not a hardship at all.

I trailed my fingers over his shoulders, the soft cotton of his shirt teasing my flesh, down his arms to his hands. Then I pushed him over to the bed, and he sat.

I knelt at his feet and began working on his boots.

"I like you there," he said. "You look beautiful kneeling before me."

I hadn't thought about the submissiveness of my position until he mentioned it. I had only wanted to please him. Restless legs syndrome suddenly struck my knees and legs, screaming at me to rise. I ignored them, staying in the kneeling position, as I pulled Ryan's boots off. Afterward, I peeled his socks off, baring his feet, which were oddly beautiful for a man. Then, I was able to follow my instincts and stand. I took his hand and pulled him off the bed. Now I stood before him, facing him, his brown eyes staring down at me with electric heat. I began unbuttoning his shirt, and as I did, I let my fingers trail over the warm beauty of his bronze skin. I fingered the chest hairs, the hardness of his muscles, his abs. I trailed over each nipple. They were already hard, yet they hardened even further at my touch. When all the buttons were undone, I parted the two layers of fabric, baring him to my view, and pushed the shirt off his shoulders.

I skimmed my fingers around his soft leather belt, the hard metal of his belt buckle. And beneath it, the bulge that awaited me. Slowly I unbuckled the belt and pulled it off of his jeans with a flourish. I unsnapped them, unzipped them, brushed them over his hips until he was standing in a blue denim puddle. He stepped out of them. Only his boxer briefs covered him now, and his cock was bulging out of them, a small dab of fluid visible on the light-green cotton.

I gaped at him. I had seen him naked many times before—he wasn't even totally naked this time—but every time, he was even more beautiful, more magnificent.

But his patience was wearing thin. After a few minutes of my gawking, he said, "Do I need to repeat myself? Undress me."

His words made me shiver. I had been on my own for so long, never answering to anyone other than bosses. I'd always had great bosses—until Mark, apparently—so I never had to follow orders from anyone I didn't respect.

There was no doubt that I respected Ryan Steel. Hell, I was hopelessly in love with him.

But never before had anyone been so blatantly commanding to me. Other than my father, who I'd fought off.

Why had I never thought about disobeying Ryan Steel? Why did it never enter my mind to deny him when he demanded something?

I wasn't about to deny him now. I swept my hand behind him, caressing the globes of his well-formed buttocks. Then I slid my thumb under the waistband of his briefs. Slowly I moved them to his hips and slid them over his thighs, his cock pointing out.

Ryan Steel was large. Not that I had anything to compare him to, really, but he was large. Today he seemed even larger than normal, and another bead of pre-cum pearled on the tip of his cock.

"Lick it off, baby. Lick my cock for me."

I slid my tongue over the glistening drop, licking and playing. I had grown accustomed to the salty male flavor. So accustomed that I savored it, enjoyed it, relished it. I swirled my tongue over his cock head again, and then again, before pushing my lips forward and taking his shaft into my mouth. I had never been able to go down entirely to his base, but I was getting better. He didn't seem to mind. His groans told me that.

I was still amazed at how much I could please him, how much he enjoyed what I did. Me. Ruby Lee. Former virgin with no experience.

It was so powerful.

I moved my lips on his shaft while I fingered his balls, touching them, massaging them, squeezing them lightly. I itched to explore him further, so I let his balls go and slid my hands up his firm thighs to his hips and around to his gorgeous ass. He was flexed, the globe so hard under my caress. I ran my fingers through the crease, and he jolted slightly when I touched his asshole.

I gasped and let his cock drop from my mouth. I wasn't ready to go there yet. Before he could ask for something I wasn't ready to give, I moved my hands back to his hips and plunged my lips upon his cock once more.

I continued to suck him, kissing him at the base and moving my hand along with my mouth so he would feel like I was taking more than I was. I increased my speed, thrusting back and forth along his erection.

"God, baby. So fucking good."

I wanted him to come in my mouth again. I wanted to do that for him, give him everything I had.

I was expecting him to stop me, turn me over, and thrust into me as he'd done so many times before. But it dawned on me that I was still fully clothed. As much as I had wanted to experience him naked, now I wished I had shed every garment of my own. Because right now, what I wanted more than anything in the world was for him to plunge that big hard dick right inside my pussy.

He didn't hold my head this time, which surprised me, as commanding as he usually was.

Instead, he pulled away. "Baby, I don't want this to end yet."

He had never had a problem coming twice in one night. But it was late, and we were both tired.

"Whatever you want, my love. I'm here."

"I want to fuck you. I want to fuck your tits."

I widened my eyes. "What?" I had no idea what he was talking about.

"Take off your shirt, baby. Do it the way you did it that time when I came to your apartment, so angry and upset about finding about my mother. It was so hot the way you tore your buttons open."

My fingers shook as I grabbed my shirt collar. I yanked it opened, but only one button gave.

"Baby, please. Like you did last time."

I summoned all my love for Ryan, all the passion, all the desire, the lust, the soul-wrenching devotion, this time grabbing the bottom of my shirt and yanking.

The fabric split this time, white buttons flying and clattering against the wall and floor.

Ryan took over then. He yanked my bra right off of me, tearing it in two. He gazed down at my breasts.

"Such beautiful tits, baby. I love pinching them, sucking on them, twisting them, playing with them. But tonight I want to come between them."

Still I had no idea what he was talking about.

"Lie down on your back," he commanded.

I complied, still wearing my pants and shoes and socks. He didn't seem concerned with them at the moment.

He straddled me, right below my breasts, and stuck his cock in between them.

"Push them together, baby, so they make a tight sheath for me."

My nipples were hard as rocks, straining, aching for his teeth and tongue. He clearly had something else in mind. I pushed my boobs together, over his cock, so that it was squeezed between them. He began moving forward and backward, lubricated nicely from the blowjob I'd given him.

"God, that feels so good, Ruby. You have the greatest tits."

They weren't as big as Jade's, but they were okay. Right now, he seemed to be enjoying them immensely.

"Have you ever had a pearl necklace?"

I shook my head. "No. The only nice piece of jewelry I have is the bracelet you gave me."

He chuckled, and then groaned. "I don't want to laugh. Feels so good."

Why didn't he want to laugh? I totally didn't understand.

"I'm going to come, baby. Come from this titty fuck."

My breasts were so sensitive, my nipples so hard. Even though I didn't know what the hell he was talking about, I was up for anything.

He continued thrusting between my breasts while I squeezed them together. Faster, faster, faster. He closed his eyes and groaned, and then he climaxed, squirting my chest and my neck.

He leaned back and let out a low moan. "Baby. Oh my God." He lay down next to me. "You like your pearl necklace?" he asked, grinning.

"Ryan, I don't—"

Then I laughed out loud. The drops of cum on my neck and chest. Those were the pearls. How naïve I still was. But he didn't seem to mind.

I smiled at him. "I think the more pressing question is, did you enjoy *giving* me the pearl necklace?"

"Baby," he said. "I enjoy giving you everything. And right now, I'm going to give you one hell of a giant orgasm."

CHAPTER FORTY-SIX

Ryan

How beautiful she looked, my cum splattered on her alabaster neck and chest. I knew I should get up and get a wet rag and cleanse her, but I couldn't. I wanted to see my mark on her as I stuck my tongue between her legs.

I quickly disposed of the rest of her clothes. When I spread her legs, she glistened with more cream than I'd ever seen.

"Baby, you're drenched."

"I know." Her fingers were on her nipples, playing with them, twisting them. "I can feel it. This whole thing drove me crazy, Ryan."

"I'm about to drive you a lot crazier." I dived into her succulent pussy. Sweet vanilla musk. Sweet Ruby.

Her folds were red and engorged, ready for me. For a split second, I regretted the pearl necklace, wishing I had saved my cock to thrust into her.

But I could live with the outcome. She tasted so good, smelled so good. Although I wanted to devour her, I started with long slow strokes, from her perineum to her clit and then back down. Her sweet little asshole beckoned, but I would leave it alone for now.

Her pussy was more than enough of a tasty treat for me tonight. Already I was starting to harden again, and I had barely begun licking her. She moaned above me, still playing with her ruby nipples.

"That's right, baby. Pinch those nipples for me. God, you're so hot." I licked her again, and then again, savoring every sweet morsel she offered. I pushed my tongue into her tight hole, and she began to move her hips, grinding her flesh against my face.

"Ryan, yes. Feels so good."

She had taken damn good care of me tonight. It was time for me to let her come. I clamped my lips over her clit and sucked while inserting two fingers into her pussy.

She locked around me, coming all over me.

"Yeah, come. So hot. So fucking hot."

"Fuck me, Ryan. Please. Fuck me now."

She didn't have to ask twice. I was hard again, of course, so I moved forward, removing my fingers from her pussy and replacing them with my cock. Perfect paradise. I had found the perfect paradise between the legs of this unlikely woman.

No. That wasn't fair, and it didn't do her justice.

I loved her so much. Was completely and hopelessly devoted to her.

And as I pumped in and out, making love to her, becoming one with a woman who had become so important to me, so vital to my very life, I shouted out words, words so very foreign to me.

"Ruby, marry me!"

★ ★ ★

We didn't talk about my question—which hadn't even been a question. It had been more like a command. We were both so exhausted after more orgasms that we fell into slumber beside each other.

When I woke up, Ruby had already gone, leaving me a text.

Had to get into work to see about that vacation time. Love you.

We hadn't known each other long enough to consider marriage. What had made me say those words?

Simple. She had become vital to my existence—a drug I craved physically and emotionally. I could no longer exist without her, and I wanted to marry her. I wanted what my brothers had with their wives. But I feared Ruby would not be ready yet.

She was still so new to all of this. Would she want to settle down? To experience only one man her entire life?

That thought filled me with jealousy. Being the only man who had ever been inside that sweet pussy was a huge turn-on, and I was determined that no one else would ever touch her.

I would see her later, and we would talk. For now, I had to contact Joe and Talon and see if they were up for another trip to the Caribbean.

★ ★ ★

"I don't know, Ry," Joe said, sitting at his kitchen table.

Melanie had gone back to work, and Talon had come over. We were having a late breakfast of corned beef hash and eggs.

"With Melanie being pregnant and all," Joe continued, "I don't know if it's a good time for me to leave."

"Believe me, I understand. But this is big. Bigger than any

one of us."

"No one wants to put an end to this more than I do," Talon said. "But have you considered that Mathias might be sending us on a wild-goose chase?"

"Yes," I said. "And so has Ruby. We're not going into this lightly. But at this point, we have to follow every lead. Especially if we can save the women and children—and men, for all we know—being held there. I'll be honest. I don't want Ruby going. I want her safe. But this is her father, and I can't stop her from going. If we have to, we'll go alone."

Joe shook his head. "We can't let the two of you go alone."

"Jade would understand," Talon said. "She wouldn't be happy about me leaving, especially because we might be putting ourselves in danger, but she knows how important it is for me to end this, once and for all, and to see Mathias behind bars where he belongs."

"Melanie would understand too," Joe said. "But this is different for me. I'm going to be a father. I can't take any chances with my life. My child needs a dad."

"Hey," I said. "I plan on all of us getting out of this alive. Talon, we all know you've been through way worse. And I'm not talking about your time in captivity. I'm talking about what you witnessed and had to do overseas."

For a moment, Talon's eyes took on a haunted look, but in no time he was himself again. "For a long time, I didn't care whether I lived or died. Now I want to live. But damn it, we can't let what happened to me happen to one more person if we can stop it."

Joe finally nodded. "You're right. I know you're right. Let's do this."

"Okay." I sighed in relief. I didn't want to do this without my brothers. "We need to check with our foremen and let them know we're going to be gone for a few weeks. I can have Marion over at my office to make all the arrangements."

"What about Marj?" Talon said. "You know she's going to want to go along."

I shook my head. "Absolutely not. It's bad enough that Ruby's going. But at least she's a trained police detective."

"I don't particularly want Ruby going either," Joe said. "Though I see her point. This concerns her as much as it does the rest of us. I agree with Ryan. No way is Marj going."

"There's only one way to get around that," I said. "We can't tell her we're leaving, which means Jade and Melanie are going to have to keep it a secret, at least until we're gone."

Joe nodded. "Melanie will do it."

"So will Jade," Talon said. "She'll hate it, but she'll do it if I ask her to."

I stood. "Okay. It's settled. I'll have Marion take care of the details, and in the meantime, I have someone I need to visit."

"Who's that?" Joe asked.

"Larry Wade. I'm going to float this new information in front of him and see if I get any bites."

"Great idea," Joe said. "I'll go with you."

Talon went rigid.

"You don't have to go, Tal," I said. "Joe and I have got this."

"Look, I'm probably going to come face-to-face with Mathias on this trip of ours. I need to get used to facing those men. I'm going with you."

CHAPTER FORTY-SEVEN

Ruby

Ruby, marry me.

Those words haunted me. I hadn't been able to get them out of my mind.

And to top that off, I was also out of a job.

My request for vacation time had not gone over well. In the wake of Mark's death, the department was a mess. They were shorthanded, and they didn't think they could accommodate any vacation time for me with such short notice, especially since I'd just taken time for the previous trip to Jamaica. Even after I told them the whole story, and I was sure they would see it my way, they didn't budge.

So I had done the only thing I thought I could. I quit the force.

I had been a member of the Grand Junction Police Department for eleven years, detective for only a few months. These people had been my friends and my family when I had no others until Melanie and the rest of the Steels had come charging into my life.

Maybe it was time for a change. I could marry Ryan Steel and never have to worry about money again in my lifetime. I loved him so much, but his proposal had come in the throes of lovemaking, and neither of us had so much as mentioned it afterward. Did he even remember saying it? I wasn't sure.

I also wasn't the type to depend on a man—or anyone else, for that matter—for my support. I'd been making it on my own for the better part of the last two decades. Being dependent on another person didn't sit well with me.

If I married Ryan Steel, it would be because we both wanted to spend our lives together, not because I needed his money.

Luckily, I'd saved a lot over the years. I'd lived well beneath my means, my only extravagance being my gym membership, which wasn't much, and the recent trip to Jamaica to celebrate Melanie's wedding. If I continued living as I had been, I'd be able to make it about a year before I needed to find another job, and that wasn't including what I'd set aside for retirement.

Yeah, I was in pretty good shape.

Still, it had hurt to leave the force. But they'd given me no choice. I had to go after my father. I had to do what I could to stop him.

And God, I hoped I could finally do it.

Before I'd left, I'd contacted the guys in research about fingerprinting the book and note Ryan had found under my sofa. They were pals of mine, and they promised to call me the minute they had results. They also indicated I could contact them anytime if I needed anything, but now that I was off the force, would that be against policy? I didn't want to get anyone in trouble.

I sighed. I was giving up more than a job and a family. I was giving up a lot of resources that I might need on this journey.

Unfortunately, I didn't have a choice.

Though I knew Ryan wouldn't approve, I was now at the door of my apartment. I needed to pack up for the trip. I entered stealthily, armed. I'd had to turn in my department weapon, but I still had my own, which I kept locked up in my car at all times. I did a quick search of the premises. Everything appeared fine, and I felt safe—for the time being at least.

I had grown more and more confident that I had been advised by an anonymous source, most likely my father, to steer clear of my home so the book and paper could be planted. Wendy Madigan hadn't orchestrated the planting, as the evidence implicated her.

Then again...I knew enough about Wendy to know that she never did what anyone expected. But surely she wouldn't implicate herself.

No, this had been my father. He was up to something, and I was beginning to wonder if he was helping me in his warped way.

He'd murdered my boss, and while Mark hadn't deserved to die, he'd clearly been in league with my father, at least for that one small portion of his scheme. Mark was a good cop, so the only thing that could have gotten to him was a threat against his family.

Or money.

It might have all come down to money. I'd seen good people do bad things, all in the name of money.

The Steels had it. Wendy had it. My father had it, though he appeared to be running out.

But money had never been important to me. That's why I had lived such a modest life, saving most of what I'd earned.

Was money truly the root of all evil? I didn't think so, but one thing had become increasingly clear. With money, almost anything was possible—good or evil.

I gathered my passport and other travel stuff as quickly

as I could, stuffing everything into a large duffel bag. I wasn't sure exactly where we'd be going. Ryan would take care of that. All I knew was that it would be somewhere in the Caribbean, possibly near Jamaica, possibly not. And I couldn't neglect the possibility that my father was sending us on a wild-goose chase.

"Damn it," I said aloud. "If only I knew for sure that you were telling me the truth."

My bedroom door creaked, and I gasped.

"I assure you"—my father's voice—"I have told you nothing but the truth. This all ends now."

CHAPTER FORTY-EIGHT

Ryan

Jonah, Talon, and I sat facing the warden of the prison. We'd been ushered into his office after we asked to see Larry Wade.

"We don't usually give out this information, but you three have been in to visit Wade quite a few times since his incarceration. Plus, there are extenuating circumstances. We were going to have to contact you, anyway."

"What information? And what extenuating circumstances?" Joe asked. "I want to speak to my uncle."

"We'd let you if we could," the bearded man said, "but Mr. Wade was murdered last night."

My veins turned to ice. Not that I gave a shit that the motherfucker was dead, but now another source of information had dried up.

Talon looked visibly relieved. He hadn't wanted to face Larry again. He'd had issues the first time he'd tried it, but my brother was nothing if not strong, and he would have done it. Now he didn't have to.

"Murdered?" Joe asked.

"Yes. And it appears to have been an inside job."

"Another inmate, you mean?" I said.

The warden cleared his throat. "No. Not another inmate. Mr. Wade was in a solitary cell...on suicide watch."

I widened my eyes, and Talon's looked like they were going to pop out of his head.

"Suicide watch?" Joe said.

"Yes. Our psychologist had determined Mr. Wade was a suicide risk. Plus, he'd been routinely attacked by other prisoners. He was fading fast and succumbing to severe depression. So he was put in solitary on suicide watch."

Joe scoffed. "Putting prisoners on suicide watch. Give me a break."

"They're still people, Mr. Steel."

"If you knew what this so-called person—"

Talon gripped Joe's arm. "It's okay, Joe. We don't need to go there."

"We're well aware of what Mr. Wade was accused of. However, he was still innocent until proven guilty in a court of law. He hadn't gone to trial yet."

Joe stood. "I guess our business is done here. We won't be getting any more information out of our dear old uncle."

"Please have a seat, Mr. Steel," the warden said. "I'm afraid our business is far from done here."

"Look. If you think I'm going to shed tears over the loss of that piece of shit, think again." Joe motioned to Talon and me. "Let's go, guys."

I stood as Joe headed toward the door, but a large guard blocked his exit.

"What the hell is going on here?" Joe demanded.

"Have a seat, like the warden said," the guard said.

"Are you fucking kidding me? Get the hell out of my way."

"Joe," Talon said. "Let's just see what the guy has to say."

Joe rolled his eyes. "Fine." He plunked back into his chair. "What is it?"

"Like I told you," the warden said. "It was an inside job. But not by another inmate. A prison guard killed Mr. Wade."

"And we should care because...?" Joe said.

"You should care, Mr. Steel, because I have sworn testimony from two of my guards that you paid them off to rough Mr. Wade up."

Joe's eyes widened. "That's bullshit."

"That's not for you or for me to say. Now, that said, normally we look the other way when this happens. A few beatings don't concern us. But a murder? We have to investigate that."

"I can assure you that my brothers and I had nothing to do with Larry's murder," I interjected.

"Maybe not. But one of my guards murdered Larry Wade. It couldn't have been anyone else because no one else had access. And oddly, one of my guards has since disappeared into thin air."

"So what?" Joe said.

"So this," the warden countered. "It seems pretty plausible that this guard might have been given a sum of money to do Mr. Wade in. A *large* sum of money. And you three certainly could have come up with a *large* sum of money."

Joe stood again, raising a fist. "Don't you dare try to hang this on us."

"We already have evidence that you paid a couple of guards to rough him up," the warden said.

"So? That's their word against mine. And that doesn't mean I had him murdered."

"No, it doesn't. But it does mean I can have you questioned, and I will."

"We don't have time for this," I said. "We're going on a trip. A very important trip. You can't hold us here."

"You're right. I can't. But the police want to question all three of you. Don't leave the state until they do."

Joe rubbed his stubbled chin. "Christ."

"It's not your fault, Joe," I said.

Talon punched some numbers into his phone. "I'm calling Jade. We need an attorney."

"The police expect you sometime today," the warden said.

"My girlfriend is a detective on the force," I said. "I can assure you this will all come to nothing."

"For all of your sakes, I hope you're right," the warden said. "But we have to investigate. Good day."

We all stood, and the guard moved from the doorway, letting us pass.

"I'm sorry," Joe said, once we were alone. "This is on me. I did slip a guard a benji. On two separate occasions."

"Don't blame yourself," I said. "We all wanted to see him get the shit kicked out of him."

"You were just taking care of things," Talon said. "Just like you always have, big brother."

"I wanted him to suffer for what he did to you," Joe said.

"We understand that," I said.

Joe rubbed his forehead. "Shit. I swear to God I never paid anyone off to kill him."

"We know, Joe," Talon said. "He's no use to us dead."

"Look," I said. "We'll talk to the cops, assure them we had nothing to do with Larry's murder, and then we'll get out of town."

Talon eyed his phone screen. "Jade just texted me. She's getting an attorney at the top criminal defense firm in the city to meet us at the station. Everything will be fine."

I sighed. "All right, then. Let's get this over with."

CHAPTER FORTY-NINE

Ruby

"How did you get in here?"

"The same way I got in the other night."

"So *you* left the book."

"I did."

"You should know. I'm armed."

He smiled, and a spooky recognition oozed through me. His smile resembled mine, right down to the slightly lower gumline on the left side of his mouth. I'd never noticed that before.

"I am no threat to you. I never was."

"Oh...except for the time you tried to rape me."

"That was unfortunate. I was a different person then. I regret it."

"Well, you won't get the chance to try it again." I pointed my gun at him.

"Kill me, Ruby, and you'll never find what you're looking for."

"Maybe all I'm looking for is to send you to hell."

He smiled again, and I gulped back nausea at the resemblance.

"Then do it, Ruby. Pull that trigger. Murder me in cold blood."

I laughed. Actually laughed! "Cold blood? Are you kidding me? This would be the most hot-blooded murder ever committed. But I assure you, I'd get away with it. You broke into my house. Pure self-defense."

"Then what are you waiting for?"

What *was* I waiting for? I aimed the gun right between his eyes.

"Kill me, though," he said, "and you'll never discover the truth."

"I know all the truth I need. You raped Gina. You tortured and raped Talon Steel. You tried to rape me. You've had something to do with the disappearance of those girls I met in Jamaica. You tried to have Brooke Bailey killed for insurance money. And God himself only knows what other heinous acts you've committed or had a part in."

"I had reasons for everything I did, including letting you live all these years."

"I've often wondered about that," I said. "Why didn't you have me taken care of long ago?"

He smiled. "A father's pride."

I scoffed, even though I knew he could have killed me at any time. Still, his statement rang with morsels of truth. "Please."

"It's true. You're strong and determined. I've watched you since you left. I helped keep you safe."

"I kept myself safe, you shithead."

"Did you never wonder why, as a fifteen-year-old girl, you were never caught? Never arrested? Never violated?"

"I stayed under the radar."

"Yes, you did. With a lot of help from me."

That was bullshit. He was playing mind games. I had taken

care of myself all those years. So I changed the subject on him.

"I'm not interested in your reasons for anything you did." I cocked the gun. "Say goodbye, Daddy."

Continue The Steel Brothers Saga with Book Nine

Unraveled

Coming February 13, 2018

MESSAGE FROM HELEN HARDT

Dear Reader,

Thank you for reading *Twisted*. If you want to find out about my current backlist and future releases, please like my Facebook page: **www.facebook.com/HelenHardt** and join my mailing list: **www.helenhardt.com/signup/**. I often do giveaways. If you're a fan and would like to join my street team to help spread the word about my books, you can do so here: **www.facebook.com/groups/hardtandsoul/**. I regularly do awesome giveaways for my street team members.

If you enjoyed the story, please take the time to leave a review on a site like Amazon or Goodreads. I welcome all feedback.

I wish you all the best!

Helen

ALSO BY HELEN HARDT

The Sex and the Season Series:
Lily and the Duke
Rose in Bloom
Lady Alexandra's Lover
Sophie's Voice
The Perils of Patricia (Coming Soon)

The Temptation Saga:
Tempting Dusty
Teasing Annie
Taking Catie
Taming Angelina
Treasuring Amber
Trusting Sydney
Tantalizing Maria

The Steel Brothers Saga:
Craving
Obsession
Possession
Melt
Burn
Surrender
Shattered
Twisted
Unraveled (Coming February 13, 2018)

Daughters of the Prairie:
The Outlaw's Angel
Lessons of the Heart
Song of the Raven

Misadventures Series:
Misadventures of a Good Wife
Misadventures with a Rockstar

DISCUSSION QUESTIONS

1. The theme of a story is its central idea or ideas. To put it simply, it's what the story means. How would you characterize the theme of Twisted?

2. Discuss Ruby's character. How has she changed since we first met her? Were you surprised that she ended up quitting the police force? Why or why not?

3. What do you think the real relationship between Brad Steel and Wendy Madigan was or is?

4. Do you believe, based on what we know so far, that Bradford Steel is alive? Why or why not?

5. Ryan and Ruby have evolved quite a bit in the bedroom. Discuss Ruby's reaction to this and her conversations with Melanie. Is Ruby losing herself or finding herself?

6. Rodney Cates mentions that one of the people Theodore Mathias trusted was Brad Steel. What did you make of this revelation? What might the relationship between the two men be?

7. Discuss literary devices used in the story. Any foreshadowing? Other devices? What is the significance of the story's title?

8. What does the future hold for Jonah? Will he be arrested for

accessory to the murder of Larry Wade?

9. Will the Steels and Ruby find the mysterious Caribbean island? What might they find there?

10. Discuss the symbol on the ring. What meanings might it have other than those alluded to in Twisted?

11. Ruby deduces that Mathias is running out of money. Do you feel this is true? Why or why not? Where might the money have gone?

12. Jade promised to tell Brooke the truth about Nico Kostas/ Theodore Mathias. Discuss what Brooke's reaction might have been.

13. Ruby theorizes that Wendy has a reason for everything she says, even the lies. Do you agree? Why or why not?

14. Are you ready for the Steel Brothers Saga to end?

ACKNOWLEDGEMENTS

Twisted turned out to be the perfect title for this book in the Steel saga. From the twisted symbol on the future lawmakers' rings to the twisted mind of Wendy Madigan—and many more twists in between—this book, more than any others in the saga so far, finally begins to bring the many secrets surrounding the Steels to light. I loved writing this installment of the saga. I've left a cliffhanger, of course, but soon the mysteries will all be solved.

A very special thank you to my husband, Dean, who is a district lecturer for the Grand Masonic Lodge of Colorado. Your knowledge of symbols helped me immeasurably.

Thanks so much to my amazing editors, Celina Summers and Michele Hamner Moore. Your guidance and suggestions were, as always, invaluable. Thank you to my line editor, Scott Saunders, and my proofreaders, Amy Grishman, Angela Kelly, and Chrissie Saunders. Thank you to all the great people at Waterhouse Press—Meredith, David, Kurt, Shayla, Jon, Yvonne, Jeanne, Renee, Dave, and Robyn. Special thanks to Yvonne Ellis for the beautiful cover art for *Twisted* and for the whole series.

Many thanks to my assistant, Amy Denim, for taking care of business so I can write. I couldn't do it without you!

Thank you to the members of my street team, Hardt and Soul. HS members got the first look at *Twisted*, and I appreciate all your support, reviews, and general good vibes. You all mean more to me than you can possibly know.

Thanks to my always supportive family and friends, and to my local writing groups, Colorado Romance Writers and Heart of Denver Romance Writers, for their love and support.

Most of all, thank you to the diehard Steel fans who have eagerly waited for the conclusion of the series. Things will be *Unraveled* soon!

ABOUT THE AUTHOR

#1 *New York Times*, #1 *USA Today*, and #1 *Wall Street Journal* bestselling author Helen Hardt's passion for the written word began with the books her mother read to her at bedtime. She wrote her first story at age six and hasn't stopped since. In addition to being an award-winning author of contemporary and historical romance and erotica, she's a mother, an attorney, a black belt in Taekwondo, a grammar geek, an appreciator of fine red wine, and a lover of Ben and Jerry's ice cream. She writes from her home in Colorado, where she lives with her family. Helen loves to hear from readers.

Visit her here:
www.facebook.com/HelenHardt